GOODCOPBADCOP

JIM ALEXANDER

Planet Jimbot
Glasgow

All characters and events in this publication, other than those clearly in the public domain, are fictitious and any resemblance to real persons, living or dead, is purely coincidental.

ISBN (print): 978-1-9164535-0-0
ISBN (digital): 978-1-9164535-1-7

GoodCopBadCop is a legally deposited book at the National Library of Scotland, Edinburgh.

To the best three things that have happened to me. David, Euan and Neil.

1.

Horrible things, criminal things, happen all around you. If only you could see beyond the tip of your nose.

The end of the road.

You can go about your life, not in the least aware of what's going on—turn a literal blind eye to the black eyes and gouged thighs—and even if something does break through, permeates the senses—even if you witness something that terrifies and upsets you, you can dispense your civic duty with a bullet point phone call.

You can pass it on.

And when you get home, be sure to have a slow sob in your lover's lap; later you'll have a story for dinner parties, for all the neighbours to hear carte blanche your now God-given right to rant on all things law and order. But the point is you don't have to care, it doesn't have to trouble you further, not really.

It's not your responsibility.

There is the dirt and filth of the city. People, who will do anything, say anything, in the pursuit of a chemical hit. People who wish to profit at someone else's expense.

People who wish to do harm. Desperate people. Violent people. Dishonest people. People who don't understand. Good people turned bad.

Hate crime.

Stick your head out of the window. Close your eyes as your physiology adjusts to the biting cold. Listen. Let your mind conjure up the images to go with the chill. Try to absorb all the bad things going on right now, out there. A man slaps a woman's face harder than he intended and finds he cannot stop. A trusted relative strokes a boy's hair, allows his fingers to linger; the child reaches out for affection, and there it is, a line is crossed. At a pond in a local park, poisoned dead ducklings float in a slow circular pattern. The streets—you've heard of them, perhaps even spoken of them in hushed tones—which offer no safety, respite, no love or financial security, only the opposite. Do or die; the fight for survival; the right to live out some kind of life.

This is the point you leave the room and I come in. You can trust me. Go on, sit back while I do all the work. You can look away. You could argue, but that would mean looking me in the eye.

Relax, I'll clear up the mess. Without a further thought, it's okay to return to the slow, inexorable process of rotting away while tucked up safely in your bed.

Right now, a human heart and severed hand lie discarded in a Glasgow alleyway.

2.

Interrogation No. 1

The door was open.

I was sitting patiently in Interview Room 3, Helen Street Police Station, Govan, Glasgow. A B5-sized notebook was on the table in front of me, not the most riveting of company. Eyelids heavy, I was feeling quite sleepy. Several microsleeps later, the last of them ending with a sudden, maddening straightening of the head, a uniformed police officer walked in alongside our suspect.

'For the purposes of the interview,' I said, speaking in the direction of the recording equipment on the table, which was tucked against the wall furthest from the door. 'This is DI Brian Fisher and I'm joined by PC Philip Murphy and suspect Adam Walker.'

The suspect was cuffed, wrists clamped, hands to the front. He was still wearing his work uniform. The officer, having guided him to the side of the table opposite me, placed his hand on the suspect's shoulder and exerted downward force. Even so, the suspect seemed to glide into the chair, like a python charmed back into its basket. So beguiling was the motion, I had this strange thought that his posterior wasn't actually touching the seat, but floating a smidgen above. It struck me he had the poise of a ballerina. Not that I knew of any ballerinas. Except maybe the ones from the film *Black Swan*.

Once settled, the suspect looked up, straight into my eyes. It was then that he recognised me.

I wanted to give him some time. Didn't want to catch him unawares.

I nodded to PC Murphy. 'Two cappuccinos,' I said, before hurriedly adding, almost tripping over the words, 'if it's not too much trouble.' But I sensed that it already was.

'Sir?' PC Murphy said, his questioning tone running longer than the actual word. He gave me a nod in return, but it was a different kind of nod, mechanical and controlled—one that might have masked his true feelings when faced with the mundane, servile nature of my request, if it weren't for the noticeable grinding of his back teeth.

I liked PC Murphy and I wanted him to know this, which was why I was smiling at him.

There was a judicial pause as the question of rank, the recognition of where we both were on the food chain of law enforcement, sank in. PC Murphy quickly acquiesced with another, in terms of tone, more decidedly neutral, 'Sir'.

And off he went.

'PC Murphy is kindly leaving the room for some hot beverages,' I said as way of running commentary for the tape.

As the door closed behind us, it did so with an extended squeak, reminiscent of our rodent friends next door. It was the type of noise that could really get under your skin, if you let it.

'Door hinges,' I said, making my eyes big, 'gone unhinged.'

Simultaneously I flashed our suspect what I hoped was a reassuring smile. Where I was concerned, if it were up to me, it was smiles all round.

'Cappuccino okay for you? Mr Adam Walker, isn't it, just to confirm?'

In terms of questions, I'd decided on a particular opening gambit; a two for one deal.

Our suspect Mr Walker had five options. Answer both questions in the correct order; answer both questions in the wrong order; answer one of the questions, but not specify which one he was answering; answer the other question, but not specify which one; or answer neither. Rather predictably (the stats said seven out of every ten suspects did so) he chose the last option, while throwing in a steely stare for free (eight out of ten).

'We can delay things of course, while we wait for your lawyer,' I said. 'You have asked for a solicitor? Are we arranging one for you? No one tells me anything in here.'

I got a twitch out of him for that. I was all too aware with his previous non-response he had already set down a marker. It was too soon for him to change tack, not this early, surely?

And then, what do you know, he surprised me. His face broke into a smile, although not a friendly one, to the point I could see a full set of incisors. And that's not all.

'Your mouth's receding.' I waved my finger in the direction of my own gum line. 'I mean, I see you have gum disease. You need to watch that.'

'When you brush,' I said, miming brushing my teeth up and down, 'you need to go up and down, not side to side like they taught you. Always taking your time. It's not a sprint.'

I experienced a slight rush of panic. I should have asked PC Murphy not to add sugar to the cappuccinos on account of the gums situation. But I couldn't turn back time, and even if I could, would probably do so for a more worthy cause such as going back to save JFK or prevent myself from eating that smoked sausage a Monday or so ago.

My hands parted and danced as if about to reveal the contents of a magic trick. 'Anyway, you and me, tête-à-tête, an informal chat,' I said. Besides, there was a camera attached to the back wall looming over his shoulder. I didn't need to point it out for both of us to know it was there. It was the guest at the party that no one had invited, but it wouldn't be a party if not there. 'This can be anything you want it to be.'

'My full title is Chief Inspector Brian Fisher,' I said. 'But you can call me Brian if it makes things easier for you. That would certainly be my preference.'

Now that introductions were over, for me it was confession time. 'I need to come clean,' I said, 'Not my choice, you understand—in fact third out of three—but Room 3 is the only room available.' I shrugged long and hard. A sigh followed. 'Afraid to say the other two are out of commission.'

I considered leaving it at that, but there was no point in leaving us both, for different reasons to be fair, in a state of suspense.

'Room 1 is in dire need of a lick of paint. There are patches on the walls,' I said. 'Room 2 has mice. No idea where they're coming from, but as you can imagine it's a bit embarrassing in a place like this, having something unauthorised come and go anytime they please. We've put traps down, but these guys are good.'

It was on me before I realised, I was chuckling to myself. This wasn't some affectation on my part. In a way I really admired those critters.

I continued. 'Plan was vermin control booked in for today, painter and decorator Thursday, except someone on our end got their wires crossed. And it doesn't take a detective to tell who's just walked through the door, a painter and decorator from an exterminator.'

My stomach rumbled. I wondered, is there another noise that placed you in the here and now? That convinced you that you weren't dreaming? Corroborated the fact you weren't in a fugue state? Nothing confirmed reality more than the growling of one's stomach.

And the sensation that came with such cold, hard reality made me queasy and oddly nostalgic for those fuzzy microsleeps of only moments before.

I smiled at our suspect Mr Walker. No response. He just sat there, handcuffed, wrists clasped, tenseness extended around the shoulders and neck muscles. The pointy features on his face appeared even more so—with the inadequate lighting, you had to overcompensate and see past the areas of shade, but it didn't necessarily show you in a good light.

'Anyhow,' I recapped, 'Room 1 is currently under renovation. Room 2 is under siege. You know what, it's never a good time, so sometimes you just have to take the plunge and make a decision—give the walls a much needed makeover. Sod's Law, I suppose, that we've done so at the same time we're questioning a would-be serial killer.'

I gave our suspect the look over. A momentary rub of the thumbs constituted his only movement, the only sign he wasn't made of clay. It would have to do for now, I decided; otherwise I was wasting my time. Otherwise I could be out getting my suit dry-cleaned, or directing traffic, or passing Desk Sergeant Phil's retirement sheet around the office.

***

Twenty-four hours prior to the interrogation, that's when the heart and hand were found in a Glasgow back lane. Bath Lane to be precise. Both were wrapped in newspaper. The hand was severed above the wrist. The heart had been messily removed, but the fact it was removed at all and relatively intact pointed towards medical training. The hand didn't constitute the finest of cuts either. You could see bone sticking out. But perhaps I was being a little overcritical here.

By the time I arrived in my unmarked car (a sensible, well-maintained Kia Rio), several policemen were already standing around both heart and hand, forming a kind of cordon. Approaching briskly, I was on first name terms with one of the officers.

'Hullo there, Frank,' I said.

'Good morning, Chief Inspector, sir,' Frank said.

Frank was the kind of chap who nervously and instinctively saluted anything that approached him. In my case, I was never that much into airs and graces. I wanted to put him at ease. 'Frank, it's me, call me Brian,' I said.

Each newspaper wrapping was unfolded, exposing their grisly contents.

I crouched down.

If I was to describe myself, I'd say I was slight in frame. Not malnourished, just on the tall and thin side. All to do with genes, you'd think. My suit, trousers, and coat were baggy on me, but I liked to think fashionably so.

'Tell me, Frank, is your mother well?' I said.

'Doing okay, thanks, sir,' he said, hovering over me, standing perhaps a little too close for total comfort.

'She asks after you sometimes.'

'Always good to hear,' I said. 'And your Uncle Tommy?'

'Still alive, sir. Still plays the harmonica, even though he complains it hurts his teeth.'

I was splayed, palms down flat, head twisted and lowered, ear brushing the ground and eyes fixed on the stump, so better to examine it. I wasn't sure what I was looking for. Checking for distinguishing marks—I could have made a case for that—but it was a severed hand no matter what angle you looked at it. I was within sniffing distance, but that particular box had already been ticked when I got there.

I found myself reading the newspaper. It was the *Evening Times*. The headline read something on the lines of, 'Man Wields Pet Hamster as Murder Weapon.'

Eighteen hours prior to the interrogation, CCTV images were obtained, which caught a man in Bath Lane wearing a raincoat, hood up and pulled tight over his face. For the most part he had his back to the camera, hunkering down, in one quick efficient movement placing two objects wrapped in newspaper down on the ground. He may or may not have been wearing latex gloves. Objects deposited and mission accomplished, the man walked off.

Fourteen hours prior to the interrogation, a police dog named Sasha trotted into the general vicinity. Best snout forward, handler at the ready, Sasha sniffed around an overloaded city centre rubbish bin; her investigative prowess coming up trumps. On closer inspection, the bin, having been unceremoniously turned upside down and emptied of its contents, gave up recently discarded scrunched up latex gloves.

Spare a thought for that German Shepherd, black and tan, rewarded back at the dog unit with a clutch of bone-shaped biscuits. Enthusiastic tail wagging. Big booming bark. A case of happy panting all round. Well done, Sasha!

Six hours prior to the interrogation, forensics having already had its way with the gloves, I was making enquiries at Queen Elizabeth Hospital, the pharmacy department . I was barely done with the front desk when, in full view, a male dressed in pharmacy technician overalls made a break for it.

Less than an hour prior, back at the station, two days earlier than expected, a painter and decorator arrived with stepladder and tin of emulsion paint destined for Interview Room 1.

***

And we were back. Nothing else mattered in the world to me at this moment in time, only the man sitting across from me with his sharp features and lifeless eyes. The sole focus, what he might or might not say. That and the comfort, or otherwise, of my interview room chair.

'Chair could be comfier,' I said. To underline the point, I leaned back in the seat, which was stiff and unwieldy and squeaked at the brackets. I allowed myself the self-indulgence of dwelling on a twinge of accompanying stabbing back pain. 'Brutal,' I said. 'I blame government cuts.'

Undeterred, I rummaged around in one of my trouser pockets. From there I produced a little key, like I was some forgotten character from *The Lord of the Rings*. I placed the key down, then used the tip of my finger to guide it along the table next to the notebook.

And I wasn't done there. From my other pocket, I fumbled past some loose change and a half-finished packet of chewy mints in order to produce a pair of scrunched up latex gloves, which only earlier that morning I had purchased from Boots. You never knew when something like that might come in handy. I did my best to fold them out, placing them down the other side of the notebook to the key.

Finally, there was a flutter, a glimmer of interest to be had from the pair of great white shark eyes facing me.

It was like I was a druid.

I was performing a strange ritual that only a select few could hope to understand. I opened up the notebook and folded it back on a fresh blank page. I dutifully ripped out the page at the perforations. I placed the blank page above the notebook's designated area, giving it its own space on the table.

Surveying what I had created, notebook, gloves, key and blank page, I had to confess it was perplexing. I thought this must be the work of a madman and by implication that I'd turned quite insane. A feverish druid. An unstable alchemist.

But then I looked up and saw something in our suspect's eyes. Something someone like me could finally relate to. If I hadn't quite opened a door, I'd created one either of us could walk through if we so chose. Perhaps to meet in the middle, having entered from opposite sides.

I stretched my arms out either side as far as they could go.

'I'm a great believer in luck, you know,' I said.

I underwent half a notion to yawn, but quickly checked myself. I hunched my shoulders, bringing my arms in, palms out, elevating my hands.

'And you,' I said, 'let's face it; the fates have not been kind. Latex gloves that leave no prints, much like the ones I have here,' I said, nodding towards the gloves deposited on the table.

'Disposed of in a city centre rubbish bin,' I continued.

'Situated less than a mile from a crime scene consisting of a ripped-out heart and severed human hand.'

At this, the suspect Mr Walker noisily cleared his throat. I was no throat surgeon, but could tell he was getting purchase, dislodging whatever dark matter lurked there, before, just as suddenly, he stopped.

I hesitated. 'Yeah?' I asked.

There was no response from Walker.

'You have something to say?' I said.

There was no response from Walker.

'Thought, ah, you might have something to say there.'

There was no response from Walker.

So on I went. 'Now those gloves were made in Panama. They have—now I know this …' I flicked through the notebook until I got to the first page with writing on it. I lifted the page up for the benefit of our suspect. 'I wrote it down,' I said.

In fact, it was the only thing written anywhere. Swinging the page back into my line of sight, all the while fighting the compulsion to use my lips to make a helicopter noise, I read, 'its own unique carboxylated open-chain aliphatic latex polymer.'

I put the notebook back down with a satisfying whump. 'Who would have thought the science of latex gloves could be so, so interesting? Maybe we could have a National Latex Glove Day? I'd be up for that.'

'A single batch of latex gloves made in Panama.' With such a revelation, only one thing could and should have followed. However, a massive, unprecedented amount of willpower later and I still hadn't burst into the song of the same name by Van Halen.

Willpower. Staying on the right track. It was all about willpower.

'Panama,' I said, 'just like the canal and the city. But, unlike both of them, despatched to the Queen Elizabeth

Hospital in Glasgow. If not an outright error, then the only pharmacy department in a hundred-mile radius anytime recently to receive them. One of those gloriously random occurrences ...'

Walker coughed. It was a terrible sound, conjuring up the image of a bottomless pit that allowed no echo and no hope of escape.

'... the system ...'

There followed another cough.

'... sometimes ...'

Another cough.

'... spits out.'

I was beginning to suspect trying to read this fella was the equivalent of making sense of Sanskrit inscribed on cheap toilet paper, but if I was anything, I was a trier.

'That's where I come in,' I said. 'I'm making a routine call. I'm hoping to find a pharmacist, someone I can fire a few questions at, and at the same time show off my new comprehensive *Mastermind* subject-baiting knowledge of latex gloves—and—'

I pointed a finger, which on reflection seemed a pointless thing to do since he was the only other person in the room. 'That pharmacist—pharmacist technician to be precise—was you.'

For a moment, his eyes subconsciously darted to and fro like the pixelated dots that passed for video games in the early '80s.

'At the hospital desk, I caught your gaze. You were dressed in blue overalls, as you still are. We stared into each other's eyes, just like we're doing now. We could almost be back there. Except for the handcuffs.'

Lifelessness exerted control over his gaze once more.

'Before I even open my mouth, you panic, you turn, make a bolt for it.' My fingers tapped a beat on the table. 'You trip. You fall. I mean if that's not bad luck, then ....'

He dropped his head, as if bowing at a martial arts contest, but was the act intended to signal the end of the bout, or merely the beginning?

'We checked out your flat,' I said.

He looked up.

'That always gets a reaction. Sinking in—yes, we've been rooting around in your stuff. Your personal things. It's got to be done, I'm afraid. We found a box of latex gloves. Panamanian in origin.'

'Property of Queen Elizabeth Hospital.'

'Obtained, I'm surmising, without the hospital's blessing,' I murmured as something of an afterthought. 'Minus the pair you had already used, of course.'

Taking my time now. Letting the words spread and percolate through the air around us. I sat back in my chair, which immediately creaked, reminding me of the pitfalls of doing so, but having committed to the act, I wasn't going to back out of it.

'And—' I said, trying not to sound like some cheesy daytime TV presenter (and failing.) 'We found an empty notebook, not unlike the one I have here, also on the table, minus a single sheaf of paper, which had been torn out. This might mean something. It might not.'

'What we don't have is a body to go with the heart and hand. I mean, tests are in; it's official, they belong to each other.'

I leaned forward, but with no corresponding noise this time to come from the chair. I was on a roll here. I plonked my elbows securely on the table. My face wore an almost conspiratorial expression.

'Just you and me until the cappuccinos arrive,' I said. 'Come on, Mr Walker—can I call you Adam?—under that strong silent exterior, I bet there's a voice just dying to break out. Let me guess, you wanted to do something memorable? Maybe they'll call you the 'Hand on Heart

Guy'? I'm trying to do my best here. It's all a bit lame. You need someone who fancies themselves as something of a wordsmith for a snappier turn of phrase.'

I paused to breathe.

'But between you and me, Mr Walker, I don't think people will write many books about you. There's just not enough story. Why take so much care to hide a body, but do something as careless as to discard latex gloves in a city centre bin? Were you playing with us? Were you trying to get one up on us? It's everyone these days. Show me someone who can't resist making some kind of statement? Not clever, Adam. Not clever at all.'

'There's not enough material. We have a man's hand. We have a man's heart. I know you want to, so tell me. Where is the rest of the body?'

Nothing. Frozen in time. I had my fox stunned and staring at the spotlight, when ideally I wanted him running free without a care in a woodlands estate. I wanted him to run, like a fox, so I could catch him all over again.

Diligently, I held up the little key pinched between finger and thumb.

'Cat got your tongue?' I said. 'OK, OK, perhaps what's called for is a little trust.'

I stretched over the table and using the little key unlocked Walker's cuffs with the smallest of clicks.

He wasted no time raising both hands so better to examine them. He flexed his wrists to remove the numbness. The handcuffs were still attached to one of his wrists, hanging there limply and ineffectively, like a lynched man, noose around his neck and left dangling from a tree. His mind was racing. It was as plain as a pikestaff. He realised the possibilities.

There was still my voice. Still my voice to focus on. 'You'll find in this room all you'll ever need. Second pair of gloves, second sheet of paper ...'.

'More than just a heart. More than just a hand. But crucially not more than one victim. You planned on going on and on—and except for all that misfortune, that run of terrible bad luck—you might very well have done so. The frustration of it all. Doesn't it want to make you scream? Howl at the moon? Two is better than one, that's all I'm saying.'

I smiled at the guy. Part of me felt drawn to him; to applaud the underdog present, I think, in all of us. I couldn't help it. I felt for him. When it came down to it, fundamentally, we were both human beings. Just for a second, I rooted for him.

'If I'm wrong in all of this,' I said, 'then granted I apologise unreservedly.'

Thus far in, some guttural emissions apart, it's fair to say that not a single word had passed his lips. Suddenly, without warning, he belly-flopped onto the table; his hands reaching out for my neck. No longer reaching, he had a hold of my throat. Both thumbs positioned just below my Adam's apple. He squeezed.

He was fast. It was all so fast.

He squeezed some more. Cutting off the oxygen. In my mind, it was like the frame of a house falling in.

I couldn't even say I gasped out a decent amount of air before everything went black; before I completely lost consciousness.

My crumpled body slumped back onto my seat; head lolled backwards listlessly like a broken toy. Dead to the world.

Even though I was gone, I still knew what was happening, or at least I could piece it all together. Intuitively. You could call it an out-of-body experience, but limited to the interview room only.

I knew each of the rooms so well. Whenever I could, I would reach out, always careful to make my actions appear natural, never premeditated, and stroke one of the walls. Over the years it had become something of a pre-interrogation ritual. I'd worked at the station for so long.

Walker stretched, pressed down, and slid the single sheet of blank paper towards him. He spat on the page; a big dollop of spittle and mucus plopped down. The gloop had a wine red taint, which was where the gum disease came in.

Using his forefinger, he traced out the chewy blood-speckled spit into the number '2'. If there were an orchestra playing inside his head, it would be going full pelt. But if he was the conductor, there was something missing. His gaze fell onto the gloves.

Meanwhile, there was still me. I wasn't completely adrift, something was stirring inside. Something was going on inside my brain.

My skull jolted.

I rolled my head from the chin outwards, releasing a satisfying crack of the neck. My body shuddered. It filled out my suit. Ringed eyes opened with raw intensity, rendered bloodshot. Face cloaked in dust made from dead human skin. My hair was ruffled. My swollen tongue recoiled from stabbing canines, only to find grinding molars. The hairs on my arms stood on end and pressed against the sleeves of my shirt.

A fire raged in my chest. After that lot, the back pain was a piece of piss.

I was the fucking cat's pyjamas.

Starting at my belly, moving up my ribcage, taking my throat hostage, there was laughter. As pure as it was cruel as it was real, I was creasing myself.

'Hullo again,' I said. The walls of the room seemed to grab my words and toss them around like food in a skillet. My voice was deeper. My voice was everywhere, burrowing under the skin, then restless. Like a clutch of angry parasitic nematodes, soon as in, needful to burst out again.

'I suppose now, given my return to rude health, you'll not be proceeding to the glove stage, then?' I asked. 'But waste not, want not.'

I grabbed them from the table. A couple of strategic pinches later followed by a satisfying snap of thin rubber, the gloves were on.

As for the state of mind of our suspect, to say the least, he was in a state of vex. The previously moody silent treatment and gruel-thin air of menace, usurped only recently by the throttling of my carotid, had now given way to something else.

He'd thought he was in control. That the whole ritual played out previously was just for him. Now it was like his whole world was turned upside down, with the real prospect it may never turn back round again.

There was fear and trepidation in his eyes. A subset of survival instincts having kicked in, he motioned to twist and vacate his chair and make for the door.

'Nobody move an inch!' I barked.

I kicked away the table.

On the periphery the recording equipment, a helpless witness, went tumbling and crashing. Chairs freshly vacated remained standing, embracing the role of the primary silent onlookers. All that was missing to fill them was a pair of showroom dummies.

'Where do you think you're going? Hello, I'm over here. Hello?'

My voice exerted a strange control over him. He was a fox frozen again in the headlights. But even as it started, the whole charade was already played out in my mind.

It didn't matter that he was no longer moving. I threw myself at him. I hurtled into him, was on top of him.

He was on his back. We struggled; a mess of writhing, kicking, pneumatic limbs; slippery like wet soap. I was giddy with it all. Eventually, using both my hands, I pinned him down.

My mind was barbed wire. Tearing and screeching. Cats boiled alive.

My mouth roared and exploded, discharging a tsunami of saliva. 'Are you listening to me? Am I wasting my breath here? Is it you against me? Against the world? Against your mother hoping you'd amount to something more than a tragic waste of space? A waste of fucking air? You tiny, tiny fuck.'

His head flopped to the side. He opened his mouth to speak, before closing it.

I saw his ear, occupying space, which took everything in while giving nothing away. I hated its shape. It taunted me. I hated the fact it existed at all.

I dipped my chin and bit his earlobe. Snarling like a hungry dog, my teeth pulled and snatched.

His eyes darted once more, his line of vision desperately trying to capture what was happening to him. There was terror etched all over his bread-pudding face.

I bit clean through. A piece of earlobe popped into my mouth. The sensation of it against my cold tongue was warmer than expected.

I straightened up and allowed a weeping Walker to squirm free, bleeding freely from one ear.

'Prick,' I said. It was either this or *bon voyage*.

Walker, his arms and legs pushing up in unison, clambering like a crab, ushered himself into the corner. To his credit, he was traumatised but consistent. He still hadn't said a thing.

I stayed where I was, effectively squatting on the floor, removed from the mess and violence of before, or so I hoped. I tried to enjoy the peace and silence, what was coming my way. I closed my eyes and slid the tip of my tongue along my front teeth. A sluice of saliva carried the fragment of ear from one side of my mouth to the other.

'Breathe, just breathe,' I said.

A whimper came from the corner.

'I'm talking to myself, not you,' I snapped at Walker. Some of the anger was kicking back. Some hate and revulsion and loathing, but not enough to stem the inevitable calm.

There was reverie; a tweeting of imaginary birds.

I relaxed and felt myself again.

I smiled at Walker while maintaining the distance between us, waiting patiently for him to take a peek and not go through the motions of recoiling from me.

'Compare this room to the Universe,' I said. 'This tiny, cramped room. Compare it to the planets, stars, the cosmos. We're so unimportant. No different to dust. We're ants. Brains too small for our bloated, useless bodies.'

'Adam, I'm talking to you now.'

I wanted my voice to come across as unthreatening as possible. I only wanted to reassure him.

'Our lives over in the blink of an eye. Does it matter what we do? In fifty years, a hundred, once we're gone will anyone even care? I'm as aware of the futility of existence as the next man—or woman. I just want something to cling to; to prove that you, me, we can make a difference. It's not completely meaningless.'

'I just need some words, a location; the name of a street maybe.'

Walker was no longer crying, although it was difficult to tell from all the sweat and beads of blood that remained on his face. In fact, I'd go as far as to say he seemed deep in thought. He stared into my eyes and recognised in me something ... unrecognisable. He thought by dint of taking another life, he had elevated himself above the laws of human nature; that he was somehow different, occupier of some higher plane. He looked into my face and realised he wasn't.

My transformation had an effect; bringing to him a transformation of sorts as well. He was in awe of me.

An air bubble had formed on the bite mark on his ear. He motioned to say something, you could see it. It was as plain as the nose at the end of his face. Slowly, surely, he began to speak. At this point nothing else mattered. It was him and me.

We filled the room.

The door to the room squeaked open. From our suspect Adam Walker, there may have been words. There may have been as much as three syllables, rendered almost inaudible by the pitiful squeak that was the protest song of the door.

PC Murphy walked into the room with a couple of frothy cappuccinos carried in one of those cardboard cupholder trays. He had a look on his face, as if half-expecting me to send him back out again.

'Sir?' he said.

Accompanying this, again, was that questioning tone of his.

It did nothing to stem the shock on PC Murphy's face, which was understandable, registering the scene in front of him.

Meanwhile, in Interview Room 1, a painter and decorator took a step back and licked his lips on reviewing a job well done in the form of a freshly painted wall, in aqua blue.

Meanwhile, in Interview Room 2, a trap snapped shut, but there was no mouse. For all anyone could say, it could have been a ghost.

As for myself, I got to my feet and walked a little unsteadily in PC Murphy's direction. I couldn't take my eyes away from the cappuccinos. I raised my hand up to my throat, and before I knew it, I'd made a gulping, swallowing motion.

Having undergone a brief hiatus, my tummy resumed rumbling. The here and now. A reality check it may have been, but it made for poor timing.

I turned my head to share PC Murphy's view of things and blinked as I took in the carnage.

'What can I say?' I said, shrugging my shoulders, for a better thing to say or do, 'Interview Room 3.'

***

One short statement later, having left the dubious comforts of Interview Room 3, I found myself gravitating towards a quiet corner in the main office. If you were just visiting, on first impression of the surroundings, it could have been any kind of office setting; people typing, on the phone taking and fielding enquiries; asking, then demanding, then pleading for IT support. It was just that the subject matter was that much grimmer. And the buttons on the uniforms that much shinier.

I was woozy. I just needed a minute. My teeth were a little bloodstained.

'Bad gums,' I explained to a passing, utterly disinterested colleague.

I glanced at the nearby noticeboard. Up there among the local ads for karate and badminton classes was a ragged piece of scrap paper, which read, 'This is Govan'. Really, no further explanation necessary.

My stomach rumbled ominously. Sergeant McShane, sitting at his desk, caught my eye. Mouth open as wide as humanly possible, he was in the act of slowly, deliberately lifting a mince and onion pasty to his gaping mince-and-onion-pasty-sized cakehole.

This was in direct conflagration of the warm food desk policy prohibiting the eating of hot, steaming pasties and the like at your workstation. After all I'd been through, this proved the last irrefutable straw, breaking the largest of donkey's back.

Legs pumping like fiddler's elbows, I dashed to the toilet. I barged into the nearest available cubicle. Like a torrent of bad news, I emptied my stomach into the bowl. I looked down. Floating amongst the dark orange gloop of carrot chunks, sweetcorn, and clumps of barely digested macaroni and cheese, was our suspect's earlobe. On closer examination, everything considered, it was in pretty good shape.

The faster time moved, the slower it seemed. Instinctively, I moved to flush, but luckily, in the last available transient moment open to me, I hesitated. Clearly, to not flush, this was the right thing to do.

***

Elsewhere, in Bath Lane, there was police tape, having formed a quadrilateral perimeter. The tape surrounded a couple of police chalk outlines, in close proximity one to the other, intended to represent specific shapes.

A human heart and severed hand.

3.

The Partick Cat

W*hy shouldn't you cook a lobster dead?*

After the events of Interview Room 3, changes were afoot. The camera never lies, but at times it could be an unreliable witness. The picture was jumpy and of generally poor quality. The fault had been reported several times, but the department responsible had already spent its entire budget just two months into the financial year. I'd said it a hundred times; the lighting in that room did you no favours. An inadvertent spillage of a hot frothy liquid on the machinery didn't help matters either.

There was lost time. Crucially around the point the suspect was unrestrained. What they could discern from the recording was a mixture of clicks and hissing. There was shouting, which for all anyone could know, could easily have come from inside a tunnel.

Between me and our suspect, you could see there had been a struggle. The big chiefs discussed the possibility of the suspect having thrown himself forward and somehow, in so doing, manoeuvring the handcuffs, key in the lock, some strategic jerks later, which ultimately freed him, so allowing him to tussle some more. They hypothesised every scenario, tried to work each out, feasible or otherwise, stopping just short of suggesting an act of God. While they chattered on, at no point did they ask me anything, and I never volunteered any information. What could I have said anyway that would have helped things along, or stymied the more bizarre theories being bandied about, or even made much in the way of sense? I could have told them the truth, of course, as if that would have got us anywhere.

In the end, they were too many 'somehows' to make any of it stick. The general rule, when they count six or seven 'somehows', is that you get referred to six or seven sessions with a police psychologist.

Oh, by the way, I was taken off the case, but we did find the rest of the victim's body. The trio of syllables uttered by our suspect did mean something after all; having permeated the ether, or at least the inner workings of my ear; having formed the words 'Holmlea Road'.

It was enough to lead us to the body, minus one heart and one left hand and, as it happened, minus one right foot.

***

The following day, if it even qualified as such, I woke up at 4.42 a.m. My head was splitting, the frontal lobe of my brain pulsating, akin to the effects of caffeine withdrawal. Except that I'd given up coffee two years ago, but to be sure of the exact date I would need to check my diary. The cappuccinos at interrogation, at least where I was concerned, were just for show.

The morning, such as it was, was uneventful. I opened the fridge door, which whined mercilessly at the hinges, reminding me of something I didn't need reminded of. The fridge light flickered for a few moments before coming to a decision to remain firmly on. This activity was down to wanting milk for my muesli, but it was the smell of raw meat that hit me first.

In my refrigerator, there were no vegetables. This was never a good sign.

On the subject of muesli, my clear preference is for the economy brand. The closer it resembles and tastes like rabbit food, the better. Luxury muesli leaves me cold. I always thought this fact alone best betrayed my working-class roots.

Out the door at 5.32 a.m., I decided to leave the car. No Govan trek for me today, so the plan was to walk from my flat in Butterbiggins Road and see where that got me. On the way into the city centre, there was nothing much to report, bar one abandoned shopping trolley.

I ventured on. The city was quiet at this time; populated by junkies walking the streets, twitching, waiting impatiently for their dealers to get out of bed. That or the alkies, bodies popping in fits and starts, anticipating the moment Tesco Metro opened its doors, and even then, the excruciating realisation, no matter how they pleaded, that no one will sell alcohol to them before 10 a.m. (half twelve on a Sunday). Or the first wave of commuters headed for the early trains. In the first two instances, the drug addicts and alcoholics, I was on first name terms with all who met my eye.

I reached George Square and sat on a public bench dedicated to Barry Kaye, a pillar of the community. Genuinely selfless, only interested in helping others, the type of human being that of late had regrettably slid out of fashion. Sitting there, I liked to be reminded every so often that they were good people in the world; people like Barry, who only wanted to help youngsters from troubled homes reach their potential. Help them make something of themselves. That is, until one of them planted a machete into poor Barry's head. There was always one bad egg looking to ruin it for everyone else.

It was raining now, which combined with a bracing wind pushed me back up to my feet. I resumed my walk to the station.

Twenty minutes later, I popped into Baird Street. Inside, officers and support workers went about their everyday work, along the way shouting out snippets alluding to outstanding cases, and I was content to just sit at a spare desk and listen.

'The Partick Cat, a burglar with a unique MO, has struck again,' one voice went.

'Just announced,' went another, 'a crackdown on the unlicensed sale of weapons.'

Another voice. 'Yet more reports coming in of rival gangs fighting with samurai swords and broadswords.'

It struck me how regimented office chat had become. People talked in terms of newspaper headlines or, perhaps more to the point, tweets.

'Alex Salmond arrested for impersonating Captain Kirk out of Star Trek—again,' yet another voice piped. 'Wait, I got that wrong,' the voice corrected itself, only to correct itself again. 'Wait, I was right the first time.'

'The least of his worries,' someone else chipped in.

Now that was better. There was the banter. Humanity was still breaking through.

And so they went on. All those voices competing, every chirp and cheep, distinct from each other, but all coalescing somehow, forming an unlikely choir of reported crime. Truth be told, it was giving me a sore head. I had my orders, having only been based here since yesterday, but was already experiencing feelings of deep-rooted nostalgia for the ordered insanity of Govan.

Harmony of a kind was ruthlessly restored when someone from Despatch approached to inform me that the 'Partick Cat' was now one of my cases. (To be honest, I think I was sitting on her chair and she was looking for an excuse to get rid of me.)

I didn't need to be told twice. I vacated the building, grabbing an unmarked police car (a Kia Picanto) on the way. I drove out to the scene of the Partick Cat's latest burglary; a Dennistoun address, situated in the east end. It was a tenement block. A ground floor flat. The Partick Cat had long since expanded his (or her) base of operations, no longer confined to Partick or even the west end of Glasgow.

Having parked and now on foot, I passed a hedgerow. Sticking unceremoniously out of the shrubbery was an empty bottle of Buckfast.

It was still early. Standing outside the tenement door, to satisfy my curiosity, I pressed the tradesman buzzer. With an irritable drone it released the lock, allowing me to pull open the door and enter the block.

Indoors, I stared momentarily at the grey, cold stairs that greeted me, which led up to the first floor and beyond. It ignited within me a longing so deep and intense. It felt for a second like I should find a dark corner to sob uncontrollably in. But certain moments were flexible, determined by various choices, and this was this type of moment. So I chose to keep it together.

I knocked on the door and a crestfallen young man of around ten years old answered.

'You find my PS4?' he said hopefully.

I flashed the boy a little smile and put a consoling hand on his shoulder. In return he gave me a stare like I was the Devil.

'What's your name?' I said.

'Trevor,' he said. 'Three games gone as well.' He sniffed

loudly. 'brand new *Red Dead Redemption* and the new *FIFA* and *Batman*.' He scrunched up his forehead, which was old before its time. 'Eh,' he said, 'and a *Grandmas v Zombies* game I borrowed from my uncle, which I never ever *ever* even wanted to borrow, but my Ma made me.'

'Mum or dad about, Trevor?'

This sparked a flurry of activity—you'd think by the sounds that someone had left scones too long in the oven—with much screeching, slamming of doors, and probable waving of arms, culminating in Trevor's mum, who went by the name of Mrs Gray, appearing and ushering me into the flat. Now inside, I surveyed the scene, gathered intel, and basically came across as a right nosey so and so. It was all in the job description.

This is what I learned. In the wee hours, the Cat had climbed in through the kitchen window, which had been left on its latch. For someone with the prowess of the Partick Cat, the family may as well have put up a big welcome sign in bright neon lights. As the occupants slept, he filled his bag of swag. As burglars went, the Cat was tidier than most. He hadn't wrecked the flat; anything but. There were gaps, you could see the telltale indentations in the carpet where expensive electrical equipment should have been, but otherwise, he'd left the place as he found it. Maybe even straightened a few cushions.

True to his MO, the Cat stole handpicked pieces of jewellery. To our knowledge he had never taken anything below a retail value of one hundred and fifty pounds. He'd even pilfer pets, if they were on the pricey side. Labradors, Boxers, Persian cats, a macaw; he even appropriated an iguana once.

I stayed for a cup of tea and a chocolate Hobnob and compiled a list of missing items. I reassured Mrs Gray that we'd do our best to retrieve the stolen goods. Chances of a successful outcome were statistically next to negligible, but on this I did not dwell. Instead we talked about the weather.

The shock of it all hadn't sunk in for either mother or son, but it would come around right enough, as sure as day followed night, but for the time being my job here was done.

I took my leave of flat and tenement and walked out into diagonal rain. On the street, two youths participated in a gang fight. One carried a samurai sword and the other a broadsword.

One thing that really upset me was delinquents fighting with swords. The carnage it left in its wake. So many broken lives and sliced digits. And I realised I was in the process of swapping one depressing set of statistics for another and that it was enough to make me weep.

It really, really upset me.

***

When a lobster dies, its body goes into self-destruct mode, releasing an internal chemical that begins to decompose its insides, rendering it inedible. If you want to eat it, ideally, you need to cook it alive.

Radges! Radges with swords! For fuck's sake!

For the moment, they seemed content to indulge in various idiot savant gesticulations. That and barely intelligible threats laced with the keywords 'numpty', 'mother', and 'insert-your-own-expletive-head'. Then there was the occasional twirl of a blade like they'd watched five minutes of *Games of Thrones* and next thing they're thinking they're the Knights of the Round Table (Dennistoun branch).

Someone could get hurt, mind, so time for some police intervention. I grabbed the bottle of Buckfast from the hedgerow, noting that it was just under half empty.

Buckfast was a fortified wine licensed by Buckfast Abbey in Devon, South West England. Sweet and strong, full of caffeine, easy to drink, and—in the jump of a heartbeat—got you as pissed as a rowdy newt. It had long been a favoured drink of the local Neds, fuelling street violence and all kinds of fucked up chicanery. It was a massive social problem.

So much so, a local Member of Parliament travelled all the way to Devon to meet up with Benedictine monks. True story, these were the jokers responsible for the brewing of said diabolical beverage. The MP canvassed the monks passionately, articulately, and compellingly for a reduction in alcohol and caffeine levels.

In response, they gave her the silent treatment.

I ran towards the duelling youths, who were both in their late teens. All the while furtively unscrewing the lid of the bottle, having already decided which one of them would pose the most problem and which one would be putty in my hands. They were sufficiently spaced apart for me to weave in between them. I raised the bottle of Buckie like I was toasting the Pope, or the Queen, or some quasi-hybrid.

'Polis,' I shouted in my best Glasgow Ned patois. 'Drop your weapons, or I'll stick this bottle right up each of your arseholes!'

'Until your fucking pips squeak,' I added, probably unnecessarily.

'There's two of us, ye dafty,' piped up the samurai sword-carrying youth, 'and only wan of those.' To prove his point he struck a Zorro pose, pointing out with the end of his blade the solitary bottle held in my hand. I would have been more impressed by his well-honed detective skills if not for the fact I wanted his tongue served to me in a club sandwich.

The broadsword youth on the other side of me had

lowered his weapon so it hung pendulously between his legs. This was as submissive a posture as it got. It told me *his* bottle had crashed. The only thing stopping him from bolting was the gang mentality; you run out on your mate, word got round, your name was mud. You could then look forward to getting the shit kicked out of you on a daily basis with no end in sight.

'Can you no count, wan, two?' The would-be samurai continued the wiseass banter in a bid to prove his brain cell count approached double figures. To underline the point, because that's what he seemed to like to do, with his spare hand, the prick gave me the finger.

Well fuck that, I thought.

I moved like a panther.

With a forward jerk of my arm, the contents of the bottle went flying out, sticky projectile alcohol hitting the faux-samurai's face.

It leisurely rolled down his cheek. Samurai was taken by surprise but couldn't resist a quick dart of the tongue to taste the sweet liquid. More importantly, one delayed reaction later, he realised that it was in his eyes. He was blinded.

I was on top of him, one hand pinching his wrist, forcing him to drop the sword. My other hand was wrapped around his throat. Squeezing tighter, tighter still.

From under his tracksuit top, I could hear his heart hammering.

Samurai was choking, struggling; then he went quiet, body gone still, no fight left in him, resigned to the fates, and I was fighting the compulsion to bite off the bastard's nose and crush his skull.

Instead, I asked him a question in my best people-hating hiss. 'Where did you get that fucking sword?'

I released my grip; his voice was a rasp against my hiss. I was patient now and happy enough to wait for him to finish pissing himself. 'McMenemy,' the boy samurai said, coughing and wheezing like a fifty-a-day man. 'That's where I got the sword, man.'

His mate helped him to his feet. They made a sorry bedraggled bunch, but they were young, they'd get over it, unfortunately.

Confiscating their weapons, I kicked both of their arses. Broadsword in one hand, samurai sword in the other, I chased the boys down the street.

Point made, I stopped and watched them run for a little while longer, but didn't wait to see them disappear into the sunset. I had bigger fish to fry.

***

Why freeze the lobster beforehand?

It was five in the morning. For many, 5 a.m. in October in Scotland still qualified as a night raid. True to form, it was dark and freezing when we set off. We could have been on the dark side of the moon, except we had an atmosphere, but only just.

I was the only plain-clothes member among six police officers crammed into the back of the van. I surveyed the faces of the squashed uniforms in there with me. Some I knew better than others. The officer who appeared to have forgotten to put on deodorant; we were getting to know him far better than any of us would have liked.

We arrived outside McMenemy's spacious abode in Hamilton. Based on the tip-off volunteered by one of the sword-wielding youths, we had a warrant but didn't have a name for the operation yet. Operation 'Shite-for-Brains' came one suggestion from PC Ferris. Hardly professional, but as quips went, it was good for morale.

The back of the van opened and police macaroni spilled out. I glanced up and down the street, which was empty—no signs of life. The two most gung-ho members of our troupe, carrying a battering ram each side, were already at McMenemy's door. One swing was all it took. With an almighty crash, like God Himself was knocking on the door, the hinges were off. The raiding party assumed single file and marched into the house. As if a demolished door wasn't enough of a calling card, some officers, as way of announcing their arrival, shouted out random nonsense.

On cue, McMenemy, who was in his fifties but had the appearance of a man in his eighties, stood in the hall. Mercifully, he was dressed in his pyjamas. Some of the sights I'd seen on night raids. I am always grateful for a man in his pyjamas.

McMenemy had a resigned expression, like ahead of him he had a week's worth of washing up. I gave him a little nod.

McMenemy knew the drill. It had been hammered into him often enough. As a matter of routine he put his hands out, wrists touching, anticipating the cuffs. McMenemy was well known to us primarily as a small time drug dealer with a big time drug habit of his own, but otherwise a pretty decent guy to talk to. He followed rugby union and no time for football, which made him unique in the West of Scotland criminal fraternity. He was also a massive Rod Stewart fan, which made him less so. His reason for turning to crime was all too common. Compared to the penury of normal life, it was the easy option, until you got caught, and even then ...

PC Evans called me into the living room. The entire room—couch, coffee table, the whole kit and caboodle—was festooned with all kinds of unlicensed weapons. Firearms, swords, daggers, axes, spiked clubs, a tomahawk ...

I even spotted a pair of knitting needles, although for

all I knew McMenemy may have taken up knitting as a hobby. Apparently, over the last couple of years, knitting had seen a marked rise in popularity amongst middle-aged men. Very good for stress, according to an article I'd read in the *Glasgow Herald*.

I was wearing gloves, of course. From the pile on the coffee table, I picked up and examined a sawn-off shotgun. Put it down. Picked up a pair of heavy-duty tongs.

McMenemy was still mooching around the hall. I popped my head around the living room door to talk to him, snapping the tongs together for effect. 'Branching out are we, McMenemy?' I said. 'They do say a change is as good as a rest.'

I didn't wait for a reply. Back in the living room, peeking out from one of the mounds of weapons of mass nastiness, if I wasn't mistaken, was a PS4. Upon closer inspection, wedged in beside it, were some games—the new *FIFA* and *Batman* games, *Red Dead Redemption*, and there could be no mistaking or forgetting *Grandmas v Zombies*. I returned to the hall to speak to McMenemy who was scratching his neck, his hand flapping like an undernourished Labrador's paw.

'Didn't take you for a console games man,' I said to him.

'Uh,' McMenemy said. He was out of sorts already, my last remark only adding to his confusion. Then it came to him with what could have been a jolt. 'Oh, computer games, nah, nah, it's for my nephew. He's three a week on Tuesday.'

'Three,' I said, 'a terrific age. The world is his oyster, so you'd hope.'

It was time to change tack. 'Your nephew, he wouldn't know anything about the Partick Cat now, would he?'

A little intelligence had returned to McMenemy's eyes. But only his eyes. His mouth was at an odd angle, lips pursed tightly, and he may very well have been biting the tip of his tongue.

You spend enough time in their company, you find everyone guilty of one thing or the other, eventually.

'No, wait, my apologies,' I said, 'what I meant to say was *you*. You wouldn't know anything about the Partick Cat, now would you?'

There was a shout from the back garden. The other officers falling over themselves to answer the call. I, on the other hand, was not for budging and neither was McMenemy.

I was struggling for breath. It was a stress thing. I knew the air was there, all around me, but there was a barrier between me and it.

McMenemy's eyes bulged, while there were stars in mine.

Truth be said, I was feeling a little unsteady. A change was coming over me.

***

The freezing cold stuns the lobster, putting it into a near-comatose state. This makes for a more humane way of cooking it. Quicker yet would be to stab the lobster in the head, right behind the eyes.

It was official, McMenemy and I were the only fuckers left in the house.

My fellow officers were congregated on the back lawn. Parked there, if I heard the cacophony of noise right, was a full-sized replica WWII two-ton German tank SDKFZ 222 'Helga'. (And if I hadn't heard right, I would find out about it later back at the station.) Trust me, that type of thing could fetch an estimated five grand at auction under the Proceeds of Crime Act.

This, if you're into that sort of thing, was a steal. You

could pick up all kinds of bargain-basement giveaways at the shopping experience that was the Proceeds of Crime Act. It wasn't unknown for various members of the criminal fraternity to throw their hat into the ring and take a punt.

No, it was just me and the manky, junkie, pyjama-wearing, Rod Stewart-loving, born-again weapons dealer. For some fucked up reason, I started appraising his pyjamas. A wicked combo of thick brown and thin blue stripes. 'Such sartorial elegance, McMenemy,' I said. 'Still beating off the young beauties with a shitty stick?'

The dick actually opened his mouth, about to begin the process of polluting the air with some ill-thought out quip no doubt, just begging for a smack in the fizzer. But self-preservation prevailed and not a peep came out of him. It was time, I decided, to raise the ante. 'The Partick Cat,' I hissed. 'I won't say it a fourth time.'

McMenemy's face was chalk-white. Twitchy. He was staring down the (sawn-off) barrel of the gun of a lengthy jail sentence, but that wasn't what was bothering him right now.

'Don't know him personally,' he said. 'He's a friend of a friend of a friend, if you know what I mean.'

'I don't have a scooby what you fucking mean,' I said, 'and if I was to confess to anything, it's that I'm bored with this conversation to the point of losing my mind, or lapsing into a coma, or bashing your face in with a sizeable chunk of concrete—all just to keep me from dozing off.' I flashed a tiny smile, the type to reassure people that I was not joking. 'Capish?'

'Try Pete's Plaice, the chippy, they know him there,' McMenemy said, gulping erratically; his Adam's apple doing somersaults.

Hollers and whoops came from the back lawn. Some of the mad bastards out there had climbed into the tank.

I stepped forward, put the cuffs on McMenemy, and then kneed him in the balls.

McMenemy dropped down to the floor, whimpering and in a flood of tears. A strange looking drool leaked from his mouth as he waited, impatiently I bet, for the explosion in his groin to subside.

I crouched down towards him. I got in close, so there was no mistaking on his part what I had to say. 'Stay there, don't move, someone will come for you in around ten minutes.'

At this, hollering and riotous laughter emanated from the back lawn. 'Make that half an hour,' I said.

I left them all to it and took my exit through the remnants of what had been the front door.

I was out and walking at a fair pace down the street. I knew of Pete's Plaice, the 'chippy' in question, or fish and chip shop to give it its full title. Pete's Plaice, so the boast went, purveyors of the best deep fried white pudding this side of the Western hemisphere. Although let's face it, if it wasn't bolted down these guys would happily deep-fry it.

Interrupting my train of thought, I was aware of a wasp buzzing near my right ear. Wasps. Fucking vicious, ugly, narky bastards. No choice but to get out of their way. You couldn't reason with them. My kind of creature.

Walking towards me, pushing a pram, was a female in her early twenties. As she passed, I saw a little baby's head and fingers poking out from the blanket and was gripped by the notion that there must be some Class A drugs stashed away in the pram somewhere. I did my best to shrug off the feeling. It wasn't easy.

Meanwhile, the wasp had flown away. All told, it was lucky for mother, child, and flying insect that I was in a hurry.

I continued walking. For want of a better way to spice

up the inner workings of the mind, as way of variety, I thought of a shoplifter I'd nicked a month back. Alive and well as far as I was aware, but in the quiet moments, that didn't stop me imagining his rotting body lying in a shallow grave, cockroaches making a new home of his skin. Everything about him was dead and decayed, except for the eyes, eyelids still flickering, still somehow alive ...

I wanted to exhale then take in a lungful of air, but something compelling inside stopped me. An aversion to anything fresh.

I bit deep into my knuckles. I drew blood. It was all I could do to stop screaming and calling everyone and everything around me every dirty unclean whore bastard name under the sun.

It was the job. It was the job that got to you every time. There wasn't anything I could do about that. So I composed myself and held it together, because the job right now was taking me to a fish and chip establishment called Pete's Plaice.

***

Why do lobsters scream?

I played a mental game. In my mind I went through the six types of carpet—loop carpet, cut and loop carpet, Saxony, cable carpet, plush and velvet carpet—brain fully exercised as it imagined each of them vividly, jumping from one to another. And then I was calm. You could say I was feeling like a different person.

A young couple, same sex, hand in hand, walked past me and I flashed them a huge, wide, pearly-white smile. I swore I could feel my eyes twinkling in their sockets. Sometimes, feeling good about yourself caught you unawares, but the onus had to fall on you, and you alone, to embrace it all the same. A blooming flower. A baby smiling. A giant panda chomping on bamboo. In such a splendid frame of mind, I entered Pete's Plaice.

Straight off, the pungent smell of grease and vinegar hit me, strong enough to strip paint and torch lungs. An assault on the olfactory system, there's nothing like walking into a chippy. It's like another country.

A girl barely in her teens was in charge of the fryer. Sliced potato sizzled loudly in the burning fat; a collection of thunderclaps; the noise I guessed acid rain must sound like. I was in her line of sight.

'What you havin'?' she said.

'Oh,' I said, giving it a few seconds thought, 'a portion of your best chips, please, to sit in.' I made a face; big hungry eyes. If I was capable of thirsty eyes, that would have come next. 'And a cup of tea, please.'

There were some tables in an adjoining room, so I took my fried booty and ambled through the open archway and sat in the far corner. My new vantage point gave me a reasonably good view of the counter/food frying area.

I was completely relaxed when I noticed my plate hadn't been cleaned properly.

There was some congealed black pudding on the edge, a remnant of an earlier meal, and I hated the idea of black pudding. I'm no vegetarian, but the idea of pig's blood—a vital ingredient, it makes the pudding black—made me uncomfortable.

Adding to my consternation, the tea was served in a Styrofoam cup. I took a sip and visibly bristled at the polystyrene aftertaste.

Still, I consoled myself, that was the 'Greasy Joe' experience for you. In any case, it was the grease that kept the building, walls and all, from falling over. I sat and noiselessly ate a couple of chips from my plate, against my better judgement using the cutlery provided. The chips were a gamut of taste and texture sensations, chiefly of the chalky, hard-edged and mushy-in-the middle variety.

There was only one other person in the seating area; a gentleman in his late fifties, thinning hair, white-speckled beard, particularly thick about the chin area. He scooped up some fried egg and in an instant, like a mongoose, fired it into his mouth. It was an egg fried to the point of no return, or at the very least to the point of incredibly chewy. The man masticated for dear life and I feared it would take more than incisors and saliva to break down that particular beast. A warped version of a Bob Dylan song suddenly popped into my head, '*A hard yolk's a-gonna fall.*'

My phone rang. I answered and, if the scent of the chippy hadn't inflicted sufficient damage to my senses, my ears were assaulted by the other end of the line, courtesy of a bombastic PC Ferris. 'Detective Inspector Fisher, sir,' he yelled, 'you're missing the party!'

In the background, each of the raiding party was screeching, trying to drown out everyone else. I just knew those jokers were still on the back lawn, like a monkeys' tea party, clambering in and out of that tank. I swear I could hear the uncorking of a champagne bottle.

I glanced at the other man in the seated area of Pete's Plaice and noted his intensity of chewing had not let up. I decided I couldn't allow the hullabaloo over the phone, which threatened to burst my eardrum, to continue.

'I'm sorry, eating chips, can't talk right now,' I said firmly but quietly before ending the call.

And not a millisecond too soon, I spied through the archway, having just walked in, a man in his mid-thirties wearing a leather jacket, sleeves rolled up to the elbows. He strode with purpose, a swagger no less, shaking jazz hands as way of greeting towards the young lady behind the counter.

She lifted the counter hatch and through he sauntered. The man in a leather jacket headed towards the door leading to the back, which I'd clocked on arrival, but from my present vantage point, could no longer see.

I thought, should I stay put or make a move? Absentmindedly I tossed another chip into my mouth. I swallowed instantaneously. Too late, I hadn't realised how crispy, jagged and pointed it was. It was a foreign object. Next thing I knew, there was a cruel, sharp, barbed pain in my throat, showing no signs of letting up. My hand, cradling, protective, was up at my throat, massaging, but no matter, I was choking.

Choking to death—or so it seemed—on a chip.

***

Lobsters can't scream as they don't have vocal chords. The sound you hear instead is of steam escaping from its shell. It's like the noise the air out of a football makes when deflating.

A chip! Stuck in my throat! For fuck's sake! Well, not today!

I ground my teeth, ground down my whole body. Images in my head. A rent boy self-harming. The head of a German shepherd wrapped in cling film and kept in a freezer.

I swallowed like I'd never swallowed before. As way of protest, the jagged edges of the fried projectile sliced and ripped, but however defiantly, went down like a captain with his ship. I was winning! A few excruciating moments later, the psycho-chip was clear of my throat and at the mercy of my stomach acid. Result!

Plate in hand, I was on my feet. A man's relentless chewing the only background noise as I headed through the archway.

At the sight of me, the eyes of the girl behind the

counter widened. She worked in a Glasgow chippy, so surely had seen far worse. I didn't say a word, but rather pointed out the black pudding blemish on my plate. She shrugged and assumed a blank expression, which appeared to come naturally to her.

Both of us seemed reluctant to speak. We were in some kind of chip shop stand-off. Then I flashed my badge and in a heartbeat she opened the till, presumably to give me a refund.

I was a DI on a mission, so I lifted the counter hatch and walked to the door at the back. I had no idea if the girl was watching me do this, but she gave out no cries of warning. It would be a surprise if she was still there when I got back.

I tried the back door, which was locked. That is, up until the point I employed my trusty size tens to kick it in.

Once inside, I ascertained the lights were out, but at least the broken back door behind me let in some light. At the back of the room stood two sturdy tables bedecked with treasures—granny's best jewellery, various laptops and tablets, gaming systems, power tools, wallets and purses. Tied to a table leg was a Pekingese, wearing a shiny collar. The toy dog's squashed pooch face, carrying with it an air of resignation, did not seem out of place.

The common denominator attached to each item was a retail value of one hundred and fifty pounds and over. It looked like I'd interrupted a fucking stocktake.

Suddenly there was movement from the corner. Christ, this guy was quick, light on his feet—just like a Partick Cat!

Before I could react, a Terramundi Money Pot came crashing down on the back of my head. The Terramundi cracked open, releasing about five hundred pounds worth of two-pound coins. It felt like I was hit by a bastard cannonball.

The back of my head erupted. I was down on one knee, fighting the wooziness, for a second there trying not to blackout. From around my ears, blood dripped in slow motion.

Still, through the pain, I was aware of the sound of footsteps, however muffled, shuffling away.

So what was a fucking DI to do? I gritted my teeth and straightened my buckled legs. Twisting and grinding my hips, I hunched my body, and with a fearful amount of effort propelled myself forward. Quasimodo-style, I bounded after the Terramundi-Pot-back-stabbing irredeemable bastard.

I was hobbling, but I was moving. I exited Pete's Plaice. I looked around. I looked up. What I saw was the Partick Cat making his getaway, climbing up a drainpipe.

I blinked twice to clear my head. I flexed my fingers like I was a fucking pianist, knuckles in unison making a satisfying crack.

I started climbing the drainpipe, too. I was in goddamned pursuit.

As I scuttled up, it wasn't long before the weight, so brought to bear, caused the brackets to loosen perilously. Time moved in instalments and before I knew it ...

There was a God Almighty creak as pursued and pursuer combined brought the drainpipe down.

Me and the Partick Cat came down with it, except he was near the top and I was the size of a fat man's arse from the bottom.

It was a matter of a few feet, but even with less of a fall, my sick, embittered body felt the impact. It was like I was wrapped in barbed wire bubble wrap.

Still, you should have seen the other guy.

I dragged myself up and staggered forward. The Cat

was not moving. His head was gashed; face smashed; body disjointed and spread out in funny looking angles. He would live, but it would be painful. There seemed little point in beating him up.

And now I had a closer look at him, yep, I could confirm, nice jacket. The sleeves-rolled-up-to-the-elbows look did him no favours, though.

A groan slowly emerged from him. His eyes fluttered open, allowing us minimal eye contact before they closed tight again. This close, you could see crow's feet, spread around his eyes like weeds on a path, giving me cause to adjust estimated age from mid-thirties to early forties.

'What gave me away?' he croaked.

There was pain and sweet, bitter disappointment in his voice; a need to know. There was anguish. For me, over and above the satisfaction of having captured the bellend, of course, this was the icing on the cake.

I crouched, I leaned, so he could hear my whispered snarl all the clearer.

'A *Batman* game, a *FIFA* game, what else, *Red Dead Redemption*, and ...' My lips slapped noisily together '... fucking *Grandmas v Zombies*!'

As an afterthought, I suddenly regretted not putting red sauce on my chips back at Pete's Plaice.

I decided to go home and make up for this by boiling alive a lobster. That and buying a PS4. (I'd need to check whether I could order both online.)

4.

Mrs MacPhellimey

I woke up sore and stiff. At least this time it was a bed that I was waking up in and not some bare, soiled mattress. Not a garden hedge, either.

As an added bonus, it was my own bed. I felt like I had not only won the lottery, but put all my winnings on a five thousand to one winning ticket for an unfashionable football team to finish top of the Premier League.

Over the last few days there had been developments. All sorts of lines were being drawn. The 'T's were getting gigantic crosses and the 'I's even bigger dots. I'd always been a loner and it's not as if anyone was questioning fundamentally the quality of my police work.

And yet, there was talk. Talk of being assigned a partner. Talk of a date being finalised with the police psychologist. Talk of me being called to a hearing over my conduct on a recent case (which ended messily, I would be the first to admit). If someone were to sit down and review all of these developments together, then surely I'd come up as a bad stat—a source of concern.

Did I have a favourite, and appropriately obtuse, way

of describing the police force? You know the Lernaean Hydra, mythical beast of Ancient Greece, where you would cut off its head and in its place two would grow back, and so on? Well, with the police, it was the opposite. You sliced off two and only one came back. That would do it.

So I crawled out of bed, had a shower, skipped a shave, and got dressed. Then, I did what came naturally to me. I followed my chosen vocation.

I investigated my next case.

Such conviction took me to the sometimes leafy suburb of Bishopbriggs, where I stood in front of a detached two-storey house. If I could have described the scene, it was on the same lines as the priest standing outside a building in the movie poster for *The Exorcist*.

The weather was just like any other day in Glasgow. Overcast. Black foreboding clouds choked the sky.

I knocked on the door and ten seconds later, a lady nudging her seventies with a mushroom cloud for hair, opened the door. Her name was Mrs MacPhellimey.

Mrs MacPhellimey was sprightly on her feet, especially nimble for a near-septuagenarian, and before I knew it, I was ushered into the living room and waiting armchair. You could hear the springs creak every time you shifted in the chair, but good lord it was comfy.

Comfy, wasn't that the perfect word? And what better way to describe comfy than by using the word comfy itself?

As I re-ran the 'c-word' in my mind, before finally letting it go, Mrs MacPhellimey alighted to the kitchen. She returned with a tray carrying a teapot, milk jug, sugar bowl, and two tea cups. She placed the tray down on the coffee table and poured me a cup, careful not to add too much milk. Using petite sugar tongs, and demonstrating great dexterity, she lifted a sugar lump, popping it with a flourish into my cup, so creating the most satisfying 'plop' I had heard in quite some time.

'Ah, Nirvana,' I said, purring with appreciation. I took a sip. The tea flowed down my throat and wrapped me in a fuzzy, weather resistant fleece. 'Really warms the cockles of your heart.'

'More tea, Inspector?' Mrs MacPhellimey said.

Up until this point, I'd only had a sip. I thought furiously for something to say.

'Brian ...' I said. 'Please, call me Brian.' I introduced a pause to proceedings, hoping to reinforce the sincerity of the request, before caving in, adding, 'Yes, yes please, I don't mind if I do.'

I visibly gushed, watching on as Mrs MacPhellimey took full charge of the teapot and, leaning slightly forward, oozing elegance out of every pore, 'poured' a drop of tea into my cup.

Not only was the teapot just the quaintest thing, but our teacups rested on flower-shaped lace doilies. It was like the coffee table had commandeered a time machine and transported itself back to the 1950s. While taking in the sweet majesty that was Mrs MacPhellimey and her post-war splendour, I couldn't help but detect more than a hint of a glint in the old lady's eyes.

From the side pocket of my suit jacket, I took out a small constabulary notebook. I knew e-notebooks were all the rage these days (personally, I blame *CSI*) but I was a traditionalist at heart. In the presence of a time-travelling coffee table, anything else would have been a gross aberration anyway. Held in my other hand, a small pen was at the ready, poised to scribble down if not actual nuggets, then certainly gold dust.

I was sitting at one end of the coffee table and Mrs MacPhellimey sat at an angle from me on the couch. She clasped her hands in what you'd best describe as an adorable picture of concentration. But duty not only called, it intruded. It was time to start the ball rolling.

I made statements of fact, followed by a question. 'You phoned the police and reported that your husband of fifty years was missing.' I looked down at my notes. 'One Ernest MacPhellimey. When was the last time you saw your husband?'

'Two weeks ago,' she said.

I was about to ask another question when Mrs MacPhellimey pressed cradled hands against her chest. I reacted instinctively, my first thought to go to her aid, the majority of my person already having left the chair. Mrs MacPhellimey, though, motioned with fluttering hands for me to sit back down.

'I'm perfectly well,' she said. 'It's just Ernie—that was his name, you see—he was such a devoted husband. There was nothing—*nothing*—he wouldn't do for me.'

Mrs MacPhellimey took a long rasping breath. I waited for her to continue her statement, but she seemed to be drawing out the moment. It might seem odd to some that she was describing her husband in the past tense. But, if you were to ask me, when you attained a certain age, you earned the right to use whatever tense you liked and yaboo-sucks to any impudent naysayer who would claim otherwise.

'Yes, two weeks,' she said, eventually. 'And I don't know how I've coped without him. He's the one up in the middle of the night to switch off the electric blanket.'

'Electric blanket,' I said, while writing the words down on my notebook. 'Mmm hmm, you don't want it on all night. Gets all stuffy and uncomfortable.'

'To the point of insufferable,' I added with what I hoped was appropriate levels of gusto.

Quickly, Mrs MacPhellimey was up on her feet. It was as if the springs in her couch had ejected her like one of those James Bond characters, usually a villain, unfortunate enough to find him or herself sitting on the front passenger seat of 007's car.

She vanished back into the kitchen. Some clattering, banging, a couple of bumps, and a single taking of the Lord's name in vain later, she appeared with a two-tiered silver-finished cake trolley. Mrs MacPhellimey pushed the trolley, which glided along on little wheels. She was headed in my direction. Doggedly. Silently. Not a squeak. I doubt anything on God's earth could divert her from her chosen path. All that was missing was the theme music to the movie *Jaws*.

The lower tier of the trolley contained a mixture of fruit scones and little cream cakes. Occupying the top tier was a big round Black Forest gateau, which took up every millimetre of an unfeasibly large serving platter. To get from one side of the gateau to the other, you'd need to go through passport control. Such was its girth, my eyes almost popped out of my head, a reconstruction of Wile E. Coyote's first sighting of the Road Runner.

'Now, you look like a young man in need of a feed,' Mrs MacPhellimey said. 'Cake?'

I shifted in my chair. I sat on my hands. I wasn't sure where to look. 'Ah, no thank you,' I said. 'A small to medium-sized scone will do me, if you have one.'

I was trying to watch my weight, conscious of having put on a few pounds, it was something of a personal mission statement. With such an offering of larger than life gateau, I feared, Mrs MacPhellimey had already made good her shot across the bows of the good ship DI Brian Fisher. Any pretence of a small to medium-sized scone had long faded. If it was a battle of wills, and I would hope it was not, then she was surely winning.

'If I may, I'd like to take a look around the house,' I said.

Perhaps a tad presumptuously, my arms reached out to

take hold of either arm of the chair and I began slowly to raise myself up, only for Mrs MacPhellimey to dart and jink past the trolley and around the coffee table, hunching forward to face me at close quarters. I hovered, bum cheeks clenched, frozen in the moment, so close to the off-cream seat cushion positioned just below me, and yet so far. It was like an interrogation.

She eyeballed me, hinting at a ferocious intensity. It seemed to me that there was a great deal of toughness to be found behind that seemingly sweet exterior of hers.

'For what?' she said.

I was nonplussed. She was giving me the first degree. I had to remind myself that first and foremost I was a police detective. That this was what all the years of training, all the experience amassed on the job, all the hard work was for.

'Umm, eh, ah, ooft ...' I said, before editing in my mind for articulacy. 'For clues,' I said, finally.

At this point, there was real concern that this would be the day I finally saw someone's head detonate. The shape of Mrs MacPhellimey's mushroom cloud hair only added to the suspense. Her body, every part of her, shook like a slowed-down pneumatic drill.

'You don't mind, do you?' I said this while fully acknowledging in my own mind that in all probability the clear opposite was the case.

She returned her hands to her chest, but this time, miraculously, the action accompanied the sweetest and lightest of expressions. In the time it took to flick a switch, she had gone from outraged berserker to calmness personified.

Mrs MacPhellimey was an angel again.

'Of course I don't, my dear,' she said. She smiled and from this I could see her antediluvian dimples. 'While you're at it, give the place a root around. You couldn't possibly give me a valuation for the house? You don't mind do you?' she said.

A half-chuckle emanated from her throat. Her smile revealed a set of teeth a little too large for her mouth. 'Far too spacious for one person and I've been thinking of selling,' she said.

I slinked off to the kitchen area. Unsurprisingly, given Mrs MacPhellimey's already well-established MO, the kitchen wasn't the most modern I'd seen. Still, it oozed charm. That and some off-brown mahogany.

'I'm a Detective Inspector, ma'am,' I shouted back in the direction of the living room. 'Not a property surveyor, but I'd say ...'

How could I deny her, especially as she'd used my own words against me? I peered out of the kitchen window, which gave me a clear view of the back garden. Tall fencing, I noted. Obviously these were people who enjoyed their privacy.

Prominent on the lawn was a large mound of recently dug dirt. Either the MacPhellimey household was being visited by giant moles, or there was some other perhaps more plausible explanation? The mound followed a slight diagonal; was longer than your usual garden heap; say top to bottom around six feet in length.

'A hundred grand, easy,' I said.

Having given serious thought to a price for the property, I'd taken into account as way of bonus the '50s charm of the decor, but discounted the potentially troublesome prospect of having oversized moles in one's backyard.

Returning to the living room, I found it devoid of human presence. (Perhaps, there was the odd ghost floating around.)

'In the loo!' The voice of Mrs MacPhellimey wafted down from the top of the stairs, situated in the hallway.

'Won't be a tick!'

As I stood there, I let out a long involuntary sigh. I was alone, but wasn't quite alone. My head dropped and all of a sudden my sights tracked and centred on the cake trolley. I took it in—in its most exquisite and savage form—the impossibly large chocolate cream and fruit gateau.

Moments passed. Time enough for the grabbing and tearing and munching. I heard the soft scrape of slipper on carpet descending the stairs, but this didn't seem to matter. I buried my face into the rich, spongy, sweet mush.

Mrs MacPhellimey returned to the living room to find me on my knees, head bent down like a pig in a trough. All that was left of the monster cake was a line of crumbs, a pathway which led directly to me. I had red in my eyes, like I'd spent too long bathing in a swimming pool, that classic cocktail of chlorine and urine.

I had filled out my suit, but in this instance with good reason. Like a wiper blade on the windscreen that was my mouth, my tongue removed the remaining gateau-induced debris from my gums.

'Inspector, are you all right?' Mrs MacPhellimey said.

She sounded genuinely concerned, and not just because there was cake lodged up my nostrils.

I'd let my guard down only for a second, but sometimes that was enough. The sin of gluttony had come a-calling, but whatever elemental compulsion had possessed me to eat a monster gateau whole, it was gone now.

I shuffled my knees along living room carpet, until now facing Mrs MacPhellimey.

I held out my hands to my sides as way of apology, only to notice that they too were coated in fragments of cake. It was messy. It was impossible to hide the evidence incriminating me as a top trolley gateau thief, so

I decided to come clean and make reparations for my crime.

'I'll do the dishes,' I said.

***

Twenty minutes later, face still flushed with embarrassment, I left the house.

Upon leaving, I assured Mrs MacPhellimey that the police would leave no stone unturned in the search for her missing husband.

As I walked down the front garden path, right on cue, walking up it was a plain-clothes officer I recognised as Detective Sergeant Julie Spencer. My instincts told me that this was no ships-passing-in-the-morning-noon-or-night incident. No, this had the feeling of something more permanent. It was all about possessing insight, the intuitive powers of a detective. This, and the fact I'd read my e-mails that morning.

'Sir,' she said, 'I'm DS Spencer.'

She was five-foot-eight. She had straight hair, which ended roughly halfway between ears and shoulders. Blue eyes. Early thirties. Was she attractive? I don't know. On such matters, I never professed to have much of a clue. Not that it mattered. I'm not a Neanderthal. That was clearly below the standards expected of my profession; I had no idea why I'd even thought of it.

'We've been assigned together, sir,' she said. 'As a team,' she added unnecessarily. (She was police. Adding unnecessarily, even from time to time, is what we do.)

I pursed my lips. It felt like there was an anvil sitting in my stomach. An anvil that consisted solely of sickly mush. Inexplicably, for a second, I worried if it would spread through my body like some rapacious, grungy Black Forest fungus.

'First thing you can do, DS,' I said, 'is enter this house.' I swivelled on my heels and pointed out the building I'd just that minute vacated.

'Caution the occupant,' I continued, 'one Mrs MacPhellimey, and arrange for a warrant to dig up her back garden. I strongly suspect you'll find her husband buried there, deceased, previously reported missing.'

'She may have had accomplices. Help to dig the grave. But I doubt it.'

DS Spencer said nothing, but the clear and present danger was if I stood there long enough, she'd eventually think of something to say. I handed her my notebook, total content: two words: 'electric' and 'blanket'.

With that, in stark defiance of my bloated belly, I bounced and resumed my journey down the path and onwards towards my parked car.

5.

UI

I knew the drill. I wasn't some police cadet, a funny colour of green around the gills. DS Spencer would catch up with me soon enough. At some point, sooner rather than later, we'd have to investigate a case together. We'd have to share the same car. Maybe, in the more quiet moments, we could work together on the same crossword. But for the time being, I was giving her little errands to follow up on, like, for want of a better example, closing the MacPhellimey case.

I asked her to visit a school as part of a community policing initiative to educate young impressionable minds that a knife, chib, or hammer wasn't ideally the best way to settle an argument.

I asked her to follow up on a particular brand of ladies' tights worn over the faces of the perpetrators of a recent post office heist. (I would have been the first to put my hand up to any sexist charge, but this just happened to be the thing that came up at this particular time. For the record I had no issue whatsoever with myself, if it came to it, investigating ladies' tights.)

I asked her to accompany a dog catcher and muck in where dangerous dogs were concerned. She protested she was more of a cat person and, I have to admit, I sympathised, before sending her out regardless.

I wanted her out of the way, if only in the meantime. I had some odds and ends I needed to work out on my own. For a start, I was currently UI—currently 'Under Investigation'.

To help with enquiries, the one concerning myself, I found my way back to the station—the one I call my own, Helen Street in Govan. Although, not to a part of the building I was familiar with. Helen Street was built to hold petty criminals, homicidal maniacs, terrorists and, it would appear, police officers.

I stood at the door bearing the sign 'Anti-Corruption Unit'. The room itself was situated in an otherwise isolated area on the first floor. I was as aware of the stories as much as anyone. The parable in action that was ACU.

If, for whatever reason, you had cause to walk by, you could feel cold icy air waft out from under the door, no matter the state of the weather outside. You could, that is, right up until the point they fitted a draft excluder.

And here I was, taking a deep breath, putting my hand on the door handle, another deep breath, pushing down with my hand, another deep breath, pulling the door towards me, another deep breath, mentally preparing to walk through.

Let's do this, I was thinking furiously, to coincide with another deep breath ...

I entered the room and was confronted by three Wise Men. First impression as I closed the door carefully behind me was that the room itself was surprisingly cramped. In the middle of the floor, an empty hard-backed wooden chair, there for the entire world to see, detached and unloved, even in a confined space such as this. Not that the world would ever have cause to see it, that is. This chair was for certain eyes only.

Three pairs of eyes to be exact. Dominating proceedings, on the far side of the room, was a long, broad table with its trio of occupants.

I sat on the chair. I glanced up, moving quick-fire from one Wise Man to another. Rat-tat-tat. One was in his forties, the other two in their fifties. None of them would ever see a full head of hair again. But further comment would signal overindulgence on my part. As far as I was concerned, I was in a room with, left to right, Wise Man 1, Wise Man 2 and Wise Man 3.

Wise Man 2 opened the folder and, in a pique of concentration, scanned the top page. As he read, he mouthed some of the words. Finally finished, peering at his wristwatch, he blinked furiously.

'Thank you for attending, Detective Inspector,' he said. 'And on time, too. We don't usually get that.'

'Happy, sirs, to help with any and all lines of enquiry,' I said. My hands gripped the sides of the seat. My thumbs followed the grooves in the wood.

The focus changed to Wise Man 1, who at least took the trouble of leafing through the contents of his folder.

'Appreciated, Detective Inspector, everything is appreciated,' Wise Man 1 said. 'You are of course aware of the serious allegations made against you. The validity of which may not only mean dismissal from the force, but could very well result in criminal prosecution.'

If any or both of these happened, it was only a matter of time, I supposed. Still, you could prepare for the hangman's noose as much as you could, but it would never be enough; you could never properly prepare for the real thing. I'd been called to this internal hearing, small and perfectly formed as it was, for an entirely different case, but I now found myself wondering if news had filtered through of the events of Interview Room 3 from several days ago and the unfortunate incident involving a missing earlobe.

It was Wise Man 3's turn to speak. 'You are here, Fisher, to allow us to establish the facts. That is the primary concern of a meeting such as this. It could very well be when you walk out of that door, I'm hoping in no more than forty-five minutes, we may never have cause to meet again.'

'At least not professionally,' Wise Man 1 said, leaning back to the point his chair was tipping. He did so in order to take Wise Man 2 out of his sights and give Wise Man 3 the full benefit of an arched eyebrow.

I released my grip of the chair. I could feel myself relax a little. Whoever these men were, one thing was sure, they were an absolute riot.

Wise Man 3 had a resigned expression on his face. Wise Man 1's face lit up like he was a boy who had unexpectedly been put in charge of the sweetie shop.

Wise Man 3 sat forward, hands clasped. He enunciated his words carefully. 'Perhaps you could give us your version, Fisher, of the events of eight Wednesdays ago?' he said.

'Oh,' he suddenly continued, 'we believe you have a reputation to witter, to go on and on, but "*in your own words*", alas, means exactly that.'

From the top table came three successive sighs. It was the sound a clock would make if designed to exhale rather than tick.

'So just describe things as you see fit to describe them.'

Eight Wednesdays ago could, under normal circumstances, be as vague and non-specific a term as it first appeared, but I knew exactly what incident he was referring to. And I was thinking maybe news of the 'ear incident' hadn't reached them?

No exceptions, maybe everyone in the station had left it to someone else to inform someone in the know—that 'know' being the three Wise Men. Or maybe they were holding this particular ace up their sleeves, set to transpire over the next forty-five minutes, waiting for the moment when I was on the ropes and ready for the killer punch? Or maybe news had reached them and they didn't care, or considered it irrelevant to the case at hand? Or maybe they were waiting for me to come clean myself, and the longer I avoided doing so, the longer their faces would go as way of expressing their extreme disappointment? So much supposition; it was the road to madness, of endless sleepless nights, and I'd had enough of those already. Maybe I should just let the hearing play itself out, see it through to its natural or unnatural end and save the endless speculation for then? Maybe ...?

I'd been speculating internally in real time. I realised that too great an interval had elapsed and there was now the very real danger we'd ventured into 'uneasy silence' territory.

'Where should I start?' I said.

'From the beginning,' Wise Man 3 said.

If that's what they wanted, well who was I to argue. I angled my head a little upwards and to the side. I had a wistful, faraway expression. I took a long breath and allowed the oxygen to permeate my brain.

'The working day in question began,' I said, 'when I was called out to a nuclear submarine based at Faslane Naval Base.'

How cold it was that morning, or so I recalled. The sun shone as bright as it could, but it seemed so distant, so far away. It was important, I thought, to set the scene as best I could.

'I approached the base, which as you'd expect was heavily fenced off. Outside, there were tents. There were placard-waving protestors, a hotpotch of Greens, CND; all the usual 'anti-establishment/pro-anything-that-says-it's-not-the-establishment' groups.

Lots of 'V' masks. There were kids that should have been at school.'

'Security was expecting me, so I was waved through and given directions to one of the docked submarines. There, I was greeted by a civilian dressed in pale green overalls, holding an upside down mop in his hand.'

Wise Man 2 raised his hand like he was stopping traffic. 'I've been waiting for this bit,' he said. 'It does say 'man with an upside-down mop' in your official report, but I wasn't sure if this was a typo?'

The two other Wise Men looked questioningly at Wise Man 2.

'A man with an upside-down *map*, for example,' Wise Man 2 said. More convinced by this response than I would have thought they should have been, the men nodded in unison before returning their collective gaze to me.

'A mop,' I said.

Wise Man 2 picked up his pen to make a correction on his notes of a correction, which, as it turned out, was incorrect. The voices had lost their novelty. It seemed a waste of energy to try and distinguish who was speaking; to focus on anything but the words. On raising my head, all I could make out was an amorphous blob. A dark, formless shape with noses and eyes that occasionally poked out. This for me was what the three Wise Men had quickly become.

'So where in all of this were the Ministry of Defence police?' a voice said.

'I asked the man with the mop—a Mr Souter—the very same thing,' I answered. "Vamoosed," he said.'

'He informed me that as soon as the MOD police see

a fourteen-year-old in a 'V' mask, they get skittish. They take off in packs.'

'Really, Detective Inspector Fisher?'

'Really,' I said. 'They obviously didn't consider the ongoing situation to be a security risk. There was a civilian worker inside the sub banging on the submarine walls and generally making a nuisance of himself. The submarine at the time wasn't armed with nuclear weapons—at least I assumed it wasn't. So I'm thinking the MOD police had made a conscious decision to leave the matter to a civilian counterpart.'

'I should add,' I said, 'I did wait for several minutes for anyone remotely official to turn up. By then, even the guy with the mop had made his excuses and left.'

'Most irregular. You couldn't make it up. A nuisance, you say?'

'That was what I was told, sir,' I said. 'That and the fact the worker in the sub was a painter and decorator by trade, contracted to do what painters and decorators do best.'

In the back of my mind, there was the inescapable conclusion, going round in circles, patterns, recurring themes; the pointlessness of existence when faced with the full futility of fate. How many painters and decorators in the world? How many?

'One can only assume,' a voice went, bringing me back to reality, with a dryness that, appropriately enough, could crack paint.

I continued as effortlessly neutral as before, at least on the outside.

'I found, though, having moved through the cramped corridors of the sub, using his incessant banging as my guide, that this painter and decorator was also an arsonist. He had set fire to the sub. Taking cover behind an open metal hatch, he was about five-foot-six, pot-bellied, short curly hair turned white too soon, eyes maybe a little too close together. I could see in his hand, muzzle perched at the door, a WWII Luger. I later found out his name was Francis Telfer. He was clearly agitated.'

'Painter ...?'

'Yes, painter. Short for painter and decorator.'

'Ah, I see, please go on.'

'He shouted at me not to take another step. A lit cigarette was stuck to his bottom lip, an obvious no-no considering his surroundings.'

'Smoke was beginning to fill the corridor, it was a slow creep, originating from a room in between the pair of us. That's where his flammable painting materials were. That's where the fire was.'

'En route, I'd picked up a fire extinguisher. So I said, "Maybe one more step?" And from there, things just escalated.'

'Francis popped out from behind the door, aiming the gun at me, screeching at the top of his voice; his vocal chords must have been stretched to the limit. Even so, he did agree to my request.'

I could have gone into more detail. What he screamed at me was something on the lines of, 'OK, Christ God feck, just one more step then!' His voice reached such a high pitch, I was sure dogs would be writhing in agony for miles around, blood pouring out of their ears.

'Of course, I needed to attend to the room on fire ...'

There were so many specifics in my head. More than the Wise Men needed to hear. How I took a deep breath and turned the wheel to open the hatch. I was greeted by a wall of heat and billowing smoke. I could feel my eyebrows singe. The flames congregated in the corner, like a pack of wild animals, fiercely protective of territory held, and hungry, always hungry to take over more. If I'd arrived any later, it might have been too late to contain the fire. But I hadn't, so I released the contents of the fire extinguisher. The foam descended on the flames like teenage fans heading in the direction of the latest teen pop sensation, before smothering the life out of it.

'... Because of my actions, the fire was quickly under control.'

'As for Francis Telfer, if you ask me, I'd say he was stir-crazy and had been for a while. Apparently, he'd kept the WWII Luger—handed down by his late grandfather, who had fought in the war—in an empty paint tin.'

I noted movement from the corner of my eye. Wise Men moving as one; like a single shape; like smoke without fire. The middle head dipped sharply like a bouncing ball, staring at his notes intently and questioningly. His mouth was moving as well.

'Wait a minute,' he said, 'a Luger, you say? It states in the case notes it was a Beretta Modello.'

I wasn't sure how to respond. Did he genuinely want to spark a Luger/Beretta Modello debate?

'Never mind,' he said. 'My main point is—this painter and decorator, so why was he waving a WWII firearm around inside a nuclear submarine in close proximity to a fire that he himself had started?'

I nodded in agreement. Such a movement of the head made me feel quite giddy and liberated. 'Sir, I asked him that very same question,' I said. 'Telfer clearly was in a state of pique. His weapon was elevated to eye height and he had this sort of frantic concentration on his face, staring through the sight of the gun.'

'"Been robbed three times in the last six months," he explained. "You've got to take your own precautions. Police are never around when you need them."'

'It was then that I ascertained his name and said, "What's the problem here Francis? Can't we talk about this?"'

'And then I edged a few steps further forward.'

I could have told them that he'd worked as a taxi driver for fourteen years, but that was already in my report. So, yeah, he was used to working in poky conditions. But being cooped up in the sub, everything had that echo, picking up any noise, every scratch, even paintbrush on metal ...

He'd made a mistake, he gave me that, but he couldn't afford to lose his job. He wanted to negotiate. He wanted to speak with the Prime Minister.

'It was at that point that I apprehended him.'

Lips emerged from the amorphous blob. 'Yes,' the voice said. 'Would you care to elucidate?'

'It was over in a flash, really,' I said. 'He went quietly.'

'Can you account for the damage to Francis Telfer's knees? Also, some scarring around the groin area?'

'I'm sorry, I ...' my mind was sprinting, speeding away from me. 'He may have tripped, visibility was poor. There was a lot of smoke ...'.

***

There was a lot of smoke.

Telfer couldn't see the wood for the trees. He couldn't make out, at least not straight away, that I'd undergone a change. He held his Luger tightly, to try to compensate for the fact his hand was shaking. He used his other arm for steadying purposes.

This close to him, close enough to reach out and touch, I was a big enough target. Holding the extinguisher in both hands, I lowered it down until it nestled in between my legs, like it was some motherfucking, God-slaying, phallic death machine.

I could feel my face twisting, spasming. I realised I was trying to smile.

'The Prime Minister,' I said, 'that might be a teensy bit outside my jurisdiction. Will Kofi Annan do you? He'd be even trickier. António Guterres?' I spoke with an air of menace. 'Say hello to Ban Ki-moon!' I swung the fire extinguisher, which connected with a satisfying smack into Telfer's balls.

Telfer collapsed onto his knees. The noise of this was much amplified, it seemed much crueller as it carried through the corridor. He was a beaten man.

After the fire, there was the cold realisation. A life turned upside down. There was the sound of sobbing. For want of a better description of the miserable wretch now cowed in front of me—

'Fuck-brain,' I said.

***

'There was a lot of smoke,' one of the Wise Men repeated, appearing not too dissimilar to be a puff of smoke himself. 'Hmm, mm ...' The voice trailed off. A turn of the crankshaft later. 'Was the gun loaded?'

'Technically, yes,' I said. I scratched my nose. I straightened my back. I tapped my feet. 'There was a bullet same age as the Luger, but as it turned out, it had rusted to the barrel.'

'I escorted Telfer back outside the sub where two MOD police were waiting for us. They both looked harassed, firearms on their persons, but they were present nonetheless, having upgraded their interest in our painter and decorator-cum-submarine arsonist.'

The Wise Men didn't need to hear this, that it was all too much for Telfer. His legs gave way beneath him. The MOD police were handily placed to stop him falling, though—I watched them drag him off. His shoes scuffed on the ground.

'Normality ensued and, as if on cue, next to the sub, a familiar face reappeared,' I continued. 'If this was a world, I decided right there and then it was one to be inherited by men with mops.'

There was a pause. A weighty one. Just me and the big puff of smoke.

'Pizza,' I said.

The Wise Men, to a man, were slouched. Single hands supported sides of faces. The voices were a little bored, a little confused. 'So by that I take it, after the incident in Faslane, you went for a spot of lunch?'

'No,' I said. 'That's one way of describing a human body after being thrown from the top of a six-storey building.'

Fingers emerged from the collective smog to scratch three noses. Three backs straightened up simultaneously. Three pairs of feet tapped lightly. If there was an initiation to be had, then it was official, we were all Wise Men together.

'I should explain,' I said.

'Please do.'

'After Faslane, I was called out to a trio of linked homicides,' I said. 'When I arrived at the murder scene, I gave a little wave to the forensics team.'

Forensics for me, I have to confess, really stand out in their white suits and masks. Outside the lab it was especially incongruous, but strangely sinister as well. It was like the world we knew, and had come to know, was being superseded somehow. I don't know, replaced. I bet, though, as uniforms go, a real pain to keep clean in a wet, muddy residential street in Glasgow. I found this to be a consoling thought.

'Always good to keep on the right side of forensics.'

Three Wise Men grunted. I was thinking, maybe they had their own thoughts on all things forensics?

Probably.

Probably not.

'I was in Castlemilk,' I said. 'The victim had been thrown from the roof of a six-storey maisonette block. There was a large dispersal of blood and bone, jaw and teeth, across the street and pavement. A rag doll was at its epicentre.'

I brought my fist down with force, for effect, onto my open palm. 'Businessman—and I use the term as loosely as common decency allows—Bryce Coleman was planning that day on taking a month's break in Benidorm,' I said. 'But not before the settling of old scores first.'

From the top table there was a collective intake of breath. 'Okay,' a voice said, 'it's not as if we weren't expecting this. Pre-warned is, ah, well ... pre-warned, basically.'

'With Coleman, the one striking aspect, so I had been told, was that he was almost bald, virtually hairless, even his eyebrows lack motivation. But what he lacked in facial hair, he made up for in criminal amoral dexterity.'

Did I just make a connection between being bald and amoral? I hoped not.

I continued. 'He had the foresight, and in this respect was ahead of the curve, to launder his dirty money through a 'legit' company, a taxi service called Inverarity Cabs.'

'From this foundation he built his crime network, which in hand built his business network, which in hand built his civic reputation.'

'He's never been one to miss a photo opportunity with a twinkly-eyed pensioner or a troubled youth grateful for any kind of attention from an otherwise uncaring world. He does a lot of work for charity and doesn't like to talk about it because others are in place to do just that for him.'

To be fair to the Wise Men, they said they'd let me speak—and I was on a roll here.

'Coleman uses his fleets of cabs, network of nursing homes, saunas, and various other business interests as an infrastructure for organised crime. They say he must have ten hands, his fingers are in so many pies. Transportation, smuggling, distribution, drugs, the sex-trade, extortion, contraband cigarettes ...'

'Need I go on?'

The thing was, I was sure the Wise Men not only *did not* want me to go on, they actually wouldn't have wanted me to start in the first place. I felt like I was a character in a Dickensian novel, the kind that quickly and rudely comes to understand his place in the world. Lowly and encumbered.

With this in mind, and suitably browbeaten, I made my peace offering. 'Feel free to place the word 'allegedly' at the front of anything I've said,' I said. 'But it's true, isn't it? The police, media, nobody will go anywhere near him.'

'Allegedly,' I added post-haste.

One of the Wise Men interjected. 'It's not as easy as that. There is the black and the white, and there are the greys.'

They were creatures, formless beasts; one body, three heads. Doing what three heads normally do.

'He's untouchable,' I said.

'Well,' I corrected myself, 'he does appear to answer to someone, a shadowy figure, much like yourselves.'

Incidentally, I didn't say that last sentence. Not out loud at any rate.

'Apparently not,' a Wise Man said, 'or we wouldn't be having this meeting, would we now?'

They had me there. Or they would have had me there, if having me there was the name of the game.

I massaged the back of my neck. My shoulders ached like they'd suddenly decided they no longer wished to be part of my body.

'And it had happened before,' I said, but not before allowing a weariness to wash over me, while at the same time trying to steer things back on track. 'At least according to urban legend. The modern urban legend that is Bryce Coleman.'

I chose to let my words float over them, before falling, resting on them like snowflakes or, possibly more accurately, dust. I'd said enough about Coleman, even though there was still plenty left to say. I was determined that I didn't need to explain, not to them. They knew already all right.

They knew that Bryce Coleman had a score to settle and that he was no stranger to making a point. To making an example of someone. His henchmen would escort the victim to the top of a tall building. Head first; they'd throw him off the roof. As for Coleman, he'd be in position down below on the ground. As the victim plummeted, Coleman would be looking up. He was nimble on his feet. If need be, he would take a speedy step back, or a swift sidestep. Last thing he wanted was to be hit by a hurtling projectile of skin and bone. What he did want, what he was looking for, who knows. Maybe he wanted to see the victim's face one last time in all its tortured and terrified glory. To read something from it. He had the best possible view, so determined to a pathological degree not to miss anything. The best view in the street, victim's mouth wide open, forming a scream that realistically, given the circumstances, he would never finish.

It didn't take a wise man to tell me all this was conjecture, based on hearsay, but what was beyond doubt, though, were the events of eight Wednesdays ago. That morning, within not much more than a mile from each other, three people died. All thrown from a very tall building. All having made a mess of nice, decent residential areas. Three stains across the city, not to be removed any time soon. And when the time comes to scrub the detritus away, people would still know it was there. Something instinctive, a muscle memory, they'd step over all the right spots.

What I did know was I left one crime scene in Castlemilk to stand at another one in Croftbank Street. Pulped and smashed matter was everywhere. I was careful where I put my feet. I stared at my reflection in a random pool of the victim's blood.

'One of the victims,' I said, 'the one at Croftbank Street, was a fifteen-year-old. Why? I don't know, maybe a drug deal gone wrong, or a poor school report, or both?'

'The fifteen-year-old in question was Bryce Coleman's godson.'

The Wise Men sat very still. I had to look up to remind myself that, besides me, there were others in the room. And I had to concentrate to make out the faces from the swirl. I tried so hard it made my eyes squint.

'Who else would have killed him?' I said. 'Who would have dared? That's why I knew it had to be Coleman, no one else.'

'In the course of my investigations, I then went to Glasgow airport.'

There, I reflected, the sky was solid grey. No spectrum. No other colours allowed anywhere near. As a Wise Man had said, 'there are the greys.'

Likewise, the main airport building was a block of grey; it blended in with the natural environment. It's why, I suppose, us Scots are such a colourful people, full of inventiveness and chat, to make up for all the greyness around us.

I could hear the sound of jets in the sky, either landing

or taking off, but I didn't look up. If you were in the air I wasn't interested. Outside the building, everything seemed ponderous and sluggish, like lame ants going about their laborious business in the shadow of flying thunderous behemoths. Then you walk through the doors and everything moves in fast-forward, waves of people meld together with multiple bags on wheels, moving unevenly from one point to another. Searching for the right portal to whisk them away to a place of work or a type of adventure, although you have to say, rarely both. That's where my interest lay; the period of hurry, the stress and anxiety getting from point A to gate B.

So, I scanned the area, searching the hustle and bustle, seeking one face in particular. I was thinking that if he had made it through security, he was already lost to me. If gone, then that would have been my cue to simply turn around, chalk it down to experience, lick my wounds, and find an unassuming Italian-style coffee place and order myself a hot chocolate.

That day, though, the airport concourse was generous to me. That day there was to be no hot chocolate—I spotted Coleman.

He walked with a confident stride. The kind of walk in one's mind, mix in some foreknowledge, you could attribute to someone high up in the underworld. Behind him, pushing along an overloaded trolley, which carried enough bags to make a good fist out of surviving the apocalypse, was one of his men.

'It was there that I located Bryce Coleman. He was accompanied by a known associate, Roger Wittes.'

My recollection of him, Wittes was a big man, arms of granite. At times he was given cause to use his considerable bulk in a certain way. Even so, the act of pushing along cases, each the weight of a baby elephant, seemed a bit much even for him. He was puffing hard.

Coleman turned around to Roger and yelled at him to move that big lardy arse of his. Then he told him to cut out the deep-fried kebabs for breakfast. He wasn't backward in coming forward. In fact, he was pretty rude.

'On my approach, Coleman turned and faced me,' I said. 'I knew of him; he didn't know me. I asked him for help with my enquiries. We might have scuffled.'

At this, the Wise Men came to life. Heads moved from side to side, ushering in lots of intense whispering, like a team conferring on University Challenge. But this was the University of Hard Knocks where you answered a question with a question. 'When you say "We might have scuffled," I take it you're actually meaning, "We did scuffle?"'

Keeping up the well-worn tradition of the rhetorical question, followed by a bare-bones minimum amount of pausing, the voice continued. 'At this point, Detective Inspector, we are none the wiser. Why would anyone want to confront Bryce Coleman at an airport?'

I felt my eyes mist over, like I was watching a sad scene at the movies. I wanted to find a fixed space, so I could stare at it for an extended period, but my eyes blinked, ruining the effect.

'As good a place as any,' I said. 'He was going on holiday. Maybe, for him, a time of reflection. A chance for him to look back at his life. I wanted to look into his eyes and see an emotion there. Something I could recognise. On the lines of regret, contrition, humility perhaps.'

'And did you?'

'No,' I said.

***

Blood is a funny thing. It is predictable in some ways. Without it there would be no life. Even the lowliest of creatures, the tiniest of insects, bleed something we could recognise as blood. Coleman was an insect; not one you could easily swat out of the way, but you wouldn't mind trying all the same.

My blood was boiling. It was on the rise. I looked into the bastard's eyes and could see nothing in them. It's not as if I hadn't witnessed this a thousand times. They were soulless pits, the eyes of a shark. Whatever residue of humanity that had once resided in them had been scooped out a long time ago. Maybe I could have put my arm around his shoulders, spoke kind words, expressed empathy with his situation. Perhaps I could have tried to get to the bottom of what happened in his childhood, what sickening defiling act inflicted on him had made him this way?

He was talking to me, but I'd heard all that tired gangster shite before. 'Do you know who I am? You're in a lot of trouble now, laddie. Walk away while you still have legs to walk away on.'

There was pressure in my ears, my hearing was shot. I felt much bulkier, heavier, something other than gravity bearing down. There was something in my eye.

In a way it was a curious situation. I knew so much of this man; his backstory, his mythology, his holiday plans. Everything about him was so public to me, excepting some solid evidence to finally put him away. And yet, here I was meeting him in person for the first time, here in the expanse that was Glasgow Airport. But this was no time for a firm handshake or opportunistic autograph hunting.

In any case, what a fucking let down he was. His hairless skin, the shimmering outline exposed in artificial light, there was hardly anything of him to focus on. What a dreary fucking voice he had. He really was a *C-U-Next-Tuesday*.

I headbutted him. His nose caved in. An effect not too dissimilar to an Olympic diver, triple somersault completed, splashing in the water.

From both nostrils there was a neat symmetrical spray of blood. In one sweet chaotic balletic movement, his legs gave way. He crumbled and crumpled.

He was screaming at me, although, what with the current fucked up state of his nasal cavity, he sounded like a shite cartoon character.

One of his legs just lay there, stretched out, an open invitation. Both my knees dropped down on it, which made for a satisfying crunch. Coleman yelled and cried like a baby. At least in some way I'd helped him regress back to his childhood.

As I knelt over Coleman, having left my imprint on him, an arm of granite came from behind. It took hold around my neck. It formed a vice-like grip, a boa constrictor going by the name of Roger. I gasped for air, but none was forthcoming. Line of vision shorting out. Both my hands went up to this arm of granite, grappling, grasping, pulling at it. All ineffectually.

He punched the nape of my neck really hard, so much so, it felt like Thor: God of Thunder had paid me a visit.

'Stupid bag of pus.'

I could hear Roger's words all right.

I fell. I was down on my side. I was seeing double. My eyes flitted to the concourse and I saw that we were surrounded by heavily-armed airport police. There seemed an awful lot of the buggers, but that might have been the double vision. They aimed their semi-automatic weapons at me, Roger, and Coleman. The three of us, in the wars, now partners in crime.

I remained on my side, in a foetal position; head swollen, too big for my neck to lift. 'Nothing to see,' I said, my words dragging, slurring. 'Move along now.'

My equilibrium was returning slowly back to me. The airport police took a step closer in unison and their number halved in size. A clear sign that the situation was now under control.

I started laughing, but nobody joined in.

***

'*No*,' I said.

'No,' a Wise Man echoed. There may have been a tinge of disappointment in his voice, but that was as far as it got. He didn't seem in the mood to challenge me. He didn't seem to be much in the mood for anything.

He had a long slender neck, which he slowly uncoiled. He hissed, with his extended forked-tongue. Oh, wait, or was that just my imagination?

'The airport police were slow in reacting ...' a Wise Man said, before trailing off.

Another Wise Man gripped on tight to the baton passed to him and duly took up the reins. 'You, Wittes, and Coleman were arrested. They checked out your credentials and you, Fisher, were released pending this enquiry.'

Now there came the voice of the third Wise Man. 'The man you attacked, Bryce Coleman—you did so purely on the basis of innuendo, you had no hard evidence.'

'Coleman was hospitalised with a broken nose and broken leg. What's more, his holiday plans were ruined.'

There were unforgiving stares all around. 'We're talking an unprovoked assault. We are talking grievous bodily harm. We are talking, Detective Inspector, frankly speaking, but are you out of your blasted mind?'

There was some pointing going on. Pontificating, generally, was the name of the game. My head was full of the Hydra, the Abominable Snowman, Santa Claus, and other mythical creatures. They amounted to a mixture of steam and smoke, displaying three pairs of ears. I wondered if I pursed my lips and blew with all my might, whether all that heavy gas would disperse around the room. I would breathe some of it in. Some would settle in my lungs.

'What was the point of it all?' one Wise Man said, speaking for all of them. 'You have an exemplary record. Why risk it all in one moment of madness? Over some bad guy, granted, allegedly, who will no doubt walk away at the end of this sorry state of events having sued, pardon my French, the knickers off us?'

A moment of madness, that's what they chose to call it. If only that were true. Truth is I was cursed. I was a throwback to the caveman. Fight or flight. A survival instinct so primordial, it existed in the empty space that pre-dated the Big Bang itself.

Santa Claus was no longer in the room. There would be no presents. No satsumas. No chestnuts roasted over an open fire. It was just Oliver Twist asking for more, please. Asking for a second helping of their very best gruel. It was just me and three men. Their eyes were on me, unflinching, and I stared right back at them.

My mouth twisted, it took on the shape of a crack in the wall. My mind went dark, my thoughts turned blacker than the coals of Newcastle. I was the same man, but not the same man. Still, the changes were more subtle than normal. There was no need for any more than that. The plan was not to indulge in some argy-bargy, or fisticuffs, or eye-poking—well, at least not right away.

'The thing is ...' I said; my voice was deeper. Deeper than the TauTona Mine. Deeper than Calvin Harris's love.

'Francis Telfer from Faslane had clearance. No criminal record. The thing is, I have new information. Telfer used to work for Inverarity Cabs owned by, yes, that name again, one Bryce Coleman. Coleman, no more immune to the economic downturn as any other, was vigilant, always on the lookout for fresh, new 'business' opportunities. Nothing alleged about it. He had got to Telfer. He applied pressure as only a nasty big-time gangster can. He forced Telfer to set fire to an integral part of the defence of the realm, a nuclear submarine no less.'

They were listening. I had them in the palm of my hand. They wanted to take a case like this, as cut and dry as first appeared, at least on the surface, and put a twist on it. So they could point out something everyone else had missed. To justify their expertise, their reason for being, their very existence.

And I was so very convincing. My puffed-out face, the dark rings around my eyes, everything heightened by an intensity, kicking and screaming, the one I dragged alongside me. I had identified a need in them, which I now sought to fill. I had given them their *bad cop*.

'The paymaster,' I said, before delaying, pausing for effect like some fucking judge from *The Great British Bake Off* –

'The paymaster, the *Ottoman Empire*.'

Such were the range of expressions on the Wise Men's faces, they looked anything but wise. There was so much strangeness to take in, and yet the Wise Men did not do strangeness well. They worked in circles where everything had to be ordered, where the extraordinary was clinically dissected and sculpted into the ordinary. To see my strange transformation with their own set of eyes was to not quite believe it, so I threw them something else. I threw them a bone. I threw them the *Ottoman Empire*. Which was shorthand, code for you name it: ISIS/ISIL, Al-Qaeda, Taliban, Boko Haram, Al-Shabaab. The latest, until the next one, terrorist organisation of choice.

There was silence. It would've been disappointing, less than worthwhile, if there hadn't been some silence.

Wise Man 1 was the first to respond. 'One thing is clear,' he said 'MOD police has some explaining to do. Both they and the airport police were slow to act to the growing situations around them. We will be recommending each carries out an internal review, lessons to be learned, etcetera.'

'The Terrorist Branch will be mightily interested in reading our report,' Wise Man 2 said. 'We'll package everything up, including CCTV, and send it on ASAP. It goes without saying, so all the more reason to say it—we would kindly request that details of a sensitive nature do not leave the room.'

'By sensitive, to remove any ambiguity, starting the very first moment you walked through the door, we mean *everything* that has been mentioned in this room.'

I nodded my agreement.

'DNA samples taken from the scene don't match up, Fisher,' said Wise Man 3. 'They don't point to anything of you.'

'Eye-witness accounts are muddled. Introduce panic, mayhem, who sees anything clearly in an airport?'

It was a good question. One I happily didn't have an answer for. Nothing existed inside a bubble. Even men such as these, as shut off as they appeared, had to have contacts in the outside world. All types of experts I imagined, who reported to them and kept them wise.

'If we should need any more from you, Detective Inspector,' Wise Man 2 said, 'we'll be in touch. For the time being, please, carry on regardless.'

'Forty-five minutes are up,' Wise Man 3 said, brandishing his wristwatch with a flourish.

I stood up and undulations of relief coursed through every inch of my body. It was almost intoxicating. My suit fitted loosely around my body. My eyes watered, if only for a moment.

'Thank you,' I said.

I walked to the door and could feel three pairs of eyes on my back, burning holes out of me. I reached for the door handle, expecting a final cutting word to bring my whole world crashing down. The interrogation equivalent of a sniper's bullet.

'Close the door on your way out,' the voice went.

I smiled to myself. It wasn't quite a present from Santa, not even a portion of Oliver Twist's gloop, but it would suffice all the same.

***

I left the building that was Helen Street Police Station, but I didn't get far. My head hurt, it was bad. I could no longer walk, the unremarkable vibrations caused by the impact of heel on concrete proving too debilitating, too excruciating. Again and again. Like a giant hammer crashing into a colossal gong of pain.

I brushed my nose and looked down at the tip of my finger and saw blood. My arm jutted out, hand at the ready, reaching for the protection and balance of a nearby wall. I just needed a moment to ride it through, for this God-awful feeling to pass.

Just. Needed. A moment.

It was like someone with a pitchfork, gone pitchfork-crazy, was stabbing behind my forehead, my eyes. I looked up and focussed on a cloud floating by unnaturally fast in a purple sky. I prayed with all my might for some light rain that I knew, Sod's law dictated, so long as I still needed it, would never come. And gradually, somehow, the discomfort began to subside.

I was breathing rapidly. I checked my watch. If the

world was someone else's oyster, I was ready to borrow it for a while. I made a mental note, a rushed calculation. I had in front of me a couple of hours to freshen up and still be ready for my next appointment.

Time enough to feel normal again.

6.

Home Sweet Home

My full name is Julie Elizabeth Spencer. It's difficult, jarring, not to put DS in front of there. I wasn't born a Detective Sergeant, but I have to confess I find it difficult to think of me as having been anything else.

That's pretty sad in some ways. It's okay to think so.

If you were to ask me my views on DI Fisher before I was assigned as his partner; well, if I had to be honest (and really I should), I'd say the one thing that stood out for me was that he didn't really stand out at all. He was polite, he'd always say hello. But at the same time, he was aloof. He had a rep for being a loner. I wouldn't argue with that.

First time we met, I remember, it wasn't a long conversation. It was a couple of years ago. We were talking and I happened to ask him along to our usual Thursday departmental night out. He seemed quite keen, if I remember rightly, at least initially; but later that evening he phoned me, said something had come up which meant he had to bail. He sent his sincere apologies.

The main reason I found the call memorable was that once he hung up I looked down at my phone and read that it lasted nine seconds.

No recollection of getting a word in edgeways. Not even a syllable.

Ah, wait, that wasn't the main reason. Something else happened that day. Something harrowing; something tragic. As it happened, none of us had a mind to go out that evening. As it happened, the night out was called off.

Physically, I'd heard DI Fisher described as 'a lanky streak of piss', which obviously was an inappropriate way to describe anyone. No harm to the guy, but it did kind of fit.

Oh, and yeah, a rumour was circulating around the office that he bit off a suspect's ear. If I had a pound for every time I heard Evander Holyfield and/or Mike Tyson mentioned in the same breath, I'd be at least, oh, one hundred and twenty-five pounds better off. It was 1997 when the infamous boxing ring incident happened, a memorable year in more ways than one. This was the last time I was in a relationship that lasted longer than two weeks. I think that one was a month.

I was joking there, of course. Ha ha! I was only twelve in 1997! Mind you ...

As things now stood—having sent me on various fool's errands, presumably to delay us actually getting together and investigating cases as a team—what did I think of him? I'll choose my words wisely. I'd have to say it was vexing; that it was beginning to get on my wick. There was a real danger of him coming across as a bit of a shit.

Like the real trooper I was, I did as I was told, though. With the MacPhellimey case, she was as sweet as a lamb until I arrested her. As I waited for forensics to arrive, along with a JCB Mini Digger to dig up her garden, I needed to talk her down from the top of the coffee table.

The school community trip could have gone better. I had to break up three different fights; one of them was between the teachers. In the end, I threatened to arrest the whole school. Put it this way, I don't think I'll be asked back. Not that I was losing any sleep over that.

As for investigating ladies' tights (yes, you heard that right), don't get me wrong, the assistants at New Look, Debenhams, H&M, and Primark were only too helpful, but it had crossed my mind more than once to get myself a three word tattoo, which read 'Wild Goose Chase'. 'Wild' and 'Goose' were to go on each cheek of the arse—that was a definite. Over the day the placement of 'Chase' alternated between upper arm (too boring) to sole of the foot (too interesting) to one of my eyelids (too painful).

All together it made for interesting paperwork. Unlike some of my colleagues, I wasn't one to use paperwork as an excuse to get off the streets. But I didn't hate it either. I found it therapeutic. I took solace from the fact it was all down there and recorded. Confirmation at least in my mind, looking back, that what happened had really happened. I liked the idea of detailing what I'd done with my life or, should that read, my professional life. Not that, between one and the other, there was that much of a difference. I'm just saying.

But that's just me spouting off. I wasn't trying to make anyone feel sorry for me. For the most part, despite myself sometimes, you'll no doubt have already guessed, I love my job. Proud of my rank as Detective Sergeant. Proud of what I'd achieved, all down and recorded.

I'd never been a fan of being alone, even though I'd lived alone for the last two years. Despite not being the least bit religious, I thought a lot about God, Jesus, and the Devil. I was thinking I swear too much, even though around my colleagues I didn't swear anywhere near enough.

Screaming cliché alert! My most feminine trait, to buy shoes that I'd probably never wear. We're all due at least one screaming cliché alert. My most masculine trait, that I don't shave my armpits. I mean, don't get me wrong, it's on the list, just not high up on the list. I don't like violence on TV. There's something about made-up violence that I can't bend my head around. I watched *The Walking Dead*, which I thought was a comedy, real laugh a minute, until someone pointed out to me that the shambling zonked-out characters on the show weren't folks who'd spent too long out in the sun, but undead zombies. Constantly fighting a losing battle trying to catch up on the Radio 4 podcast of *The Archers*. The two places I most wanted to visit were Strawberry Fields in Central Park, NYC—and the shoe palace of Imelda Marcos (although I heard these days most of the footwear there has turned quite mouldy).

One last thing I was grateful to my job for. It kept my mind off things; one in particular. My mother was resident of Abbey Lodge Care Home in East Kilbride. It was a nice place; nice enough building, but no denying the fact it was a home for the elderly. As you approached the building, you braced yourself, felt your body tense up. You'd see the time on the outside clock, which always read ten past two. Either it no longer worked, or no one had got round to winding it up, or someone thought it was a good thing to give the illusion of time stood still. It was always my intention to ask about it at the front desk.

It still was.

You knew what the place stood for; what it ultimately meant. You did what you thought was best for your loved one; keeping her in comfort, keeping her in care, this the person who brought you into the world, knowing full well things would never get better and that we were on the straight path from here on in.

My mother suffered from dementia. To me, she was still my mum, my constant, the one thing I had always known in my thirty-odd years of life. But, inside her, the illness had stripped away everything that once was her.

You tell me there is a God, well, I'd have to ask, how could something like God exist and allow something like dementia to exist? It was a simple enough question. I knew and accepted there were many terrible things in the world, but to have someone live a life, to embrace what it was to live a life, all those experiences, all the love, happiness and sadness, all the relationships, and then to have it taken away just like that; is there anything more cruel?

I don't feel anger. I don't know what to feel. I used to hate the unknown, but now I wasn't so sure.

On my last visit, we had some nice chairs placed at the window. I sat across from my mum. She's in her sixties. An old-looking sixties; hair turned white. She'd aged terribly since the onset of her illness. Time had eaten away at her. As I sat, hands nestled on my lap, I tried hard not to fidget.

There was so much tension coursing through me, that was the surprising thing. I was on edge. Constantly smiling, trying to be brave when feeling anything but, head threatening to explode thanks to a killer migraine.

Her head was at a slight angle. She wasn't looking at me, rather gazing into the space between me and her. No colour to her features. Her face was a grey disconnected blur. I leaned forward and thought to take her hand and for some reason, I wasn't sure why, decided not to. There was no sign of recognition in my mother's eyes. She had no idea who I was.

'Mum ...?' I said.

She straightened her head, turned and looked at me. There was something in her eyes now, but it was fear and confusion.

All there was, after this, was to lock my jaw tight and sit like a statue. Counting down the decision, seconds that lasted as long as minutes—how long to stay seated before it was time to leave? Would she even notice?

***

For the most part, I liked my job. It could be full of setbacks, nasty and cruel. I'd seen sides of humanity I would never have thought existed—and still found myself doubting they were capable of happening even after the fact.

And yet, yeah, I still tried to fall on the side of being positive. Glass half full. I think I helped protect people. I mean, I hoped that I helped people. I was sure I helped people. I liked the way kids pointed at me on the street when in uniform (although since turning DS, these days this was an all too rare occurrence). I was happy to think I did some good.

Make a decision—I made a decision. Me, DI Fisher, we were going to have a talk. I'd ask him what the fudge was going on. (I had a personal rule, give or take the odd lapse, to make a conscientious attempt not to swear before 12 noon. And, anyway, who didn't like fudge? Sweet, gorgeous, chewy while melting in your mouth fudge? Besides maybe dentists?)

And who had time for shoes, especially ones you'll never wear? Where did that come from? If I was trying to come across as more interesting than I was, cripes, couldn't I come up with something more, you know ... interesting?

Fudge it was.

7.

Appointment No. 1

Horses are strict vegetarians. This was one of the many random thoughts that popped into my head as I sat in the psychiatrist's waiting room. I was seated on a couch, as a matter of fact.

Fanta was invented by the people behind Coca Cola to sell to the Nazis. There went another one. 'Decimation' means the killing/culling of one in every ten. It doesn't mean devastation or annihilation; it's more selective than that. If you want a word for devastation or annihilation, well, there you go then, use devastation or annihilation. Another one. There came a point in my life where I realised I could do without sleep.

The psychiatrist's practice— name of Cuthbert and Associates—was situated on the fourth floor of a building on West George Street. Glancing over the literature at the front desk, it seemed they specialised in public sector workers occupying high-pressure roles. But when it came down to it, they wouldn't turn anyone away with a facial tick and a mammy complex. I commended myself; at least I was going into this with an open mind.

An adjoining door swung open. Standing there was a short woman. Unquestionably around the face, she was a Dawn French lookalike. She had a distinctive, attractively so, snub nose. In a life of surreal moments, this was one of the more surreal ones. The actress who played *The Vicar of Dibley* turned hotshot public sector psychiatrist.

'Detective Inspector,' she said.

Gingerly I got to my feet. Before she spoke I had been in a state of discombobulation, but at least she didn't sound like Dawn French. Hers were slow, carefully thunderous, monochrome words. Her voice, in truth, was more along the lines of former Prime Minister Margaret Thatcher. It threatened to shatter the illusion.

Quick to compose myself, I ambled into her office. The room was a square near-replica of the rectangular waiting room I'd just vacated, intentionally so you would have thought. This helped my normally fuzzy brain adjust in quick time to my surroundings.

Two plain brown armchairs faced each other. The psychiatrist was already seated at one, so I took the one remaining. 'Thank you,' I said. My frame sank into the cushion, which seemed to wrap itself around my person, shoring up my lower spine in a most agreeable way. Memory foam, I guessed.

She sat, body language moulded to appear as relaxed as could be. She wore a light pink herringbone fitted double cuff shirt; top button undone. For the next hour I was to be her world. Not even the advent of the end of the Universe would distract her; such was her professional devotion to me and my foibles. I could tell all this by the utterly implacable way she folded her arms. I was left in no doubt I was in the company of a professional.

'My name is Doctor Dawn Preston,' she said. 'But please, you can call me Dawn, or Dr Dawn, or DD. Whatever you feel comfortable with. I don't tend to take notes on our first session. We simply get to know each other. So, please feel free to talk about anything that's on your mind.'

Her name was Dawn! What were the chances? I was bursting to ask if people made the same connection I did, between her and the other more famous Dawn, but I thought perhaps everyone did, to the point it was now something of a sore point. Perhaps not the greatest idea to start things off by getting her back up, then. I wracked my brain for an alternative opening gambit.

'Fanta,' I said.

'Fanta?' she said. She gave me a little smile. 'Yes, soft drink of choice for the Nazi party. You'd be surprised just how many of my clients start with that one.'

Oh, she was good all right; engendered an instant positive impression. I was thinking I could open up a little. Maybe it would be good to get some stuff off my chest. You never know, unlikely as it seemed—as likely as finding Elvis on the moon working on his new album—it might do me some good.

Where to start? I began with the thing—once the Fanta observation is done with—that everyone starts with.

'I have trouble sleeping,' I said. 'Maybe an hour here, an hour there. When I wake, I force myself not to look at the time. I don't want this to build up; become any more of an obsession than it already is. I feel okay with it at the moment, but I know if I leave it unchecked, it's bound to cause complications sometime in the future. Running through my mind, more often than not when I should be asleep, sentences, ideas, fragments of thoughts, not making sense.'

'To give you an example, I arrested a twelve-year-old shoplifter,' I said. 'When asked about the bruises on his arms, he told me to "*Eff-off*". That was the closest to a fully formed sentence he got. So I need to submit a written report to the children's panel. Maybe throw in a few recommendations. Current thoughts, putting the boy into care, taking him away from his hopelessly, dangerously dysfunctional mother and abusive non-biological father; maybe there's a decent soul out there, some foster parent, who could turn his life around.'

'All the way, I go through a range of options, to going back in time, in a time machine, to smother him as a baby with a pillow. No longer a problem, the boy having never existed, you see.'

Dr Dawn the 'Dawn French' lookalike made to speak but stopped herself a millisecond before any sound escaped.

Hands held out, my body jerked into life. 'Sorry, my idea of a joke,' I said. 'Gallows humour.'

Dr Dawn's expression was not one of reassurance.

'Would you say, outside of work, you dwell on things too much? Work matters, perhaps?' she said.

My forehead creased as I thought about this. 'I have no real recollection of what I do outside of work,' I said. 'I just sort of go through the motions.'

'The shoplifter, why do you think it affected you so?'

'The fact he was a twelve-years-old. It's always the number twelve. That's the number for me, sticks out in the crowd. Twelve seems to follow me around.'

'The age of the child, yes? Can you give me another example?'

'It was twelve years ago, my last day as an officer with the mounted police. Twelve-years-old also happened to be the age of my horse. A Shire-cross named Clydebank. He was my best friend. A year's supply of dog food in the making.'

'Again, apologies; my humour,' I said, interrupting myself.

'Your humour,' Dr Dawn echoed, without inflection, her expression blank.

She wasn't one for giving anything away, which seemed to have the effect of spurring me on to say even more.

'On the morning of my last day,' I said, 'Clydebank and I were joined by Officer Bruce Gillespie and his horse Winchester, and Officer John O'Ready and his horse Tamson. We were policing an anti-imperialism demonstration held in Govanhill. It was organised by the Proper Socialist Party with a total of forty-three demonstrators in attendance. Everything was pretty quiet, so John and Bruce had ridden off in search of a coffee, leaving trusty steed and I to watch over people content to wave red flags and denounce Archdukes everywhere.'

'I heard a chomping sound. I looked down and saw some middle-aged ne'er-do-well feeding Clydebank half a sausage roll.'

'"What do you think you're doing?" I said to the guy.'

'"Giving the horsey a wee clap," he said back.'

'I asked "What are you feeding him?"'

'Ne'er-do-well looked up at me as if I'd said something mad, clearly insane, like there was life on Venus, or at a stretch, Pollokshields. Clydebank showed off his teeth as the man tantalisingly waved the other half of the sausage roll in front of him.'

'Again, that's twice you've said, "ne'er-do-well?"' interrupted Dr Dawn.

'Yes, ne'er-do-well,' I said.

'Interesting choice of word.' She made a face. She was processing things, formulating, bringing things together. She twirled her finger. 'Go on.'

'I asked him to please stop feeding the horse,' I said. 'It wasn't good for him. This was true; a sausage roll or equivalent savoury foodstuff could have given him potentially fatal colic. And, in any case, horses have a strict vegetarian diet.'

'Well, not that strict, apparently,' I said, my eyebrows darting up and down, 'not when it came to a certain horse named Clydebank and a certain sausage roll.'

'Anyhow, back to the ne'er-do-well, who was blissfully ignoring me as he continued to feed the horse. So I got down from the saddle and put handcuffs on him. That didn't go unnoticed by the other forty-two people on the demonstration.'

'"Arrested for giving a horse a wee clap," a voice shouted out from the gallery.'

'The crowd's hackles were up, edging closer, circling me, him, and the horse.'

'"Effing imperialist," one of them said.'

'"Fascist," another one shouted.'

'"Belgian," went another one.'

'All the while, Clydebank's eyes were bulging. The sausage roll wasn't agreeing with him. The eruptions from his tummy were something fierce.'

'This was my last day before starting in plainclothes and I had visions of my horse keeling over. Death by sausage roll. Not great at any time, but today of all days, this was not a good situation to be in.'

'Something snapped inside me. Normally out on a horse I was a Steady Eddie, or a Cautious Carol, but not so this time. Even though he wasn't saying anything, I screamed at the guy to shut up. Then my attention turned to the rest of the crowd. I shouted out, told the rest of them they were all under arrest.'

'At this point, my fellow officers returned on horseback, cappuccinos in hand. Nothing for me.'

'"You've arrested the whole demonstration!" officer O'Ready says to me. "Who the *eff* do you think you are? Judge Dredd?"'

I smiled at Dr Dawn. It was clear to me she wasn't sure whether I was taking our time together seriously or not. My smile was a calculated one, designed in this regard to *not* help her out.

As for Dr Dawn's expression, I'd grown accustomed over the years to a similar kind of response from officials, colleagues, members of the public; anyone unlucky enough to find themselves in conversation for any amount of time with yours truly.

It was twelve years ago when I first felt something stir inside. It was the other *me* (although I didn't realise, didn't understand, it was *him* at the time).

I didn't want to say anymore. I wasn't quite ready to braid a whole noose to fit around my neck, not at our opening session. It was up to Dr Dawn to discover the truth, to stumble onto it; or to create a truth more consistent with her professional outlook. For this to work, she had to give something back.

***

I was in another place, or at least my mind was in another place. Sometimes when I'm in a fug it's hard to tell which is which, what is fucking what.

I was sitting in darkness with the blinds open. The orange glow of a streetlight had sneaked in, stretching surreptitiously across the wall, like a possi of creeping beetles. I must have stared at it for too long. Flitting in and out, all of a sudden the genie was out of the bottle and I was ticking off in my head those in the station I'd love to disembowel and the ones I'd love to fuck. And the ones I'd love to disembowel and fuck.

You see, I had always been there, the bogeyman inside Detective Inspector Fisher, or Dick van Dyke as I liked to call him. Or Dick for short. Think about it, all those tight spots he gets into, be it confronted by Samurai and broadsword-twirling delinquents, or a blood-splattered speeding car, or a group of crack cocaine-addled pensioners? Who was the one leaping in, popping up in the nick of time and grabbing the bad guys by the knickers and eyeballs to save the day? Fucking me, that's who! Keep thinking about it, out of the both of us, just who is the *good* cop?

How else, twelve years ago, in Govanhill on my Jack Jones could I keep forty-two demonstrators and one numpty at bay? By being polite to them and minding my P's and Q's? I don't fucking think so!

It was through the sheer strength of personality of being a fucking nutcase. They were in my thrall. They knew at any moment I might pounce on any one of them and rip their fucking tongues out! That took the biscuit. That took the chocolate hobnob. That's the way to pacify the hoi polloi.

There was the sound of crashing waves in my head.

'Who the fuck do you think you are? Judge Dredd?'

At this point, officers O'Ready and Gillespie decided to get involved, probably glad of the distraction from their pish-poor cappuccinos. I left them to it, processing the crowd. My guess would be they'd suggest to the mob they get their last 'Vive La Revolution' out of their systems, and in a quiet and orderly fashion, piss off before I got back again.

As for me, I was on horseback shepherding my prisoner to a police van parked on the other end of the street. En route, we passed a baker's shop. An idea came to me and I got off my horse. With prisoner in tow, I popped into the bakery.

I bought five piping-hot bridies, just that second out of the oven. Throughout the transaction, I was the only one who was talking.

My ne'er-do-well prisoner was in a daze. The guy who served me kept his head right down.

Point of information, a bridie is a Scottish pasty, having originated in Forfar. You know the classic football scoreline *East Fife 4, Forfar 5*? It's that Forfar! Consisting of minced steak, butter, onions, and seasoned beef suet encased in flaky pastry, it formed a kind of rectangular shape, so maybe not the sleekest of designs for eating purposes, but comfort was the last thing I had in mind.

On leaving the bakery, I pushed the ne'er-do-well into a back alley and force-fed him one bridie after the other. All said, I pushed into his mouth, all five of the fuckers.

'How the fuck do you like it?' I said; equating five hot bridies to one sausage roll.

Not that, full to bursting with bridie, there could be any realistic prospect of a reply. This was as rhetorical a question as you could get.

The prisoner's hands were spinning. He gagged, a heaving sound, on minced steak and other assorted bits and pieces. And it was hot; roasting. His insides were in uproar; his lips were burning.

At the end of the onslaught, the ne'er-do-well was down on his knees, puking molten chunks back up and sobbing uncontrollably. I thought about going back to buy more bridies, but decided he wasn't worth it. (They were forty-five pence a pop.)

Instead we continued on our merry way up until the point I threw him in the back of the van and booked him. The prisoner's name, I'm not shitting you, was Michael Jackson. Maybe we should have moonwalked. Maybe I should have worn a single white glove. Maybe it was already a memorable last day as it was.

Everything calmed down after this. Everything slowed down. I handed in my uniform. I handed in my horse. It was a new beginning.

Later on that day, I had time to pop into the equine unit at Blairfield Farm to say one final cheerio to my old pal Clydebank. On arrival, I was struck by the piercing tranquillity of the farm itself. You could hear a pin drop, if ever there was cause for such a thing in the vicinity. It was enough to bring on a nosebleed.

I found Clydebank in his stable, thankfully none the worse after the day's culinary misadventure. A magnificent beast still in his prime, still with so much to give. We'd had two years together in service of Her Majesty, policing demos, patrolling the city centre, and seeing grannies across the road. In our time, we'd helped police a good few Old Firm games and been called an orange bastard by one side and a Fenian bastard by the other. Neither side bothering to enquire into our true atheist leanings. Yes, we'd been through a lot.

My old faithful. My trusty steed.

My back hunched. My eyes settled on his majestic mane. Part of me felt a twinge and I longed to kiss his throat. Longed to bite and tear a chunk out of him.

But back then, it was easy enough to keep that other part of me in check. Everything was still relative. 'First day as plainclothes tomorrow,' I said to him.

In response, Clydebank looked at me with an expression that said, 'go boil yer heid'. But that might just have been the sausage roll talking. I straightened my back and puffed out my chest and blew the beast one last kiss goodbye.

***

'Judge Dredd,' Dr Dawn repeated. I couldn't tell if she knew the character (comic book anti-hero, a Dirty Harry-styled Lawman of the Future; two movie adaptations to date, the most recent from a few years ago starring Karl

Urban. The first starred Sylvester Stallone, way back in the '90s).

'I think we'll end our first session there, a little early,' she said. 'It doesn't matter how many sessions you're down for, the first four are mandatory and subsequent ones within my discretion.' She stopped at this, smiled, and without seemingly taking any kind of breath, she then continued. 'Let's get this over with as soon as possible. They'll arrange a suitable time at the front desk. I'll see you over the next few days; maybe even tomorrow morning.'

And that was it, meeting ended with nothing in the way of advice or counselling. Nothing to chew on. Not even a declaration on which one she preferred, the Karl Urban or the Stallone one. Strangely, I felt short-changed somehow.

I didn't stick around. It was as if some preternatural force had lifted me out of my chair and ushered me out of the room. 'See you soon,' I said meekly, bleakly, as way of passing.

I realised at that point she hadn't even mentioned the 'ear'.

***

Outside, there was a swirling wind. An empty crisp packet flew towards me, its path erratic, jostled by the gusts, zipping in the air so fast I couldn't make out if it was salt and vinegar or cheese and onion flavour.

The world opened up to me as I was to discover, leaning back against the side of the Kia, DS Spencer. Her arms were crossed; this was possibly down to the unseasonably cold temperature, but more probably this was another helping of body language on display. She was calling me out; bringing to an end my attempts at stonewalling her and keeping her at arm's length, which was fair enough. I'd fulfilled my obligations for now, done and dusted.

I didn't ask how she knew I'd be here, but my rush of blood to the head (and someone's ear) at Helen Street, I guessed, was still the talk of the steamie. Half the force was on a waiting list to see a doctor, psychiatrist, or counsellor. The other half had to make do with happy pills. No big thing, all was fair in love, war, and office gossip, word of appointments got round, confidential or not.

Nothing to be ashamed about. Nothing I wouldn't happily scribble down in my diary. We were all detectives, after all. Nosey so-and-sos.

'DS Spencer,' I said.

'DI Fisher,' she said.

'I don't know about you,' I said, 'but I'm dying for a Diet Coke.'

8.

Electric Dreams

First thing to consider was that the occasional wild goose chase was good for the soul, and you never knew where it might take you. Secondly, if Stanley Kubrick was still alive and wanted the perfect location to film the underside of Glasgow, then it would be right here in Yoker at Electric Dreams.

By day, Electric Dreams was a pub. Lord only knows what it turned into at night. How best to describe it? It was like God, or more accurately, Odin, had dropped from the sky a concrete block on to some hastily placed tarmac.

Electric Dreams is surrounded by mostly waste ground with the occasional uneven patch of yellow-brown grass that never grows, no matter the weather, more than two millimetres high.

In the distance one way, there is a small, dense wood. In the other direction, there's the canal, which snakes through the north-west of Glasgow. Beyond the canal is evidence of civilisation, as the conurbation that is Yoker takes hold. From our vantage point in the car, you could see the tower blocks. People were throwing their rubbish out of top floor windows.

Behind us, there was the single track road that led to Electric Dreams. Perhaps the intention was to build a community here.

Perhaps the notion then left them, whoever *they* were, once they gazed upon the urban monstrosity, the stone monolith that was Electric Dreams. Perhaps they left it standing as way of reminder never to make the same mistake again.

It was just past lunchtime. We turned and drove up to the car park, then sat in silence in the car. It was opening hours.

When she had got into the car earlier, she hadn't offered to drive. I immediately liked her for that.

'So,' DS Spencer said, 'line of enquiry?'

'I'll take a wander in,' I said. 'Talk to our man.'

'I'm starving,' she said, 'spent so long this morning trying to pin down your whereabouts, no time for elevenses. Get us a packet of crisps, would you?'

'Hangry,' I said.

'What?' she said.

'At least you never said hangry.'

'Why would I ever want to say that?'

'Hungry and angry.'

'I know what it means.'

'What flavour?'

'The crisps?'

'The crisps.'

'Surprise me.'

'No worries.'

It was difficult to read her. Having made her point back at West George Street, I think she was now happy to let me off the leash for a little longer. After a tense start, here was a kind of peace offering. I was getting to know her;

she was trying to get to know me. Best of luck with that one, Detective Sergeant Spencer.

I got out of the Kia. My face was a picture of concentration as I tried my best not to slam the car door shut behind me.

I failed.

I walked the length of the tarmac to the main door of Electric Dreams. Ambling along, there was a strange spongy feeling to be had underfoot. The stories that tarmac could tell. At any moment, a voice at the back of my head was telling me, the ground could literally split open and swallow me whole. If it did, it was welcome to me.

It's said that I was a loner, but I wasn't really. I just didn't choose to socialise with the people that other people chose to socialise with. I reached the mainly wooden door. Peering in through a little square of frosted glass, I saw dim light. From where I was standing, the only indication of life.

I pushed open the door and it squealed like I was taking liberties. I had caused it terrible offence for daring to use it for the purpose it was intended.

Now inside the pub, I noted that the rough carpet underfoot shared the same spongy sensation as the tarmac outside. And no different to the asphalt, the stories I was sure the carpet could tell.

With such a thought in mind, Electric Dreams opened out in front of me. The interior as a whole was dilapidated, bare, no thrills; damp on the walls, paint flaking, wallpaper ripped and outdated. It was fair to say that, for the majority of regulars, décor was not the main consideration. You came here to get drunk, and in so doing obliterated the random injustices and blocked out the cruel realities of the outside world. Or at least, it was a case of here's hoping.

There was a barman standing, appropriately enough,

behind the bar. To look at him, he was slumped, moribund. He was in a zombified state.

Sitting squat on a round barstool situated at the end of the bar furthest from me was a man with a ponytail. The man was middle-aged. Not sure how old the ponytail was. To his left were three empty barstools, indicative of the scarcity of souls in the pub. For all its splendid isolation, I would have expected the pub, at this time, to be packed out. The fact it wasn't would have been a surprise to me if I actually believed in surprises.

Two other guys sat at the part of the bar closest to me. They were hunched in conversation. There was a conspiratorial air about them.

Furthest away, beyond the bar, there was the snug, just large enough to accommodate a pool table. Ensconced there were two fellas, both younger, pool cues in hand, crouched around the table, a white cue ball on green felt the centre of their universe.

I kept on walking and plumped myself on the barstool right next to the ponytail. On the subject of hair, I couldn't help but notice his was slick with grease and badly in need of a wash. Unshaven, vagrant; I'd go as far as to say he looked like he'd been sleeping in his clothes for a week.

He had the telltale odour of someone on the run for days. On the bar in front of him was a whisky and half pint of heavy, colloquially known as 'a hauf and a hauf'.

I knew him by name. He was called Ricardo.

I sat down on the stool, adjusting my buttocks until things got more comfortable. Or more accurately, tried to attain the illusion of comfort on a cold, flat, unyielding surface. I fidgeted from first position to second position, back to first position again.

My opening gambit was to address the barman, hopeful of life behind that hunched, undead exterior of his.

'Nice carpet,' I said. 'Pint of Diet Coke, please.'

Ricardo sat frozen, focussed entirely on his horizontally-ridged whisky glass. It too was greedy for his attention, like a horizontally-ridged siren.

For my Diet Coke, the barman did the necessary, though not before he shovelled ice into my glass without first asking.

'Three pound seventy,' he said.

I handed over a fiver, which he took in sluggish, humourless fashion. 'Ta very much,' I said, but the stream of niceties was proving to be one way.

'Sniff. Sniff.' The noise came from Ricardo.

'Sniff,' there it was again.

I swivelled on my seat, now facing him at an angle. 'Pardon me?' I said.

'You heard,' he said. A fact, even if I had a mind to, I could not deny.

Ricardo 'sat' his ground and eyeballed me. The tips of our noses virtually touching. His expression was thinly veiled, playfully vindictive. 'Little piggy,' he said, 'I could smell you a mile off.'

From the snug, there was the crack of a cue ball off a hoop or stripe. I was too far away and too preoccupied to make out the markings.

Barman returned with my change. His expression was expressionless. His movement was perfunctory. Such an essentially numb outlook was, I supposed, a prerequisite for working life in Electric Dreams.

'Thank you,' I said.

I took my change and sipped my drink. A rogue ice cube slipped into my mouth. I rolled the tip of my tongue, which flicked aimlessly at the cube.

To my right, Ricardo slurped noisily from his half pint.

'I'm thinking,' I said, 'been lying low for how many days now, Ricardo?'

Ricardo took the now empty half pint glass from his lips and made a show of studying it. 'And hey presto,' he said. 'You find me here. Who grassed me up?'

Ricardo put the glass back down on the bar. 'Hauf and hauf,' he said to the barman, motioning two outstretched fingers towards two empty glasses.

'You're either a brave little piggy,' Ricardo said, words intended once more for me, 'or a stupid bag of shite!'

I didn't want to look away from him. Didn't think it wise. All the same, I was aware that the snug wasn't generating any kind of noise, the area around the pool table had gone dormant.

There was a scuffing noise, the sound of a pool cue being chalked possibly, but it seemed to come from closer by.

'You know what I think?' I asked in what I hoped was a rhetorical tone, whatever that was.

'You remember Phil Oakey of The Human League?' I said. '*Don't You Want Me Baby?* You remember Giorgio Moroder? *I Feel Love* with Donna Sumner? What am I saying? I'm making them sound like they're deceased, but they're still making songs, I think, top tunes. Anyway, Phil Oakey and Giorgio Moroder, they collaborated together, created the quintessential eighties pop record, *Electric Dreams*. This morning, early doors, I popped into the station. Opening my mail, I find from an anonymous source a music CD of ... you guessed it.'

I wasn't expecting a response, and that's what I got anyway.

'The bizarre thing is that I'd only just downloaded the track a couple of weeks ago,' I said.

Nope. Nothing.

'*Electric Dreams* by Phil Oakey and Giorgio Moroder,' I prompted.

Ricardo's eyes widened. He knew full well where this

was leading. I paused, gave him the chance to take over and lead the discussion. An opportunity he neglected to take.

'This could only mean one thing. Well, to me at least,' I said. 'I recognised you as soon as I came in. Whoever, whatever, you're running from, you've run out of options. Ricardo, you're out of favours. Someone wants you off their hands, which is where I come in—and my comprehensive knowledge of '80s pop classics and dodgy Yoker bars. Electric Dreams and *Electric Dreams*. The wherewithal to make a connection.'

The silence around the pub was deafening. There was one source of sound only. It was just me talking out of my cakehole. All me.

'So, what say you and me go for a wee chat? I've got a car waiting outside. You can help me out with my enquiries; by first telling me why you're here and what the problem seems to be. Basically, throw some light on things.'

The two guys, sat at the other end of the bar when I arrived, occupied the other end of the bar no longer. They were no longer in a sitting position either. All together now, they were behind me.

I slid my glass of Diet Coke on the bar away from me. My thoughts were very much of the 'uh-oh' variety.

There was next to no time to take it all in. Guy 1 was bald with thick eyebrows. Guy 2 was slick and neat in appearance. If he were born in another time and in another place, he'd be a shoo-in for the Gestapo. Must have been a young person's look. You know how styles come and go.

A cavernous hand slammed into the back of my head. My forehead hit the bar with an almighty whack. Pain seemed to split my skull in two equal parts. A sliver of blood emerged from the resulting gash.

Next thing I was aware, my right arm was twisted around my back; immobilising me. I tried to lift my head, but only got as far as placing my chin on the bar.

Ricardo started on his new round of drinks.

'Break its arm,' Ricardo said, 'cut it, and send the little piggy wee-wee-wee all the way home.'

There was a crack, but this one came from the snug. Pool players were playing a new game of pool.

I took a deep breath.

When I exhaled, I was a different man. The kind that eats and shits pain for breakfast. My bulk shifted like the onrushing tide. My assailant adjusted his grip, sought to retain the advantage, but I was unbowed. I sat straight up on my stool, faster than a bullet, arm twisted, contorted, pain shooting through me, pulsating but, in increments, slowing down, becoming irrelevant.

Did they know who they were dealing with? Did they—

'Fucktard!' Announcing my arrival, I growled, shifting sputum from the lower recesses of my throat.

The back of my head, moving at force, hit Guy 1, as it turned out, square in the nose. His proboscis gave away with a satisfying plop and just like that I was as free as a bird.

I turned. I leapt to my feet.

Guy 1 was preoccupied, cradling his nose in both hands. He let out a mournful howl, which was fair enough—people do get attached to their schnozzles.

I landed a meaty wake-up jab on his hands-covered face. He went down in quick time.

Up until this point, Guy 2 seemed content to watch and learn, to wait his turn. Now, though, chib in hand, he was roused into action.

'Chib, ya bas!' he hollered like he was some modern-day, neddish, Gestapo-styled William Wallace.

The chib blade came at me in a flat circular motion.

I leaned back; I was rocking on my heels. Nasty consequences lay in wait for anyone in the blade's radius, but I was nimble on my feet. Swishing through the air, slicing through the ether, the blade, successfully dodged, passed on by.

Guy 2 was much like his partner; all front, full to bursting with useless bravado. Such as it was, his strategy was to come out all blazing. Showing his hand too early and leaving nothing to the imagination. When it came down to it, I wasn't too interested in using my imagination either.

Arms extended, I grabbed my attacker's leading arm in a pincer movement. It didn't take much—like kneading dough—to work and twist and cause the shoulder to pop out of its socket. My opponent roared in pain. I changed the point of pressure and broke one of the bones in his forearm. The chib fell to the ground. I released the pressure and Guy 2 crumpled and followed suit. Strewn across the spongy carpeted floor, he mewed like a deranged, unneutered cat. That and the other guy moaning, it could have been the least efficient slaughter house in the world.

'You don't get it,' I muttered under my breath, as good as drowned out by the noise around me. 'Nobody gets it.'

As for Ricardo, he made to stand up, only for a hand from yours truly to come down firmly on his shoulder.

'A word, Ricardo.' I gave his shoulder a reassuring squeeze. 'Like I said, there's a car waiting outside. Mind where you put your feet, watch out for the broken bodies as you go.'

'Oh, and one more thing ...'.

***

I'd been sitting outside Electric Dreams for a while now. The engine was off and a creeping cold had taken hold of the inside of the car. I wound the window up, but to little avail. The misery that came with plummeting temperatures was something I could do without. I was ready for action, but instead I was bored out of my head with only a concrete block with a wooden door to look at. It was my own fault. All my own doing. I could have said no, could have insisted I walk in with him, but I wanted to give him some slack. I wanted to build trust.

Now as I sat in the passenger seat in my DI's car, time passed slower than a tortoise on a leisure holiday. I grew increasingly agitated at the iciness of my breath and all I wanted to do was punch his face. (As unprofessional as that might sound.)

Then, without even as much as a drumroll to announce it, the door to Electric Dreams opened and out emerged a cross between a human being and frightened bunny rabbit. It was a face that I didn't recognise. One attached to a ponytail.

He was out of breath, wide eyed (and fluffy eared), and searching around frantically. That is, until he saw the car and sprinted in its direction.

I wound down the car window, stuck my head out and bellowed my very best 'Oi!'

He stopped in his tracks, doing everything he could not to roll back on his heels.

'Not another step, pal,' I said. 'Not until you explain what you're doing out here.'

As he shivered in the cold, his body began to stoop. 'The big man—I mean, Fisher, Detective Fisher—he sent me out.'

'Of course he did.'

I sat back. I pressed the switch to wind up the window. I felt an itch that seemed to hop from one part of my face to another, but resisted the temptation to give chase. There was an itch I was only too aware I needed to scratch, but not right now.

He opened the back door and climbed in.

'Huff, huff.'

I adjusted the rear-view mirror and watched him like a hawk from the front seat. He was gulping down air like it was going out of fashion. No choice really but to wait for the wheezing to pass.

'Huff.'

His breathing was a little more under control now. His face less stretched. His nostrils less flared.

'I'm Detective Sergeant Spencer,' I said. 'Come to help, sir, with our enquiries?'

'Ricardo,' he said.

'Of course,' I said, 'Ricardo.' My face was a blank.

Ricardo was sitting slumped, exhausted, arms hanging down, hands dangling over the back seat. 'Shit—shit—he's a fucking magician,' he said. He looked up. 'Got a message for you, huff, he said he'll be out in ten minutes, oh – and another thing …'.

'Yes?' I said.

He was wearing skinny jeans. Or jeans for a skinny person. I noticed—although wish I hadn't—he had a bulge in his pocket. There didn't seem much room in there for anything, but undeterred, he managed to squeeze in a bent, corkscrewed hand. As he rummaged, a crackly noise came from his pocket.

Through the rear-view mirror, pocket bulge and all, Ricardo filled the view. If he appeared dubious before, he looked well dodgy now.

'Careful now,' I said.

From the murky abyss, having teased it out, ever so

slowly, there surfaced a packet of fried potato product, a crumpled brown wrapper.

'Smoky bacon OK?' he said.

***

I knocked back the Diet Coke, crunching every cube of ice into obliteration, ridding the possibility of anything solid hitting the back of my throat.

Guy 1 and Guy 2 writhed and wailed at my feet. Synchronised, chaotic, noisy as fuck.

'Three pound seventy for a Diet Coke!' I said. 'In this dump?'

I was determined to get my money's worth. With two almighty glugs, I finished the absentee Ricardo's heavy and whisky. I slammed the glasses down onto the bar one after the other and looked for the barman.

There was no sign of him. After selling me a packet of crisps for a quid, his reanimated legs had taken him exit stage left.

I wasn't ready to change back. I didn't want to change back. I was resisting the warm, fuzzy cloak slowly wrapping around me, extinguishing the life out of me. For what I was feeling now was life. The scent of righteousness. The correct order of things. The reek of how it really was—of how it fucking should be.

'Hey fuckface!' a voice called out to me.

It originated from the snug.

I turned around to discover two pool players rushing towards me, cues held above their heads like they were part of some Genghis Khan billiard-playing Mongol army.

I grabbed my pint glass, mindful to tip out the one last ice cube that had got away. I smashed the glass against the bar.

The cue-twirling yobs would be in and around me in moments. Their guttural utterances filled the air. I could see the vehemence on their faces; the hatred in their eyes. It was like all my Christmases had come early.

I raised the broken glass so they had something to think about. And giving them something to think about was what I was all about.

'Fuckface,' I declared. 'That's my middle name.'

9.

Appointment No. 2

As it happened, an early slot was available. And I filled it.

Getting up that morning, I was a physical mess, but this had never stopped me before. So I stuffed myself full of painkillers to the point my body rattled and I gritted my teeth to the point of grinding them down to calcified stumps.

I drove out to the city centre, specifically West George Street, and more specifically Cuthbert and Associates, where on the road every speed bump and mini-pothole, every jump and jerk, was my accursed enemy.

I got there, I suppose that's what mattered, and was called into the office. Dr Dawn observed without comment as I sat down extremely gingerly, manoeuvring my shrieking, tender frame in slow, tiny increments, throwing in the odd 'ooh' and 'ah' for good measure like I was one of *those* plumbers in one of *those* films where he has a droopy moustache and an unfeasibly large spanner. If Dr Dawn feared it might take the whole hour session for me to guide my battered shell into my seat, she did not say.

Eventually, at last, I was sat down. My posterior had landed. The memory cushion tried its best to make sense of me, but it was an impossible task.

Dr Dawn took a few moments while she considered her opening gambit. What kind of tone was she looking to set? I couldn't help but notice she was wearing another herringbone blouse; white this time. I followed the patterns on her shirt; rows of parallel lines that sloped in opposite directions, effectively the glue that kept the pieces of fabric together. Momentarily, I lost myself in the design.

Her top button was undone again. This confirmed to me that she wasn't a stuffed shirt and I was fine with that.

In her possession was a slim, expensive-looking ballpoint, which she rolled between her hands. As for the make of pen, it was Montblanc, or maybe Aspinal of London? The truth was that most ballpoints, especially the expensive ones, look the exact same to me. Still, you can't take a psychiatrist seriously without a good pen. It's an essential psychiatrist's prop.

Also, this time she had a notebook, opened at a fresh page, laid on her lap. Dr Dawn was ready for business.

'Appointment with a baseball bat?' she said.

'Something like that,' I said, half-smiling, half-wincing. Smile and wince meeting in the middle.

'Busy day yesterday?' she said.

I breathed out through pursed lips. 'Yes, I suppose so,' I said.

'If you were to give your day a mark out of ten—one being not very busy and ten being incredibly busy ...'

'I'd say nine and a half,' I replied, lightning fast.

'How is your new partner shaping up?'

And I was immediately thinking; who mentioned anything about a new partner?

Could it have been Dr Dawn who tipped off DS

Spencer as to my whereabouts yesterday? Was she Police Scotland's version of *Deep Throat*? I raised my left eyebrow in an arch and waited a few seconds for Dr Dawn to do likewise. She did not.

Instead, I answered the question.

'Still early days,' I said. 'Still getting to know each other. But I know enough. As an example, faced with the choice of sharing a picnic together or interrogating a suspect later today, after much consideration I'd say she'd edge towards the latter.'

'Hmm,' she said. She wasn't one for giving much, if anything, away was our Dr Dawn. 'Was this the first time you'd met DS Spencer?' she continued.

'No,' I said.

'Would you care to elucidate?'

'If I must.'

Dr Dawn carefully laid her ballpoint down on the spine of her notebook.

'Well, words such as 'need' and 'must' are not ones I'd ever wish to hear in our sessions together,' she said. 'I don't want you to feel any compulsion to ...'

'It was two years ago,' I said.

I'm not sure why I cut her off. We had an hour to burn. As soon as I'd blurted the words out I was asking myself, what happened to the carefully formulated strategy to let her do most of the talking?

Anyway, I'd started, so it wouldn't hurt to finish. 'There was a missing persons case,' I said. 'A child. A girl. Twelve-years-old. You may very well remember the 'Handley' case. The Police Commissioner took a personal interest. Even the First Minister had something to say about it. Every available officer was pulled in. We were operating out of three stations on the West Coast.'

'My tummy was rumbling,' I continued.

'Your tummy ...?' Dr Dawn said. Pen poised, she raised

her notebook from her lap. She thought about writing something down, then thought better of it. Instead, she leaned back in her chair.

I took this as a prompt to continue.

'I was sitting at my desk reading the *Daily Record*,' I said. 'It was approaching lunchtime, I suppose. DS Spencer passed me just as my tummy rumbled loudly and she commented on it. Although not quite sure she was Detective Sergeant back then. Come to think of it, I wasn't a Detective Inspector.'

'Is your neighbour a potential rioter?' I said.

'I don't ...' Dr Dawn said. She was bemused. 'Hmm ...?'

'That was the *Daily Record* headline,' I explained. 'It had an accompanying photo of a youth; face obscured by a scarf and about to throw a Molotov cocktail. 'Middle East or Coatbridge?' screamed the sub-heading. You know, dramatic.'

'"You eat?" someone said. I looked up and the voice belonged to Spencer. Her hair was gathered up in a scrunchie—except that it's not called that anymore—a bobble.'

'She went on to say that she'd never seen me eat.'

'A few of them were going out for a meal the next night and she asked me if I fancied going along. She asked me if the rumours were true that I worked twenty-four hours straight. That kind of thing. I thanked her and said yes, I did eat. It didn't hurt so long as I remembered to chew. I think we even swapped numbers.'

As I relayed this to Dr Dawn, it occurred to me how terribly innocuous it all was. An exchange that lived and died in seconds. Part of the landscape; the latest addition to the vacuous hellos and cheerless cheerios that punctuated our dreary professional existences. Very little in the way of eye contact. She was being sociable and I replied in kind. A firefly moment in both our lives. But how to say this, put this across, and not come across as some stuffed shirt.

'Next day, early doors, investigating the case of the missing girl, my locus was the area where she, Lindsey Handley, was last seen. I found myself in an ordinary, painfully monotone housing estate, next to a field of long grass. The street was called Northwood Crescent. I was alone, on foot, knocking on doors, house after house after house.'

'I remember not many households were empty. Recent photo of the girl in hand, I was looking for a lead, of course, or at least a meaningful response.'

'All of us, we were working under a lot of pressure. We were under the spotlight. Mother having made an emotional appeal to the media, near incoherent, in a flood of tears. No sign of the father, who had walked out on the mother and daughter several years before but was already ruled out as a suspect. It was morning but, come midday, there would be a flotilla of needy TV camera crews and hire-a-quote journalists, nothing unusual in these types of cases.'

'And ...' Dr Dawn said.

But there was no 'and'. That was it. I withdrew into myself. I became immersed in an unnatural fog. If the good doctor was speaking to me, her words did not register. Did not permeate.

None shall pass.

Nothing getting through at all.

***

It was a colourless morning on Northwood Crescent. If you were to tell me the sky could be otherwise, I wouldn't have believed it. My fingers curled into a fist and I knock-knock-knocked on yet another door.

An unshaven middle-aged man with a narrow face, dressed in a black t-shirt stretched at the neck, opened the door. I explained who I was and why I was there. I dutifully held up the photograph of the girl. He never once looked at me. He stared at the photo in silence. His was a vacant stare. A pair of hollow eyes to go with his hollow face.

Then he simply turned and walked away, leaving the door ajar. Taken in isolation, not suspicious behaviour, but not something I could dismiss out of hand either.

Calling after him, I angled my head better to see through the gap at the door.

'Sir ...?' I said.

There was no sign of him.

I squeezed through the gap in the door and into the hall. It was at that point my phone started to buzz in my pocket. I answered.

'Brian speaking,' I said. A voice busily chirped on the other end of the phone. 'Oh,' I said. 'You've found her.'

I hadn't thought about how I'd react if the worst case scenario were to happen. The voice informed me that the Handley girl was found dead in an outlying field. She was naked, multiple lacerations to the legs and stomach.

I ended the call. As I did so, even though it would at most have been a matter of moments before, I couldn't remember if I'd thanked the caller or said goodbye.

I made another call through blurred vision. The moment it ended, I had no recollection of it or who I had spoken to.

I held the dormant phone for a moment in the palm of my hand before quickly, furtively, and conspiratorially returning it to my pocket.

I turned and with the same palm pushed the door shut.

'Sir ...' I repeated.

It was if my voice didn't carry too far into the hall. It

was as if the air was hungry for it, gobbling up the words as soon as they had left my mouth.

I walked slowly and purposefully to the living room door, where the sole occupier of the house—one Henry Roberts—was sitting in his armchair watching TV with the volume set to a ridiculously low setting. The words coming out of the box were barely audible. It took all of my concentration to try and work out what was being said.

But I had to fight the distractions. I needed to clear my head.

Mr Roberts, on the other hand, was a wholly different matter.

'Sir,' I said, 'when was the last time you saw Lindsey Handley?'

I already had my answer. I could smell her on him. It sucked the marrow from my bones.

'Stand up!' I said. It was a command, layered with dread and malice; taking no prisoners. The surrounding air would not be fucking with those particular words.

Roberts couldn't help it. Unthinking, he sprang to his feet.

It was doubtful he'd taken much notice of the unassuming figure that had first knocked on his door, but if he had, he would need to acknowledge some changes.

How he was now standing in front of a different man. Suit tighter around him, a frame that somehow occupied more space than before. There would be something in his eyes as well. Heightened sense of smell, heightened sense of everything. Now here was a face that told a picture.

I was that man; the very opposite of the pathetic, mealy-mouthed, unresponsive creature standing in front of me.

I decided to inject some life into proceedings. I punched him in the throat.

His body collapsed like a house of cards. He was down on his knees.

Holding him by both ears, I kneed him in the face.

Roberts could not have been more at one with the ground if he tried. Blood was pouring out of his nose, lending an authentic red-brown tinge to what was otherwise a crappy, uninspiring, beige carpet.

The scent of blood on rubbish carpet was in my nostrils. I took a moment to draw the curtains. After that, you could say I lost it.

It was a long morning. He had stopped breathing, but I kept on punching and kicking anyway.

I was out of breath. I could imagine all the things he had done to her, all the ways he had desecrated her. I could imagine her intermittent pleading voice throughout. At what point did she lose hope? Did she think there might be a way out of this? That she might still survive the ordeal? I was determined to ensure that Henry Roberts would be under no such illusion.

And he never fought back. At no time did he resist, despite at least part of me wishing he would.

I took a wander into the adjoining kitchen area and returned with a sharp knife.

I lost time, or maybe it was time that lost me, but sometime later I woke on a sodden, sticky floor.

Around me, a world of defecation and blood had taken shape, and the smell of copper. My jaw was sore and stiff like I'd been chewing on something really tough. The taste of grit and iron sat at the back of my throat. My stomach felt like a wasp nest.

My mind was set. I got up.

I tried not to take in any of the lurid mixture of savagery and debris inside the four walls around me. Images of the grotesque jostled and pulled at my peripheral vision. My present location could be described as many things, but you could no longer reasonably call it a *living* room.

I took what I needed from around the house. I put my jacket in a carrier bag. I went to the bathroom and wiped myself down to the shoes. I was quick and efficient. I retraced my steps and cleared my prints. I left the way I came in.

The carrier bag was a 'Bag for Life'.

Outside there was a lull. Not that there had been much of a buzz beforehand, but still, not a soul to be seen. News of the Handley girl was about to break, and then the media circus would descend. All hell would break loose. Hell on hell.

For the time being though, Northwood Crescent was a deathly, strangely quiet place to be in.

Carrier bag in hand, I didn't hang around to wait for this to change.

My car was parked on another street. As I put distance from one locus to another, it occurred to me, up until my encounter with Roberts, I had knocked on every door. Plenty of potential witnesses who had seen my face, heard my voice, knew my name.

Or rather, they had seen *a* face, heard *a* voice, and knew *a* name.

I got myself home and spent the rest of the day scrubbing. I cleansed myself. I piled my clothes into a black plastic bag, which I then labelled 'furnace'.

My tummy couldn't stop rumbling. Hunger in its purest, unrelenting form followed me around. But the last thing I wanted to do was eat.

***

'And ...'

And—I had told her enough, and even this was scratching the surface.

Even though I could recount a whole lot more, much of it stayed confined to my thoughts. It was between me and you'd have to call it my conscience. But crucially, not to be shared with Dr Dawn.

So I sat in the company of Dr Dawn, mind blank, eyes glazed over, staring off into some indiscriminate empty space.

Perhaps I had incriminated myself already, if she could place me at a certain time in a certain location. If it was, though, to come down the balance of possibilities, the spinning of a heptagonal coin, I didn't think she would. She wasn't police. Any report she might make would be chiefly concerned with my health, my present state of mind, which was fine, obviously.

Plus, we had a connection of some kind. I was sure.

So there could be no 'and'. Not on this occasion. Nothing to see here. Nothing to say here.

And yet, if you were to obliterate the word 'and'—if you removed it, ripped it from of the ether—we would all be in trouble, the world would tilt precariously on its axis. There would only be chaos, rioting on the streets, daughters having sex with their fathers. So, where there was no 'and', as was the case here, it was pretty clear to me I would need to make one up. Or rather draw on an earlier conversation and move it on to a more convenient time. My powers of recollection were suddenly pristinely clear.

'And—I phoned up DS Spencer,' I said, 'a couple of hours before the meal was due to start and told her that, regrettably, I'd need to take a rain check. I've no idea if they even went through with it in the end, after the news came through.'

I was conscious of my lips moving, forming the words,

but had no idea if any sound was escaping. 'The Handley case.'

I widened my eyes. I could feel them roll in my sockets. Like hamsters on wheels. That kind of brought me back to my senses. 'I needed an early night anyway. I was facing an early start the next day. We all were.'

'I don't think the call itself lasted very long. DS Spencer and I have never discussed it since. I mean, what possible reason should we have? Sleeping dogs and such.'

'How did you feel about it?' she said.

'Disappointed. Sorry for everyone involved,' I said.

'I was referring to the Handley case?'

'That's what I was meaning.'

I realised, from me, that she was looking for a little more gusto. So—

'Devastated,' I said. 'I was distraught. Shattered. Absolutely shattered.'

'Her killer was found to have been living locally,' I continued. 'The victim's clothing was found in his home. He was brutally killed himself, but—to date—they've never caught his killer.'

'So, it was no longer a high profile missing persons case. A murder investigation into a child killer, public declarations aside, was allowed to quietly slide down the totem pole.'

'I was assigned to another case.'

I was thinking hard. Had I left anything out? Yes, yes, probably ...

'Yes, that's about it ...' I trailed off again, which Dr Dawn picked up on before I did.

'Thank you. That all seems very comprehensive.' She crossed her arms. 'We can either sit in silence for another ten minutes or we can call it a day right now. Your decision, Detective Inspector.'

No change there, it took a monumental effort to push

through the pain barrier. Even so, I was already out of my chair before she had finished her sentence.

She called after me.

'Don't forget to talk to Sheila at the main desk,' she said. 'She'll arrange your next appointment.'

***

Not for the first time, as I walked to my car, I was left to my own thoughts. I should have been terrified. I should have been appalled.

The other *me*, he was always there. I was always aware of him burrowing, snuggling and lurking, just at the back of my head. But that day with Henry Roberts was the first time he truly revealed himself. A day of long teeth, claws, and knives.

If I were to judge myself, how would that be? That time I was still myself, but I had changed, not just physically, not just mentally.

Different thresholds. So swift to anger, so quick to get to a level of violence that was terrible, cruel, unflinching. There was no self-restraint. A severe deficit of any moral code. In its place, there was a wildness ...

But I was still myself.

I had murdered someone. He was guilty and he deserved it. Or he deserved something, but not that? I'd crossed a line and, as a result, could I allow my actions to then go unchecked?

Of course not, the situation demanded that there be some kind of consequence. I decided I needed some time, if only to try and understand why, and what I had become. Maybe I could control it better. God forgive me, maybe I could do some good instead.

But one thing I was determined to do was bring me, myself, to account.

There could be no act without consequence. I needed something; some way to exert some kind of self-control. But I knew such an undertaking would take time. I had to make allowances for a few mistakes along the way. I was very much a Work in Progress. There would be setbacks, but still there had to be checks and balances. A little wiggle room, but not too much. That day with Roberts—that killing time—that would be strike number one.

Three strikes and I was out.

10.

Interrogation No. 2

After my appointment with Dr Dawn, so came the interrogation of Ricardo Dreyfus.

Drumchapel Police Station was my next port of call. There were no issues this time with the interview room. There were no plans on the horizon to paint and decorate. No embargo placed on mice, which were free to come and go.

As I drove in, I had to contend with the crumbling shell that was my physique, trapped in my own beaten skin and aching joints. I was sick on the outside, on the inside, on all sides.

On arrival, I hobbled to the bathroom. There, I hunched over the sink and turned on the tap, even though I had no intention of applying water to any part of me. I had an unnatural craving for background noise and found the flow of the water, its impact on the white porcelain finish of the sink, to sooth and distract in equal measures.

I removed my shirt and did my best to ignore the troubled, pained expression, having hijacked my face, reflecting back at me.

I twisted my side to better inspect in the mirror a big wide expanse of a bruise, the result of an almighty whack with a pool cue. It was like a stain. Like a large country on a world map. It was remorseless, but yesterday in Electric Dreams, my attackers in turn had discovered I could be just as remorseless.

Previous to everything, I had murdered one man. In response, I'd come to terms with it. I'd gone through a twisted but compelling process that involved admonishment on one hand and self-preservation on the other. I had used up one of my three strikes.

Now, having had to contend with yesterday's shenanigans, I was relieved to report, having confirmed it in my mind, that the blessed statistic still stood.

Guy 1 and Guy 2, aka the two pool players; I had hurt them. I came out of Electric Dreams standing. In the interest of accuracy, I had something of a limp, but we can overlook that. The important thing to be gleaned among the multiple cracking and yanking of bones was that no one had died.

No one. No second strike. Nothing had got back to me. I'd followed the law of the jungle that was Electric Dreams, Yoker, and I'd given as good as I got.

The large stain-bruise on my side was the Galaxy. Lots of smaller bruises arranged around it were space rock floating around the outer edge. If my body was a universal canvas, it felt like it was the Big Crunch, the end of all existence. What was it about human beings that we needed to compare everything to something? To view such a thing, such a crippling pain, in terms of the end of the Universe?

Because it hurt, that's why. It bloody hurt. And even

here, especially here, in the barren bleached landscape of a male toilet, it all came back to one particular backdrop—enduring, unending, and so utterly depressing.

I put my shirt back on. Quickly followed—well, as quickly as the various aches and pains allowed—by my jacket.

Two more murders and I would hand myself in, or so went the ultimatum. Self-imposed.

I tried to stop looking at my reflection, which was difficult considering I was facing a mirror.

It was then that I had a wobble. Thoughts circled in a perpetual loop around my head. The less you wanted to think of it, the more you couldn't stop thinking about it. I didn't know how much more of this I could take. I wanted to scratch my face off. Scream to the world, point out the obvious, and tell them what they'd been missing. The truth was at the end of their noses.

I just needed to take some breaths. For a little while there, it was getting hairy; the thoughts in my head; the worry and angst, heated and over-cooked. Dr Dawn's voice in my head, that's all I needed.

'Words such as "need" and "must" are not ones I'd ever want to hear in our sessions together.'

I'd only been away from my favourite police psychologist for a matter of hours, but you could tell part of me was missing her already. And you know what? The panic, all that dust and heat had abated. I felt better for it. I clawed myself back. I reverted to my usual calm self; someone ready to face the world.

Or more accurately, the interview room. It was straight down to business as I joined Detective Sergeant Spencer on one side of the table. On the other side were Ricardo Dreyfus and his solicitor. I sat directly across from dear old Ricardo. His gaze was fixed on me alone, staring at me like I was some kind of crazy madman. Spencer was in charge of the recording system. The solicitor held a sheet of paper in front of him, like a newsreader ready for recital.

Whilst I had been spending quality time and navigating trips down memory lane with Dr Dawn, Spencer had done some digging. She'd flagged up a robbery from a week ago, which had all the hallmarks of Dreyfus' MO.

'Drumchapel Station,' Spencer said, clearly enunciating her words for the benefit of the recording, followed by date, time and location, 'Interview Room 1. Present are DI Fisher, DS Spencer, Ricardo Dreyfus of no fixed abode, and Mr Dreyfus's solicitor, Hadrian Jackson.'

Ricardo continued to only have eyes for me. Eyes of the bulging and wide-eyed variety.

Next to him, his solicitor noisily cleared his throat. He had his very best deadpan face on.

'My client, Mr Dreyfus, has a prepared statement,' he said. 'When my client agreed to help the police with their enquiries, he was under the misapprehension that this was to do with the search for a missing puppy from a residence in Kings Park Avenue.'

'Now my client has been informed of the true nature of the investigation,' the solicitor continued, 'I must inform you that he is unaware of any robbery of any High Street jewellers and therefore, with extreme regret, he can be of no assistance to the police in this, their present enquiry.'

Spencer and I exchanged a glance. She scrunched up her face. I couldn't hide my exasperation either. It had already been a long day.

Okay, if that's how he wanted to play it. I adjusted back to face Ricardo. I was all smiles.

'That's fine,' I said. 'Our door is always open, should anything come to mind. Happy to talk puppies anytime. Kindly tell Mr Dreyfus that he is free to go.'

The solicitor, mouth opening, turned to his client and nearly did just that, before instead giving out a disagreeable snort.

He gathered up his papers and scooped them into his briefcase. Clearly, despite my prompting, there was not to be another word spoken.

Spencer, for her part, arms firmly crossed, sat glaring at a fixed point on the far wall. It was staring all round.

This wasn't lost on the departing Ricardo. As client and solicitor went on their merry way, Ricardo Dreyfus continued to stare daggers at me.

Even when he had left, I could still feel his eyes on me, like he could see through walls. Like he had X-ray vision. Like he was a Scottish undernourished, skinny-jeans-wearing, ponytailed version of Superman.

Leading with the eyebrows, I shook my head. The fact Ricardo was a worm that had wriggled off its hook, there was nothing to do but shrug it off.

I have to confess, as little as I knew Spencer, I preferred it when she was in one of her less talkative moods as she was now. But I knew I'd have to say something, phrase a question, to bring her kicking and screaming back to me. You know what they say, you can't make an omelette without knowing how to make an omelette.

I spoke quietly. 'The High Street jewellery heist. I know the headlines. Tell me what you know.'

She sighed while absent-mindedly scratching the top of her shoulder.

'Jewellers called McConnell's,' she said. 'Just as it was opening—as soon as the shutters went up—three male robbers walked in, one holding a shotgun, the other a crowbar, the other a holdall. All three wore ladies' tights over their heads in order to disguise their faces.'

I motioned to speak.

'And before you say anything, DI, sir,' she said. 'No

one thus far has been able to identify the make of ladies' tights.'

'That's a shame,' I said. 'Brand loyalty,' I ventured, 'is a big thing with career criminals.'

I flashed a tiny smile in her direction.

She didn't reciprocate. Instead, she lowered her head and continued.

'Dreyfus has previous with a shotgun, he was caught two years ago in possession of one, which is more or less the reason why he spent the subsequent eighteen months detained at Her Majesty's pleasure. I flagged up the recent jewellery heist. It fits his MO.'

'Good work, DS,' I said. 'It's still early days. We need to keep the pressure on Ricardo. We should speak to others in the Dreyfus clan of dubious morals. Keep squeezing them until the pips squeak.'

'Rotten apples don't fall far from the tree,' Spencer said.

By that remark, if she was being facetious—or if she was just taking the mickey—I didn't much care. I rather liked her last comment and nodded enthusiastically to match.

'Yes, I agree,' I said. 'I'll need to watch the tape of the robbery.'

'There isn't one,' she said, serious in tone now. The solemnity of her words took hold of my face and gave it a good slap. 'Apparently McConnell's is under new management and they hadn't got around to setting anything up yet.'

'Apparently,' she said. A word she'd decided worth repeating.

'Who contacted the police?'

'A passer-by.'

'So none of the staff, not one, set off a hidden alarm or anything?'

'Apparently not.'

It was then that I asked DS Spencer for the name of the new owner of McConnell's the High Street Jewellers. And that's when things began to get really interesting.

***

We were back in the Kia in transit on the motorway. Spencer was certainly industrious and organised. She was driving the car.

She sort of took over and I was too sore to put up a fuss.

Too tired. I didn't even have the energy to form a petted lip.

At least we had got the potentially discomfiting subject of my car keyring out of the way. It was certainly jangly. There was a lot of stuff on there; various accoutrements accumulated. Among other things, a St Andrews Cross pin, replica dog tags, a plush-finished miniature penguin, and a penknife.

'Is the penknife legal?' she said.

'Blade is less than three inches,' I said.

'Here is a man who knows his Police, Public Order and Criminal Justice Act,' she said. 'Does it depend on how sharp it is?'

'Define sharp?' I said.

'Sharp,' she said.

The 'police officer' talk was prolonging things. The conversation had already reached its natural end. Sometimes it's just best to embrace the empty space.

She drove on. The motorway was reasonably quiet, so the Kia nudged seventy on the inside lane. The car glided agreeably, almost dreamlike, a law of physics all of its own. I looked out over Spencer's shoulder at the traffic beyond the barrier, moving in the opposite direction, which seemed to the frailty of the naked eye to be going at something like three hundred miles per hour.

'So, where to now?' I said, stretching my legs, taking advantage of the passenger seat and its two inches of extra legroom.

'Milngavie,' she said. 'A woman went missing two days ago.'

'This morning,' she continued, 'husband was sent her severed finger in a Jiffy bag. It came through the post.'

I lay the back of my head against the chair's headrest, only to come to the rapid conclusion that, as headrests go, it wasn't the most comfortable.

'Milngavie, eh?' I said. 'Nice. Nice area.'

We stopped outside the house address, 20 Tall Trees. The house was detached. Purpose-built. Quiet, respectable, very plush surroundings.

Milngavie was where people kept to themselves and regularly tended to their gardens. Jiffy bags and severed fingers were not the done thing. In my head, I could already hear the local residents protest. 'These types of things don't happen here. Not in *Mill-Guy*.'

Spencer unclipped her seatbelt and I followed suit. 'Forensics been and gone already,' she said.

We rang the doorbell and Charles Bartholomew answered. He was wearing a dressing gown. As he stood in the doorway, about to ask us in, he seemed nervous. First thing that gave this away was the gnawing of his knuckle.

Mr Bartholomew had enough of his wits about him to offer us a cup of tea, which I gratefully accepted on my and Spencer's behalf. I was never one to turn down the chance of a cup of tea.

It was a decent enough brew, courtesy of a Scottish Blend teabag if I was not mistaken, in a nice enough cup.

Both Spencer and I were on the couch. Mr

Bartholomew sat in an armchair. He looked like he carried all the troubles of the world on his sagging shoulders. Unshaven, dishevelled. He seemed terribly sad, weary; his head was down.

I was happy to sit and sip discreetly as my colleague asked the questions.

Mr Bartholomew,' Spencer said, 'can I ask, when was the last time you saw your wife? Amanda isn't it?'

'Wednesday,' he answered. 'Told me she was going shopping.'

'What type of shopping?'

'Just ... shopping. It's what she said if her intention was to be out for most of the day.'

'It must have been terrible finding a Jiffy bag in today's mail?'

'Terrible,' he agreed. 'Terrifying. Horrible. I could hear the postman walking up the path. He was whistling *Crazy Little Thing Called Love*, I think.'

'I just stood there,' he said, 'and watched the Jiffy bag being squeezed through the letter box. I opened it, checked the contents, didn't make sense of it right away, and when I did, I just dropped the bag. I was in a state. It was horrible.'

'I just sat on the bottom stair rocking to and fro for as long as—' Mr Bartholomew hunched his shoulders, which despite his best efforts still seemed to sag. He filled his cheeks with air before exhaling— 'three and a half minutes.'

'Who would do this?' he added.

To be fair, this was the question we all were asking.

'Was there a note?'

'No, nothing; just my wife's finger.'

'To your knowledge, Mr Bartholomew, is there anyone that bears a grudge against you or your wife? Any arguments you know of? Disputes? Bad blood?'

At this, Mr Bartholomew looked up, his features solidified and hardened.

I froze half-sip.

'I'm a bank manager,' he said.

'I'm a respected man,' he continued. 'A pillar of community. Ask anyone. We go to church regularly. It's something of a hike; it's on the Great Western Road, but we have family connections. Episcopalian. You might know it?'

'Saint ...' I piped in, intuitively.

'... Mary's,' Mr Bartholomew answered.

And it didn't stop there. His list of good works continued to the point I considered canonising him myself. Saint Mr Bartholomew did have a nifty ring to it.

Later, having asked all the usual questions and uttered the customary stock assurances—ever-watchful of tone, never straying from an acceptable level of sympathy and caution—myself and Spencer decamped to the local pub. The Talbot Arms, to be precise.

I wanted to get more of a feel for the local area. See if I could gain insight, some inspiration. You'd be surprised, it's sometimes the little things that make the biggest difference. The tiny things.

We sat at a round table near the window. It gave Spencer the option of peering outside, something else to look at besides my ugly mug. I had a Diet Coke with ice, served with a multi-coloured paper straw. Spencer had a pint of lager shandy.

'So, what do you think?' she said.

'He's a manager of a bank,' I mused. 'Pillar of the community, so he was quick to inform us. Former Patron of the Prince's Trust, involved in a multitude of local charities, church-goer; has some money put away. Nice house. It could be blackmail.'

'But wouldn't you expect the blackmailer to have been

in touch by now?' Spencer said. 'A note? A phone call? Something more than a finger in the post, as gruesome as that is? It's been confirmed it belongs to Amanda Bartholomew, by the way.'

'Hmm,' I said, 'No fingerprints I take it?'

'Well, here's the thing,' she said. 'The Jiffy bag is apparently covered in prints, but only from the severed finger.'

'Someone's idea of a bad joke?' I said. It was the type of question that didn't need an answer.

We'd a hit a wall. There had been nothing suspicious leading up to Amanda Bartholomew's disappearance. There was little to go on, to the point of emaciation. Without motive, a police officer's life was stripped bare. DS Spencer summed it up best: 'If you ask me, Detective Inspector Brian, the whole thing is as whiffy as a week-old haddock.'

Having delivered the epistle of the day, she drained her shandy before placing the empty glass down on the table. 'Time for another one?' she said. 'Diet Cokes all round?' On her face was a half-smiling, half-quizzical expression. It was like, even now, she was still trying to work me out.

I'd reached my limit. Any more fizzy liquid and my teeth would start to hurt. My eyes darted from one side to the other.

'No, yes, no?' she said, before unilaterally setting off.

My gaze never left her as she made her way to the bar. It was part of the job description to see people for what they were. Take Mr Bartholomew for example, was he keeping something from us? I was thinking something seemed askew, as soon as I planted eyes on him. But of course, he *was* a bank manager.

DS Spencer, Mr Bartholomew, the whole world; everybody was hiding something. The good and the bad stashed away inside of us, in safe keeping, at least for some of the time.

11.

Tiny Acts of Kindness

Matters were afoot in a lock-up garage in Clydebank. By way of description of the interior of this specific lock-up, in the corner there was a cement mixer and some cement bags; leaning up against the wall was a spade, a long hammer, and tools of a similar nature. Hanging limply from the ceiling was a bare light bulb. Taking centre stage was a dude named Bruce, stripped naked, sat slumped in a chair. There was no need to tie him down. The fight had been knocked out of him.

The lack of proper lighting—the strategically placed spools of darkness—protected, thankfully enough, Bruce's modesty, because let's face it, when all's said and done, who wants to be looking at that? He was a little flabby around the edges, showing signs of letting himself go. Give him another few years and I wouldn't be surprised if he ended up quite the fatty. For now, Bruce was exhausted, badly beaten, bruised and lacerated. He was sobbing, which was the least he could do. Where there was a fine head of healthy, thick, black hair previously, dried blood patches were now to be found.

His breathing was ragged. He was very still. Several feet in front of him was an empty stool. Between him and the stool, facing him, were three female Staffordshire bull terriers—or Staffies for short—all sat in a line. The dominant female, occupying the middle, bared her teeth.

'Christ,' Bruce muttered.

I didn't much care for blasphemy in any form, but equally one could appreciate that this was a stressful time for the lad.

'Down, lass,' I said. The lead Staffie stopped growling.

Bruce was drooling at this point. To be fair, it was the end of a long day for both of us.

I sat on the stool, legs straddled at either side. I was known to Bruce. He should have recognised me by now. Maybe he chose not to. I was a disciple, born out of place and time. I was touched and pious and, when it came down to it, let's be honest, full of spite.

'I see you've met my bitches,' I said.

Reacting to my voice, Bruce moved his head a millimetre to the side.

'Come on, man,' Bruce said, 'I didn't do nothing.'

I rolled my eyes. My hand fluttered around my chest before elevating towards my chin. 'Now,' I said, 'what's that you say? Didn't. Do. Nothing.'

I smiled. I was a spider found time to acknowledge the fly having flown into its web. 'That's a double negative, ye ken,' I said. 'That means you *did* do something!'

Tears streaked down Bruce's pitiful bruised and puffy face. My heart went out to him.

'Naww, you don't understand,' he said.

I chuckled, I hoped in sympathy, and shook my head. One's sympathy, all told, could only go so far. There could only be so many spoonfuls of the stuff. Sometimes it had to be done; the need to be cruel, not necessarily to be kind, just to be cruel.

'It's you, I'm afraid,' I said, 'who doesn't understand.'

I leapt to my feet. I held my hands out to either side like I was Robert DeNiro from one of his gangster epics. '"It wisnae me! Ye've got the wrong man,"' I said, laying on the Scottish accent. I sounded like Gerald Butler in *300*.

I resumed my normal voice, about to make, at least to my mind, a serious point. Time to outline the reality of the world we both currently inhabited.

'My son,' I said. 'If I didn't do this to you, if I didn't make you suffer in this way, someone else would be doing it in my place. And I can't allow that. It's about what turns this world of ours around. It's about debt and obligation. And someone has called in a particular debt and this, the beatings, the stripping you naked, these are the terms of payment.'

Poor Bruce's shoulders were so tight with tension, you couldn't see his neck. Slowly, he leaned forward, body creaking like a tall tree chopped down, caught in slow motion. His back was smeared in brown stuff.

The smell hit my nostrils. I couldn't help but screw up my face. 'Hoy,' I said, 'have you gone and shat yourself?'

Lead Staffie sniffed at Bruce's leg, which caused him to spring to his feet. Hallelujah, there was life in the lad after all!

I was at the garage door, unlocking the padlock. Beyond the door, I rolled up the grate. I was acutely aware of the smell coming from the bloke; it was in about my nose. It had got under my skin. I tried to make light of the situation, but really we all could do with some fresh air.

'Ha ha,' I chuckled, 'come on now, that is rank. Lord, the stench ... phew, the smell ... *'Pugh, Pugh, Barney, McGrew, Cuthbert, Dibble, and Grubb'*. I'd always been a sucker for classic children's TV. Couldn't go wrong with *Trumpton*, *Camberwick Green*, although *The Wombles* had to be my favourite. I was too young to catch them first time on TV, but we had all the discs back at the Youth Centre.

Bruce took a step forward but was so unsteady he nearly tripped over his feet. Such was his lack of coordination, it made for a truly sorry spectacle. It took everything I had not to step forward and offer him a helping hand.

But he could feel it; we both could; the stiff night air coming in from the opened aperture. It was on his naked body. He had sight of his gateway to freedom. From this, heroically, he found something from within. He gathered up some much-needed resolve. He staggered past me and out into the unlit street. It was the dark before the dawn.

Part of me wanted to cheer him on with wild and enthusiastic abandon. Instead, the cold, hard reality of the situation compelled me to hold my nose theatrically. 'Thanks for the assistance,' I said. Again, I found myself referring to his bodily function malfunction, 'my girls have enough of your scent already.'

As for the dogs, they were climbing over each other, a flurry of fine hair, all set to follow poor Bruce.

'Heel!' I said. They froze as if playing a game of Staffie statues. 'Give the poor man some dignity, some personal space,' I said, and they hung their heads with shame.

I looked out. For a lame man, Bruce had put in an impressive shift. Between him and us, there was already a considerable amount of distance.

'Run free, run like the wind,' I called after him.

'You are in my prayers,' I said.

All around the general area, much in the way of temporary fencing had been put up. The original intention, I believe, was to build an industrial village where we'd have competitively priced lock-ups, that sort of thing, in order to attract small businesses, start-ups, budding local entrepreneurs.

However, council cuts, a sad story repeated up and down the land, called a halt to proceedings, although not before having sold leases on a token amount of completed, if randomly placed, units. But for the majority, these were left in a strange limbo state of mid-construction, creating something of a ghost industrial site.

The area was largely disused, discredited, and shunned. Accusations of corruption were made against one councillor in particular, who some claimed had pocketed a not unsubstantial part of the budget. Someone should pay that dude a visit sometime.

Anyway, of the few people who operated out of the odd lock-up dotted around the place, none of them would be around at this time of night.

Myself excepted.

The fencing lent the area a prison camp feel. It created a single fortified pathway. There was one way in and one way out, and consequently for Bruce, only one direction of escape.

I remembered that there was something I should have remembered. Right from the off, I meant to count to one hundred. But I didn't and who knew where in the count I should have been. It didn't matter. I wasn't going to beat myself up over it. Instead I counted to ten, grabbed a couple of things, before blithely and briskly walking out, alongside the girls.

When you came to the end of the fencing, things opened out for you. You were faced with a large expanse of muddy terrain, interspersed with opaque puddles of water of different shapes and sizes.

From where I now stood, I saw a bedraggled Bruce run diagonally across the waste ground. He was lopsided;

body twisted, ankles arranged at the most awkward of angles, arms dead and lagging behind.

Further in the distance, there was the Titan Crane, the one hundred and fifty foot cantilever giant, a monument to the past. In its prime, it was an integral part of the workings of the once fervid empire-spawning Clyde shipyards, now all but gone, withered on the industrial vine. Titan was recently rescued from disuse, lovingly restored, and now something of a tourist attraction.

Beyond this was the River Clyde itself.

The Titan Crane towered above the bleak, uncultivated landscape. Bruce, in an uneven, skewed way, predictably enough, was heading towards it. Here in the wilds of deep West Dunbartonshire, where else was there to run to?

As I watched Bruce, as naked as the day he was born, tripping and falling on the muddy ground, the force of the downwards momentum causing his face to immerse for a second in a puddle of filthy water, I experienced mixed emotions. Sad that Bruce was fast approaching his final few moments on this earth, but genuinely uplifted by the thought that the last thing he'd see was such a marvel of Scottish engineering.

Holding the meat cleaver firmly in my gloved left hand and Bruce's mobile phone in my right, I walked on. Wedged in my back jeans pocket were some rolled-up black bin bags. The Staffies, God bless, followed on, bunched up together behind me. They were unnaturally subdued; tentative; tails wedged between their legs. They could sense what was coming next.

If Bruce intended on calling out for help and pleading with the good Lord for divine intervention, then the words were lost in his throat. A clump of heavy, intrusive mud fell from his eyes. At least his sight was free of the muck. Maybe his luck was turning.

Then again, perhaps not; for what he was about to witness would surely cause him to panic wildly. Coming for him on four legs was a muscled mass of moving darkness. It wasn't one of the Staffies. This was much bigger, massive testicles. It was the shape of a devil dog.

There was a long, incessant growl which filled Bruce's ears. That was the moment, the dismantling of all previous notions of fear. Now he finally knew, as if hit by a lightning bolt of Old Testament proportions, what real fear was all about.

'Naw!' Bruce hollered. As last words went, it wasn't quite up to the standards of Lord Horatio Nelson or Colonel Walter E Kurtz.

Bruce was knocked over, down on his back on the soft and untrustworthy ground. The devil dog was on top of him.

Instinctively, adrenaline taking control, Bruce put up an arm, bent at the elbow, forearm taking the defensive lead.

The dog was toying with Bruce, devil teeth on full display, eyeing him up and down, deciding on which part of his person to attack first. But who was he kidding—Bruce in his entirety, the whole of him—was presented on a plate.

Devil dog bit into Bruce's arm with an almighty crunch, crushing bone.

Bruce's arm just dangled there. He was in shock, but this wasn't to last forever. The dog bit into his wrist, snapping tendons and shredding capillaries.

Bruce was screaming up until the point the beast's snout assaulted his throat area, tearing out chunks of now-redundant flesh. There was blood everywhere, turning the surrounding mud a strange tinge of rouge.

'My very deepest sympathies, ye ken.' I said, having finally caught up to the point I was standing over Bruce's limp body. The vessel that housed his poor, damned, about-to-be-redundant soul.

At the sound of my voice, the devil dog instantly ceased the wanton destruction. He turned and looked at me as attentively as you liked. His face was saturated with blood, covered in fragments of bone.

His mighty tongue licked clean his chops, enough to make them presentable.

I bent down and kissed him on the snout. 'Hey there, Duke,' I said.

At this, Duke broke away to join the three Staffies.

The Staffies were huddled so close together, they were practically tied in knots.

Duke merely sat, giving the girls some space, panting a little, the sheer force and violence of before now becoming a blessed thing of the past.

I knelt down to the fast-expiring Bruce. His eyes were still open and, much to my surprise, there was finally a glimmer of recognition to be found in them. It was our one major imperative as a species, to cling onto life, to fight death as long as we could. As it always should be, for all life was sacred.

Even more of a source of wonder, after the carnage of the attack, some of his vocal chords still remained.

'Fadder ...' he said. 'Please, Fadder ...'

But his words had no meaning and he was lost to me now. With a slide of the finger, I opened the phone and pressed the first number I saw on recent contacts. After a couple of rings, I spoke, using a voice that I did not recognise as my own.

'Tae whoever hears this message,' the voice said, 'wi' regards tae the owner o' this phone, ye ken, pass on tae his family and friends mah deepest sympathies.'

'He is absolved of all sin, ye ken. Consider it a tiny act of kindness.'

I waited in silence a second longer, and then brought the call to an end. I held the phone away from me. It was useless to me now. I tossed it down on the mud and it landed on Bruce's side, the opposite side to me. My own voice returned, but in a language not necessarily my own.

'Спасибо,' I said.

I closed my eyes and spots of light splashed on the back of my eyelids like I had stared too long at the sun. My head began to swim, but to falter would be to stray from the path of righteousness and I would never allow that to happen. Sluggishly, grudgingly, normality ensued.

'Thanks for the use of your phone,' I said.

The phone would be swimming with the fishes shortly, much like its owner.

Bruce was having a well-earned lie down. After everything he had been through, it would have been wrong of me to expect an answer from him. I took the bin bags from my back pocket and dropped them at my feet. We were so close to the water. I wasn't even sure if we'd need them now.

'It had to be done,' I said. 'The feathering and tarring; the ritual humiliation. It all had to be done. You said so yourself. Oh, you upset the wrong kind of person all right. We're talking a whole stack of trouble. Didn't you tell me? You told me what they'd do to you when they caught up with you, as they surely would. It was only a matter of time.'

'Ran it through my mind so many times,' I said. 'I sin, so no one else has to.'

Having swapped it from my left hand to my right, I lifted the meat cleaver, ready to take the plunge. Mercifully, it looked like Bruce had stopped breathing.

I, on the other hand, took a long and deep intake of breath. It was as if the notion had gripped me that I was breathing for two now.

'Later, I'll light a candle for you,' I said.

Swishing through the icy night air, the cleaver came down with a jarring thud. For poor Bruce, it truly was lights out.

***

It was dark. I was mindful not to look at the time, but unmistakably it was the middle of the night.

I still wasn't sleeping, which in this instance was proving beneficial. I was parked on Saracen Street, waiting on one of those nocturnal creatures that only crawl out at night.

And there he was, skulking past with unkempt facial hair and wearing a beanie hat. His name was Frankie Boy, junior member of the Dreyfus clan, eighteen or nineteen, so boy no longer. I turned on my car lights full beam.

Hand held up to his eyes, like some disco diva or Christopher Lee as Count Dracula, my quarry recoiled from the light.

I got out of the car and Frankie Boy turned and ran.

I was in pursuit.

Frankie Boy's running style was a mishmash of limbs. All the while his beanie hat bobbed up and down. Up and down. The movement was hypnotic.

Man, was he slow; I was gaining on him. I wanted him to run a little further, drain more nervous energy, so I let up some.

The joker was already out of breath. I'd put the fear of death into him.

My frame changed. My molars were grinding. With every inhalation of breath, I turned bulkier; which served to slow me down a little anyhow. Even so, when the time was right, I would make up the ground easily. And the time was right.

So how did I do it? And more to the point, why did I do it?

I leaped like a motherfucking salmon and felled Frankie Boy with an expertly judged rugby tackle. Taking no prisoners, I brought him down, thankfully for him, away from the concrete pavement and onto a grass verge. Giving him no time to collect his thoughts, or get a second wind, I was on top of him. I grabbed the side of his face and pushed down hard. His mouth, spluttering, was half-buried in the dirt and grass.

'Eat it,' I said. 'Eat the fucking dirt or I'll rip your fucking face off!'

And he knew it! He knew I would do it!

'You know me?' I said. 'You know who I am?'

'Polis,' he said, spitting out dirt.

People.

People made me do it; they drove me to it. The fight for survival and the brutality of existence; the things that most defined us. You'd think once we'd dragged ourselves out of the caves after a few thousand years or so, we'd have left all that behind. Have no more use for it. Dispensed with that inner dark part of us, as straightforward a process as a snake shedding its skin. But that was only the exterior. It was the nature of the snake to never be inclined to let go. We were still serving time in that regard, all of us.

Frankie Boy, while on the ground, started punching. With my free hand, I slapped away his most feeble efforts. Some of the punches landed on my chest. I exerted more pressure, pushing down on his cheekbone, applying more of my weight, and suddenly he got the message.

He was still and I stopped moving myself. There was only my voice.

I existed within, because I existed without. If people

no longer did terrible things to each other, committed questionable acts on each other, there would no longer be a point to me. I would be redundant. I would no longer exist. Shedded snakeskin. It was that simple.

I relaxed my arm, the one pushing down on Frankie Boy's face, although I couldn't resist pinching his cheek as I did so.

He turned his head and looked up at me. Meek, vulnerable; he was a boy again.

He would give me what I wanted. They all gave me what I wanted. I was fucking invulnerable in that respect.

'You're the odd one out, Frankie Boy, never mind the special one, you're the excluded one,' I said. 'A High Street jewellers gets robbed following the MO of one, two, maybe three of your family members. But, like a cross between a turd and a leper, you're the one they don't invite along. I know they tell you fuck all, but hey, we can only use the cards we're dealt.'

'But you catch the odd snippet, don't you?' I said. 'Walking into a kitchen gathering unannounced. Playing *Red Dead Redemption* in the next room with the door open.'

'Now, what do I discover? The Dreyfus clan all but gone missing, a huge bite taken out of the family tree, seemingly vanished from the face of the earth, or at least this side of Blantyre. Except for big brother Ricardo. I spoke to him this morning. I laid a hand on his shoulder. Which leaves cousin Tweedledum Bruce and Uncle Tweedledick William, I'd wager hidden away in some hole somewhere. Am I right? Am I not wrong?'

I nipped his cheek again, although this time applying marginally less pinch.

'Tell me what you know, Frankie Boy, it doesn't matter how muddled or cryptic, let me do the deciphering. Why should you care? There is no one here to help you. Tell me and I will leave you alone. I'll even let you keep your beanie hat!'

So ended my appeal to Frankie Boy's better nature.

12.

Appointment No. 3

'Said something about, uh, Greenland ...'.

'Greenland—as in the autonomous Danish territory Greenland?'

'Hamilton, I think I heard Hamilton, I swear to you, that's all I know.'

'Hamilton, South Lanarkshire? Formula One driver Lewis Hamilton? Broadway hit musical *Hamilton*?'

'If it was going to happen, it would be tomorrow, lucky day Thursdays.'

'Time?'

'Sometime after Uncle Wullie gets up from bed.'

***

I must have been on some kind of fast track. This was to be my third session over not many more mornings. Yes, I was on the fast track, to the point I had a nosebleed (although thankfully in this instance not literally).

Of course I could have cried off, pushed this latest appointment back. I was up to my eyeballs. I was sinking;

not swimming. But if there was a chance I could be there, part of me wanted to be there. Part of me wanted to see Dr Dawn. The other part of me had no idea why. What could she possibly positively offer me? Maybe all I wanted was a lie down on her couch. Maybe I would have settled for any excuse. Not a wink of sleep last night and I never felt as wide awake as I did now.

In her office, she was already seated when I arrived. Herringbone again. Today, a tasteful light blue.

I did my best to push all the aches and pains to the back of my mind. But here in the office of Dr Dawn, it was like a state of mind; my whole body was sore. Every movement, no matter how small, was an invitation to hurt. I took baby steps, but even so it was an effort to lower myself in the chair opposite her.

Another flurry of 'oohs' and 'aahs'. It was getting to be something of a ritual.

In all that time, she remained silent, left me to it. It was never a case of sitting comfortably, but it was time to begin anyway.

'Do you like children?' she said.

'I, ah ...'.

'The reason I ask,' she said, 'is because you had two sessions booked as community police officer at two schools. You turned up for the first one but sent DS Spencer in your place for the second.'

'I was ... busy?'

'While you still have me,' she said, 'while we still have time, shouldn't we talk through this? I would like to get to the bottom of why.'

I didn't see much point in this at all. And wasn't 'like' in this instance just another way of saying 'want' or 'need'?

But Dr Dawn had offered me her hand, professionally speaking of course. And where she wanted to lead, I had decided I was desperate to follow. I was committed. I wanted to make this a worthwhile experience for both of us. Frankly, it was good; I was coming round to the idea, no matter the pretext or context, to have someone sitting across from you prepared to listen for a change.

'Why the community policing? You'll have read the notes, I'm assuming? When I entered Interview Room 3 at Helen Street, the suspect had two perfectly formed ears. At least from where I could see.' I waited for a query-based interruption that never came. 'When I left, he only had one.'

From Dr Dawn there was a tiny nod. I had no choice but to go on. 'There would have to be an investigation of course, but failing any type of evidence that pointed one way or the other, I was told it was a done deal. In a freak accident, the suspect had tripped and fallen. He'd sliced off his earlobe against a sharp and unforgiving side of the interrogation table.'

So the report would go on to say. No one—absolutely no one—seemed interested in asking for my version of events, so I said nothing. In terms of quiet, I outdid the church mouse.

'I appropriated the missing earlobe and handed it to the doctor—although not before somehow having dropped it first in the toilet.'

'The toilet?' she said.

'The toilet,' I said.

'Hmm, all right, please continue.'

'Thanks,' I said. 'The doctor offered to sew it back on, but I heard the suspect had withdrawn consent for the procedure. In fact, he refused point blank.'

'He declined to make a statement to the authorities. That was lucky I suppose. Luck seems to follow me around. Sometimes it works for you, sometimes it doesn't.'

Was this me confessing to Dr Dawn? Or was it a case of 'fessing up to myself? I couldn't be sure. Often it came down to this, the inability to take a dispassionate view, to be objective; to not understand myself. We've all been there. Someone tell me otherwise. But at least I'd addressed the elephant in the room. The *ear*-shaped elephant. In this case, it would be an African (think about it) elephant rather than an Indian one. It's just that now I'd started, I had no idea how to stop. I just hoped I was making sense.

'Having said that,' I said, 'I was advised I should make myself scarce for a few days. Some community policing would do the trick. Fair enough, I was truly sorry for what had happened. He was disturbed, a murderer. He'd hacked and removed bits of his victim and wrapped them up in newspaper.'

'But no matter who you are or what you've done, under no circumstances can it be right to lose some of your ear. It happened on my watch, I was happy to take the blame, so I thought, yes, do some community policing and give something back.'

'I also heard, office whispers you understand, that no one else wanted to do it.'

I took a moment to run a few things inside my head. It was all about doing the Violence Reduction Unit a favour. They wanted someone to visit a local super school located in an area of super deprivation, which had become the focus for all kinds of antisocial behaviour and gang-related activity. Let's see, muggings, shoplifting sprees, and daubing graffiti on public buildings revealing classic movie twists. Things like '6th Sense—Bruce Willis is deid' and 'Darth Vader is Luke's daddy'. *Star Wars* was fair enough, but did schoolchildren of a modern age still care about movies such as *The Sixth Sense*? I thought, such an intriguing question, but after our first meeting, and the 'Judge Dredd' chat which sank like a stone, I chose this session to keep such thoughts to myself.

'Anyway, I was tasked with holding a few classes, to engage with wayward pupils, point out the error of their ways and be back home in time for tea.'

'The day came and, this being a spot of community policing, I thought it appropriate to travel in by bicycle. Unfortunately, this meant navigating the random terrors that are the Glasgow cycle lanes, which stop inexplicably in the middle of a busy road, the cycle lane equivalent of falling off a cliff. Invisible to buses, bringing out the worse in psychotic taxi drivers, unloved generally by anything on four wheels, I was on a saddle, a wing, and a prayer. But I stuck at it, only to turn up at school in a bedraggled, bashed state. And that was just me—you should have seen the bike!'

'Two senior teachers were present to greet me. They explained that the head teacher had been unavoidably delayed.' I remember one teacher, Mr Freeman, was all smiles. The other, Ms Freeman (no relation, so I was told), stared at me with wildly hostile eyes. It was the type of look a few hundred years ago would consign a witch to the pyre. Instead, I was led into the bowels of the school. 'They pointed me in the direction of my classroom: Class 12a.'

'I breezed into class. "Hullo, little people," I said, as way of introduction. The class, which was surprisingly well attended, greeted me with silence. The children were around the thirteen-year-old mark, but without exception, they all looked older. I was ready for them and their snotty noses and mucus-covered sleeves, their soulless eyes, armed, as I was, with a pointy stick and white projector screen.'

'So, I clicked the remote control and up on the screen

was the image of a kitchen knife. "Say no to knife crime," I said. In response, some of the class started whooping, which wasn't the response I was hoping for.'

'I moved on. Another click and an elderly couple appeared on screen. "Respect other people, especially the elderly," I said to them. At that, there were some boos.'

'A bottle of whisky provided the backdrop to my next statement. "Say no to alcohol and drugs." At this point, some of the pupils jumped up from their chairs, cheering enthusiastically, arms aloft as if they'd just scored the winning goal in the final of the Champions League. Even this early on, I'd made a mental note, this was not going as well as I'd hoped.'

'Then I noticed a couple of children sat on the desks to my left, one next to the other, with a small gap in-between. Both were on their smartphones, but one was stridently thumbing the keys. He had this cruel expression on his face. The other was reading a text, face as white as a sheet—he looked so terrified you could almost hear his knees knocking together. Playing out in front of me, I realised, was a textbook case of cyberbullying. Bully and victim sitting right next to each other.'

'I pointed out the children with my pointy stick. "Say no to bullying," I said. In response the bully boy got to his feet, pulled his arm back, and launched his smartphone at me. His aim, if not his manners, was impressive and the smartphone hit me in the forehead. Next thing I knew the bullied boy had followed suit; a second phone hit me square on the ridge of my nose. At this point, I dropped the control for the projector. I have to confess, I was knocked for six.'

'My head was whirling. When I squinted, I could just about make out a bead of blood forming on my nose. I was down on one knee at this point, having misplaced my equilibrium. I just said, "Class dismissed." It was a bit weak, quite pathetic, really. If I had the opportunity again, I would have said the opposite.'

'But when I looked up, I was surrounded by angry schoolchildren. In their hands were various learning-based objects, which they brandished like weapons.'

Throughout my spiel, the swings and roundabouts, Dr Dawn sat in her usual way. She never came close to interrupting. Why would she? I could be quite the chatterbox when the mood took me. But could she ever be content with one such as I; the man, the client, the patient, the detective, Brian Fisher? With her piercing gaze; she was looking for a sign. Observing. Looking for a crack. Searching for a fissure. Looking for a split.

Payback for her vigilance, I could give her the tiniest of peeks. It was like I was one of those schoolkids; awkward, jumbled limbs, so image conscious. All those strange fledgling emotions and erupting hormones. I so wanted not to disappoint. The thing was ...

She's not interested in you; she's only interested in me.

'DI Fisher—Brian—is everything okay?' she said.

Only fucking me!

As it was then, back at Class 12a, as it was now, not a complete transformation—my face was puffy, eyes a little red, shoulders straining, about to pop out of their socket—only elements of it.

Miraculously, the aches and strains had subsided, found some rabbit warren to scuttle into. I felt okay. I was doing better than okay.

'Children make for the best criminals,' I said, my mouth formed into a half-snarl as much as anything else.

'If you get to them soon enough, you can batter the conscience out of them. Take a fairly recent case of mine, a boy of nine who murdered his dad. Dad had come home after a drunken night, then proceeded to knock seven bells out of the boy's mother. The little mite then stuck a kitchen knife through pater's solar plexus. When dad hit the ground he drove the knife through dad's forehead, just like they do to the zombies in *The Walking Dead*. When I arrived on the scene, mother had a broken jaw and the kid, at least on the inside, had nothing left to break.'

'The boy held my gaze. I kind of smiled at him, but the kid wasn't for smiling back. He didn't move; he wasn't for giving anything up, even his own breath. I had every intention of arresting the boy but, before I did, I couldn't resist patting him on the top of the head. I liked his style.'

'You asked me earlier, Dr Dawn, do I like children?'

Dr Dawn seemed a little tense now; uncharacteristically so. Her back and neck pressed back on the chair, like she was on a rollercoaster going full pelt. She undid her second top button and breathed in air. There was a twitch of the chin, which I took as my cue to continue.

'So, picture the scene,' I said, 'Class 12a. Conscripted for the day, I was fending off a screaming hoard of rampaging schoolchildren.'

'One of the kids charged at me like a screaming banshee; she was roaring and stabbing me in the shoulder with the sharp end of a compass. You'd have expected the opposite, but there was a reason why it was such a well-attended class. This was where they met up, hidden in plain sight. It turned out I had uncovered one of the local gangs terrorising the area. I was looking at it and it was staring at me. It was Class 12a.'

'They came at me like mini-ninjas. Two led the way and I angled my body in anticipation so, on impact, they just bounced off me.'

'Then I heard these small snapping noises, I looked down and saw another of the little bastards attacking my hand with a stapler. I pushed him away and was reminded, if I needed any reminding, that this was a classroom, one of the most hazardous places on earth. I was stabbed by a pencil, but it wasn't sharp; it didn't pierce my clothing or skin. The kid responsible, realising his error, proceeded to furiously sharpen the pencil and stab me again. This time it tore through everything, punctured my skin. It was enough to bring tears to my eyes, let me tell you.'

'Another one of the kids then launched at me. A quick sidestep and I dodged him, but I collided with a cabinet. A few school jotters spilled out.'

'I slid down on one knee. I was surrounded by paperwork. It was as if it formed a protective circle around me. The children hesitated, didn't move a muscle.'

'I couldn't help notice that among the mess of paper was a hardback book with a black and white photo on the cover—a woman with an inordinately big mouth screaming while in a shower.'

'The title of the book was *100 Greatest Movie Spoilers of All Time*. Have to admit—and I'm not particularly proud of this—I tend to give black and white movies a wide berth. There's a colourised version of *It's A Wonderful Life*, even, in a pile of DVDs back home, but, even so—'

'I'm no different from everyone else in that respect—apart from the ones who spend twenty-four hours a day on the internet—I detest the notion of movie spoilers. The book wasn't the only distraction, and I found myself having a nosey at one of the school jotters, flicking through pages, reviewing the work inside, particularly spelling and grammar.'

'The kids just stood there, I now think as way of reacting to the sight of me checking their homework, almost waiting for my verdict.'

'Randomly, I read the sentence "*I would love to swim with killer whale's.*" I shook my head at the criminal misuse of the apostrophe. If you believed children were our future—that it was a toss-up between them and the cockroaches—you would surely have despaired.'

'All it took from me was a shake of the head. Sensing my disappointment, the spell was broken and a new wave of the little feckers advanced, this time carrying their chairs above their heads. I knew once they'd finished launching all the chairs at me, the desks would be next.'

'Quickly, I realised I needed—sorry, I'd *like*—to do something else to grab their attention. I sprang to my feet and grabbed one of those transparent shatterproof rulers. Twelve inches long, it was pliable but robust. "Kiddies, keep your distance," I warned them. I took hold of each end of the ruler, flexing it.'

'I bent it some more. The children hesitated again.'

'With a resounding crack, I snapped the allegedly shatterproof ruler. All around the classroom there were sharp intakes of breath.'

'It had stopped them in their tracks all right. Some even dropped their chairs to the ground and, for want of something better to do, they sat down on them. One of the kids with particularly clatty fingernails pointed at me and shouted, "Phone the polis, he's damaged school property." Everyone in the class started laughing; including myself. Part of the community remit was to engage with the pupils. I now considered that box ticked.'

'At this point the head teacher walked in. He took one look at the classroom. "Will you take a look at this mess?" he said.'

'As an aside, more for the benefit of the children I think, the head teacher, who was a bit of a wanker if you ask me, had more to say. He'd just seen that morning the early showing of the new Quentin Tarantino movie. Hidden in the safe all that time, apparently, was the head of Samuel L Jackson. There was this glint in his eye as he said it.'

'My mind was racing. I was thinking, was this a spoiler? Was this the source of inspiration behind the movie-themed graffiti that was choking the neighbourhood? Could the head teacher in fact be ringleader of the notorious school gang that was Class 12a?'

'As it turned out, he wasn't, but you know what I bopped him one anyway.'

I really wanted to hold Dr Dawn's gaze but then, thinking about it, was this really what I wanted to do? I feared I had waffled on too long anyway; that I had lost the thread to a lot of things; all rolled into one, like what I was doing, where I was going, and who I actually was. Then again, it was written in her job description to have all the answers, or so I imagined I read somewhere.

I held my head in my hands. My mind was a blank page. I closed my eyes and on re-opening them, I was normal again. But, with me, normal is such a variable term.

'I was booked in for another school visit,' I said. 'But if the general idea was for me to keep a low profile, it hadn't gone quite to plan. In any case, it wasn't as if I wasn't busy. Had several appointments, one with you and another with the three Wise ...'.

My voice trailed off. I was feeling nervous. I wiped sweaty palms up and down the fabric of my trousers. Where did all that bravado go, of only a few moments before? Was it that good to talk? As a species we'd been talking for hundreds of thousands of years and where had that got us? Was it really that important to get it all off your chest? Did we need to know where we were going in order to get there? Does any of it matter, especially when sometimes the voice you used, you weren't even sure was your own?

Dr Dawn was smiling. A smile I was terribly grateful for. It promised me that in the end everything would be alright, even when it was clear that it could never be. She was at all points professionally detached. She saw and listened to everything. She wrote down the occasional note. Her objective was to observe objectively, and she did that beautifully. That was the deal. The only deal in town. And part of me loved her for that.

'So,' she said, 'you sent DS Spencer to the second school instead?'

'Correct,' I said, 'and I believe it's still something of a sore point where she's concerned. Self-preservation prevails, so I actively avoid bringing it up. She didn't fare much better at her school either, so I heard, or overheard. The youth of today, eh?'

'Yes,' Dr Dawn concurred, her tone neutral. She was no longer tense around the shoulders. Her default cool as a cucumber, detached as a stand-alone bungalow manner had returned. I couldn't tell if she was agreeing with me or not.

'Thank you for opening up to me,' she said. 'It's important that I have as rounded an account of your state of minds before I submit my report.'

'We're out of time,' she said. She was matter-of-fact; the most matter-of-fact person I'd ever met.

'One session left,' she said, 'and you can come in at any time and I won't keep you waiting, I'll clear some time for you. But on your return, before I submit my report, I'd like you to first answer one question. I'd like to ask you the question now, but would prefer if you didn't answer right away. I'd like you to think about your answer first.'

'Yes,' I said, adopting a neutral tone of my own. Truth was, though, I was on tenterhooks.

'If you go on,' she said, 'what do you hope to achieve?' She shook her head; her lips pursed tight. 'No, that's not right, what I'm trying to say is ...'

'Can you still do any good?' she said.

I nodded. I was glad she didn't want a response straight

off the bat. That I could defer until our next meeting, which itself was an open-ended appointment. Like most things in life—definitely not now, maybe later, maybe never—I had no idea what the answer may be. No idea, even, *who* would be doing the answering.

'Goodbye, Dr Dawn,' I said, conscious of my lower lip trembling.

'Goodbye, Brian,' she said. Her face was very still. Part of me thought this might change, and she might suddenly blow me a kiss, but this was clearly wishful thinking on my part.

The session was clearly over.

As I made to leave Dr Dawn's office, like bobbing beanie-hat-wearing-apples in a barrel, 'Hamilton' along with 'Greenland', words which returned to the forefront of my mind. Suddenly I'd got it. I'd made the connection. It was pretty obvious, really. It was always there; right in front me, right between the eyes.

I shut the door to Dr Dawn's office behind me, carefully, diligently, like it was the most fragile thing in the world. There was no going back; there would be no quick-fire return until I had an answer to her question. But, wait a minute, another passing thought, back in the office there, during my session with Dr Dawn—

Did she just say mind, or *minds*?

13.

It's in the (Jiffy) Bag

You know what, so they tell me, Glasgow was once the great industrial city. It comes across like some city-wide mantra, reinforcing how good a place is by saying how great a place *was*. In its pomp, it was the second city of the British Empire; at a time, might I remind you, when Britain ruled half the world. Although why anyone thought owning half a planet was such a great idea, I had no idea.

Much to do with this was the River Clyde and her many estuaries, bringing in and sending out all kinds of trade. And by trade, this constituted anything people were willing to put their hands in their pockets for. There are a lot of fine old buildings around Glasgow built on the proceeds of sugar cane and slavery, but no one wants to talk about that. The general consensus is, whilst it's good to get in touch with the history of the city you call your home, it really wouldn't do to scratch too much below the surface.

Such was the level of industrial activity over the Clyde, it caused so much mess and pollution that nothing could live below the river surface. Now the shipyards had all but shrivelled up, its heyday a distant memory, life—fish and the like—had returned to the waters. As a matter of record, the passing of the Glasgow shipyards was one of regret, but a weird thought came over me. If the minnows, trout, and graylings wrote the history books instead, they'd surely have something different to say about it.

But that was then and, currently, a dismembered body was to be found swimming with the fishes in the river Clyde. Myself and PC Nimmo looked down at it from the vantage point of Victoria Bridge.

It was light, but still early. The odd early morning jogger, dog walker, and late night casino dweller besides, there weren't many people about. Which was way okay in my book. You could only take so much screaming before breakfast. Mind you, this was Glasgow. Passers-by tended to barely break stride, maybe quickly point in a dead body's direction, muttering something about it being a shame, which then reminded them, in a perverse but I think logical way, that they had some chicken in the fridge at home, which if they didn't use up today, would go off. There was little point lingering at the scene of the crime. You couldn't share a Billy Connolly joke with a corpse after all.

DI Fisher wasn't available. He had an appointment with his shrink. Another one! Well, she (I think I'd managed to piece together that 'she' was a she) was welcome to him. I was guessing 'Call-me-Brian' would have taken to a psychiatrist's couch like a pig to the mud stuff. Peel away that quiet exterior, he always seemed to have a lot to say for himself. You'd think he'd do well at *Mastermind*, if his specialist subject was 'meaningless shite'.

(Although, dare I say it, some of it was rubbing off on me, otherwise where did that observation of trout writing history books come from?) I wondered, mind you, if he mentioned those wild goose chases he'd sent me on. If he demonstrated the right amount of contrition? For one, he could start with that miserable 'wild goose chase' excuse for a fudging school visit.

Credit where credit was due, though, he came out of that cesspit Electric Dreams standing. I'd have liked to have seen with my own two eyes how he did that.

It was time—I couldn't put it off any longer—to devote my full attention to the matter at hand. The various body parts—hand, knees, feet, torso, and head to be exact—bloated, but still recognisable, floating separately on the river, but still sufficiently grouped together, carried by the currents to form a disjointed human jigsaw. (I was no statistician, but what were the chances?)

I waved at the Glasgow Humane Society officer on his boat. Someone had alerted him of the jigsaw man, and he'd then alerted the police. He was in the process of fishing the body parts out of the river.

I noticed what could have been in isolation a backside bobbing in the water. No thank you, I decided, not before breakfast. I pushed my brain into thinking this was a figment of my imagination. By sheer force of will, I drove my attention away from the water.

'Familiar MO,' I said to PC Nimmo, who was standing next to me. Nimmo was a young, fresh faced copper, UK Asian; his granddad was from Pakistan. Not that any of that was important, my great-grandfather on my mother's side was Danish, apparently, but I'd never had the inclination to go to Copenhagen. 'Gang killing,' I continued. 'Settling of old scores. It's that time of year. How long do you think it's been in the river?'

Nimmo hunched his shoulders in a non-committal

type of way. 'Umm—travelling upstream, ma'am, been in the water overnight, maybe.'

Nimmo might have been blagging big time, but on balance, giving people the benefit of the doubt was what I was all about, or so I liked to think. Mind you, he was the type of confident young man who came across like he knew what he was talking about. He could spout a staggering amount of nonsense, but with conviction.

'I can see the headline,' I said, 'The Cleaver Strikes Again'.'

'Ma'am,' Nimmo said, dubiously, 'don't you mean 'The Chopper'?'

I was quick to give him a look.

'No,' I said, 'we already caught The Chopper. Over the weekend. He had a disagreement with a traffic warden, which resulted in him chasing said public official down the street, chopping board wedged under his arm covered in incriminating DNA.'

Meanwhile, the GHS officer, having scooped everything in his purview on board, waved furiously in our direction. I took from this that all the body parts were now on the boat. There wasn't much room to be had. The victim's bits and bobs all distended and bloated and piled up too close to his feet for my liking. Nevertheless, I waved back in acknowledgment.

Nimmo took a few more seconds to process The Chopper news before giving another shrug of the shoulders. The more I thought about it, though, it was blagging. PC Nimmo had as much of a clue how long the body was in the water as I had. I might have to revisit my whole way of looking at people.

***

The Greenland in question was Greenland in Hamilton.

In terms of groceries and frozen foods, it probably wasn't the best known brand of supermarket, but I was reliably informed by an advert in the local paper, it was crammed with potentially life-altering special offers. I might be paraphrasing here.

It was half past eleven in the morning when a van screeched to a stop outside the store. It wasn't difficult piecing together what happened next. The fact of me being there helped considerably in that respect.

Occupying the front of the van were Ricardo and Uncle Wullie of the Dreyfus clan. They took a few moments to stretch ladies' tights over their faces. They used the rear-view mirror to check if they were presentable enough. Their faces looked appropriately stretched and contorted. One celebrity facelift too many.

'You ready for this?' said Ricardo.

'Yup,' said Uncle Wullie.

They barged into Greenland. There was nothing subtle about it. Ricardo carried a crowbar in one hand and a holdall in the other. Wullie carried a shotgun. Using the crowbar, Ricardo chopped the legs of the sole security guard from under him. Wullie finished the job, smashing the butt of the shotgun into the poor sod's face. I swear between them, they'd have shown more emotion swatting a fly.

Quickly, but not particularly efficiently, they turned their attention to the row of checkout counters. Checkout assistants reacted in a pretty predictable manner. Some put up their hands, while others gasped and clutched at their chests.

'This is a fucking stick-up!' Ricardo hollered, in case anyone remained unclear on the matter. He strutted and swung his crowbar about for effect like he was, maybe not the third, fourth, or fifth, but certainly the eighteenth Musketeer.

Shoppers to a man, woman, and one small person of indeterminate age, huddled behind the freezer section. There was a random scream from the checkouts.

Reacting to this, Wullie held out the shotgun in a pronounced way. His hand was shaking and so, by association, was his firearm. He wasn't exactly inspiring any kind of confidence.

'Who did that?' Wullie shouted. 'Stop screaming,' he added, as good as shrieking himself.

'Screaming makes the old duffer next to me nervous,' Ricardo said. 'You checkout motherfuckers don't want that now, do you?'

'Naw, they don't!' Wullie piped up.

Ricardo placed the holdall down onto the checkout next to him. He tried to smile through the tights.

The checkout assistant was a lady in her forties. She was taking quick deep breaths.

'Empty the till, fill up the bag, pass it along, love,' Ricardo said. He winked in a bid to lighten the mood, but someone should have had a word. Underneath the tights it looked like he was having some kind of seizure.

If you followed the trajectory past Ricardo, a straight line taking you into the bowels of the supermarket, you'd spot on display, arranged in a tall pyramid structure, Greenland's own brand of baked beans. A sign was hanging from above, proudly proclaiming twenty-four pence a tin. Life-altering might have been taking it a tad too far, but as bargains go, you had to admit, it was a bloody good one.

I stood in front of the baked beans display. My arms were tucked in behind my back. A smile ripped a hole in my face. I was the cat that got the fucking cream. And as many beans as one's digestive tract could take.

It wasn't long before a reliably twitchy Ricardo noticed me. 'What?' he said.

He blinked, looked again, and I was gone. I wasn't going to make this easy for him or for Wullie, but was hopeful they might be feeling more generous of spirit. Or more stupid, whatever was the best fit.

'It's the polis!' Ricardo said. 'The same fecker who picked me up at Electric Dreams.'

Wullie, shakily, inexplicably, seemed to be training the shotgun on the holdall, which was filling up nicely, having been passed from one checkout to the other. He threw his nephew a characteristically worried glance.

'Just leave it,' Wullie said.

Those three words only seemed to enrage Ricardo further. Steam was exiting his ears.

'After what he did to Tam and Robbie for fuck's sake?' he said. 'That's the fascist bastard cop who put them both in hospital.'

'For fuck's sake. For fuck's sake. For fuck's sake.' Either there was a strange echo wafting through the aisles of the supermarket, or this was one of Ricardo's favourite oft-repeated phrases.

Wullie motioned to open his mouth again, to urge his rash young charge to adopt a more Zen-like approach to life. But Ricardo, crowbar in hand, was already walking toward the baked beans display. Faced with such a turn of events, Wullie shrugged and mentally instructed his mouth to stand down.

'He was just like he is now,' Ricardo said, 'when, no shit, he was a different man. The fucker. Gonna sort him out.'

Ricardo announced the fact he had reached the display by tapping the beak of the crowbar on his palm. He angled his head, so he could see past the beans, checking out the tinned veg/pickles aisle. Intruding on the seemingly endless row of tins (carrots and peas mostly) and jars (pickles and beetroot mostly) was a shiny black shoe.

To Ricardo, it was like a shiny black-red rag to a bull. He raised his jimmy bar ready for the affray.

'You!' Ricardo said, as way of a battle cry.

'Yes, me,' I said, ready for anything about to come my way. Certainly anything that started with an 'R'.

The bampot was up and at me. Crowbar raised above his head.

It came down at a fair lick of speed. I parried it with a tin of baked beans I had in my hand.

My other hand was similarly tooled-up. I threw the tin down, which bounced off the top of Ricardo's foot, leaving a satisfying crunch in its wake.

Ricardo grabbed his bashed foot with his free hand. He was hopping like a mad one. He unleashed a torrent of abuse and profanity, which turned the air a dark shade of blue. By way of alternative to being pummelled by a metal club, though, I'd take potty-mouthed any day.

From yours truly there followed an 'are-you-as-stupid-as-you-look' expression, before I smacked him with my one remaining, admittedly dented, tin of beans. Cylindrical metal container ripped through tights and smashed through face. And before you could say 'vertically challenged', Ricardo was down on the ground, a crumpled heap at my feet.

I looked down at my tin, appraising it. 'Who says own brands aren't as good as the leading ones?' I said.

Meanwhile, Wullie had a decision to make. He'd heard scuffling. He set off from the checkout area to go in aid of his nephew, taking an alternative zigzag route through the cereal aisle. He did so, leaving behind a clutch of checkout assistants staring all kinds of emotion at each other.

Any attempt at stealth on Wullie's part was undermined, though, by his inability to keep his mouth shut. 'Ricardo, you there?' he said.

There followed for Wullie another few tentative, torturous steps. It was like gravity around him had tripled in strength. 'Oh Mother Mary, Stephen, and Joseph,' he muttered.

Occupying the bottom half of the middle sections of the cereal aisle were boxes of 'Bongo Pops'. Ninety-nine point nine per cent sugar and zero point one per cent fibre. Catching Wullie's eye were the zombie monkey cartoon characters that adorned the front of the box. He gulped furiously, but that wasn't enough, the saliva kept on coming.

There was a crash and zombie monkeys were scattered all over the aisle. In their place was my phizog, my head having burst through the boxes.

'None of Ricardo, Mother Mary, Stephen, or Joseph are available to talk right now,' I said, my head poking out of the cereal aisle. I twisted my neck and looked up towards a startled Uncle Wullie. As well as hard knocks, I fancied myself the purveyor of harsh truths. 'William "Wullie" Dreyfus,' I said. 'As I live and breathe. A shotgun, really? The way your hands are shaking, you can't shoot for toffee.'

With his trademark dumbfounded expression, Wullie stared at the shotgun in his hands. I would have given you short odds on it not being loaded.

Maybe it was the fact that I was in the thick of it; surrounded by as many variants of flakes, shredded squares, slabs of wheat, crispies, porridge oats, and rabbit food with bits in it as anyone could ever want to be. Maybe that was the thing that was making me giddy. But I would have sworn right there, if Wullie shot me with both barrels at next-to-nothing range, I could have caught the speeding slugs in my teeth and spat the feckers out. It was never an issue, never up for debate; I was in complete control of the situation.

'Don't you usually carry the bag?' I said.

It was time for a moment of calm. A time to reach out. A time for reason. 'Tell you what, before I arrest you, tell me all you know about McConnell's the Jewellers and I'll let you keep your dentures.'

Wullie subconsciously touched the side of his mouth. He showed all the signs of a very worried man. It was then that he told me about a white plastic bag.

Done deal. It was in the fucking bag. As it turned out, a white plastic one.

***

Time passed. Time waits for no man. Waits for no men. No man. Nomad.

There were lights; there was noise; all wrapped up in police cars and vans congregated outside the crime scene that was Greenland of Hamilton. The land was awash with police colours. Blue and yellow squares, fluorescent jackets. Police raid meets police rave.

The sorry sights of Ricardo and William Dreyfus, both handcuffed, were escorted by police officers into the back of one of the vans. Standing, watching it all was DS Julie Spencer. Her face was one of thunder.

I emerged from the supermarket with my hands in my pockets looking sheepish. I was aware that my colleague wanted to vent. With an increasing sense of dread, I came to realise the identity of the person she wanted to vent at.

'Right,' she said, stamping her feet, or so it seemed, as she made a beeline for me. I panicked. She was coming for me and I thought she was never going to stop. She was going to tear right through me.

'Got a tip-off,' I said; couldn't get the words out quick enough. 'It was last night. It was late.'

At least she had stopped now, but she was terribly close. She was invading my personal space. There was enough steam coming out of her ears to make dumplings.

'I had another appointment this morning,' I said. 'I was only in the office for five minutes ...'.

'Our old pal Ricardo and his Uncle William?' she said, cutting me off. To be honest, if I'd got out half the words I did get out before her hurried intervention, I would have still considered this a good effort. 'A supermarket robbery? In Hamilton? No back-up!' The exasperation in her voice was ever-growing.

I did consider nodding at each of her points, but my survival mechanism had kicked in, insistent that I stand like a statue and do nothing to attract even more attention to myself.

'Why didn't you tell me?' she said.

'It's in my diary on my desk in Helen Street,' I said, taking my hands out of my pockets. This was true of course; I recorded my whereabouts the old fashioned way, pen and paper. I once tried the electronic method, smartphone to be precise, but lost all my diary entries during a pursuit, which ended with a scuffle with a suspect that saw us both roll into a canal.

'You want to know my whereabouts, Detective Sergeant, you check my diary,' I said. 'It never strays from its designated place on my desk. If I'm not around, I phone in and whoever I'm put through to, I kindly request they update it on my behalf. I stay on the line just to make sure. I wait until they've confirmed they've done it.'

'Without fail,' I said, 'make my diary your first port of call.'

She held my gaze. She waited for me to maybe end with a wisecrack or a comical dance to tell her I was just funning with her. That she shouldn't take me quite so seriously. But that was never going to happen, not in this instance. I would happily extol the virtues of a traditional diary to anyone and everyone; whether they showed the tiniest of interest in the subject matter or not; the latter response being virtually always (regrettably) the case.

Another few seconds passed. I could hear ticking from an imaginary clock. She put her hand on her hair. With the ends of her fingers, she pressed down on her scalp.

'We found Bruce Dreyfus this morning,' she said. 'Chopped up and chucked in the River Clyde. We managed to acquire a clean enough print from one of the fingers for an ID.'

Close by, an engine roared to life as the police van carrying Ricardo and Uncle Wullie sped off. My thoughts were more of the Kia variety, specifically the Titanium Silver Kia Soul I had parked nearby.

'Let's leave Tweedledee and Tweedledum to stew for a bit back at the station,' I said. 'First thing, though, we should pass on our condolences in person to Aunt Morag. I think I know the address, but let's confirm on the way. Whose turn is it to drive?'

She had said her piece. Now there was work to be done.

Like a good soldier, she nodded, ready to return to the fray.

We drove through the rain to Dennistoun. The clouds were a filthy black. In the slanted, unending, lashing rain, wiper blades stuck to the unenviable task, despatching multiple conjoined raindrops, only to see them replaced instantaneously. At the same time, the car's windows steamed up, creating a wall of condensation.

Spencer was driving again. I had to confess that no one was more surprised at this than me. There were mitigating factors. She wasn't a great passenger, suffered a little from motion sickness when not behind the wheel. As for me, I discovered I was a much better, less twitchy passenger than I would have first ever thought.

Initially I think I wanted her to love the car as much as me. She didn't seem to, but I now found this fact reassuring. I'd decided I didn't want anyone to share the same feelings as me. Should our partnership be dissolved and we went on our separate postings, I didn't want the car to be subject to some Kia-themed custody battle.

I applied my sleeve to the side window in an agitated circular motion. My head twitched this way and that as I tried to make sense of the non-distinct buildings outside.

'I ...' I said, straining my eyes to such an extent, if I could, I would have had them out on stalks. 'No, the next street on.' A second later. 'No. We've gone too far.'

Spencer tightened her grip on the wheel as she did a U-turn, and before you knew it, we were back where we should have been, so no harm done.

'I think this is it,' I said.

On foot, we entered the tenement building. The flat we wanted was upstairs, situated on the third floor.

The late, dismantled Bruce Dreyfus had lived with his aunt and uncle. Uncle Wullie, as already established, was a toerag. Aunt Morag was one of those long-suffering spouses, while never condoning her family's criminal activities (all males), she just got on with things. When we entered their flat, we would be crossing into another world. This was a quasi-moralistic alternative universe, where the laws that governed the vast majority of us no longer applied. As difficult and wildly optimistic as this might have first sounded, I found it worked best if the aim was to treat each other simply as human beings and we'd all have to see where that got us. As a strategy, it worked some of the time.

There was a knocker on the door, which I happily rattled. The sound the knocking made was a brave if forlorn attempt, such was the height of the ceiling, at filling the emptiness of the hall.

As we waited for someone to answer, Spencer and I exchanged the slightest of smiles; anything less and they wouldn't have qualified as smiles at all.

The door swung open and there stood Morag Dreyfus, in her late fifties, a smidgen under five feet in height, heavy smoker, bad skin. I showed her my ID. She rolled her eyes, which didn't seem in the mood to stop rolling, like they were on a continuous loop.

'What have the silly buggers been up to now?' she said.

***

'Snorrrt!'

Morag Dreyfus had been crying, having been informed of the demise of her nephew Bruce, who she seemed to harbour genuine affection for. DS Spencer offered her a tissue from a box sitting nearby, which she took and blew into with much force. Just like the eye-rolling thing, she kept on going. I thought for a second, not certain why—some flight of fancy—that her head was about to split open, and from inside the wound would emerge a wee miniaturised man who would reach over and take my cup of tea and biscuit from me.

'Oh, no,' she said. 'Not Bruce!' By way of contrast, she hadn't batted an eyelid when informed of her husband's involvement in a supermarket heist. No discernible twitch of any kind. But the sad news involving her nephew hit her hard. She couldn't stop shaking.

'But someone left a message from his phone in the wee small hours,' she said, as if by way of protest.

Spencer and I exchanged the hastiest of glances.

'Could we hear it?' Spencer said.

Aunt Morag was remarkably composed as she played

the recording, left the night before on her mobile phone. As the message played, her expression was one of mild detachment. Such was the nature of the message; she didn't think it too out of the ordinary. It didn't frighten or spook her. As to what she would have considered out of the norm where a voicemail was concerned, the mind boggled.

The voice from the phone was quiet and carried with it a degree of remorse, I thought. By the same token, it seemed disguised, heavy on the accent, laid on a bit too thick. Also, the call was made from outside. There was wind, a swirl, sometimes forming background noise, sometimes mid-to-foreground noise, like it was toying with us, trying to decide whether to spirit the caller's voice away.

I leaned forward, listening carefully in an attempt to divine meaning from each and every syllable.

'Tae whoever hears this message, wi' regards tae the owner o' this phone, ye ken, pass on tae his family and friends mah deepest sympathies.'

I took a bite out of my biscuit, diligently, conscious of not making crumbs. A custard cream, I noted. Hadn't had one of those in a long time.

'He is absolved of all sin, ye ken. Consider it a tiny act of kindness.'

After this, there was silence, dead space. A single beep brought the communication unceremoniously to an end.

'Do you recognise the voice?' DS Spencer said.

'No, I'm sorry,' Morag said. She dabbed her nose with a scrunched-up hankie.

It sounded to me like it was the 'I am Sparta' guy. What was his name, again? The message was made at 3.12 a.m. How close was this, I wondered, to Bruce Dreyfus' time of death? Find the voice behind the voicemail and I was sure we'd be closer—as close as close could be—to discovering the answer. Film star, Gerald Butler, wasn't it? Would it be a stretch to ask him in for questioning?

'Daft as a brush he was,' Aunt Morag said, 'but a good lad, trusting lad, he'd speak to anyone. Best pals with every nutjob under the sun.'

'So young,' she said. 'Dead, you say? Found in the Clyde ...?'

She took a moment before continuing. 'He should've stayed on at college. Stuck with that apprenticeship, made something of his life. Become a bike mechanic. He loved his church group too. It got him out of the area, away from all this. God, peace, turning the other cheek and all that.' Aunt Morag's face lost all light, like it was the dark side of the moon. 'I could strangle Wullie and that ferret-faced bastard Ricardo,' she said. 'What did they do? A bad influence, both of them. Terrible, terrible. My poor Bruce.'

What could Aunt Morag do? She could only be there for her family when they wanted or needed something from her. She could beg them to change their ways, cajole and threaten them, call them every name under the sun, fall just sort of scratching their eyes out, but never to the point she would ever disown or walk out on them. Her love for Bruce was unconditional and now she wept for him and would have to bury him. He was too young.

I was up off the chair and heading to the kitchen. 'I'll make you a cup of tea,' I said.

I left the kitchen door ajar. From the living room I could hear the sobs and wails had started again, which dipped and rose as grief took hold, then released, only to take hold again, tighter this time. Grief was like that. It would go sometimes, allow a sense of eerie calm to be restored, but one never to stray too far for too long.

DS Spencer was on hand to sympathise and reassure.

Morag seemed to have access to an infinite supply of hankies, which Spencer handed over at the merest hint of a request. It was the small things that made the biggest impression.

I scanned the interior of the kitchen while putting the kettle on. I needed to act fast. Carefully, I opened the twin hatch doors beneath the sink. Inside, among the bottles of disinfectant, marigolds, and sponges on a stick, was a plain plastic bag. An unremarkable plastic bag. A white plastic bag. I reached in and grabbed it. It scrunched agreeably in my grip.

'Be there in a minute,' I said.

The kettle clicked off, making a churning noise on the lines of 'sput-sput-sput', and having reached boiling point in unexpectedly quick time. I picked up the kettle and could tell from the weight, confirmed by a brisk shake which resulted in a lack of sloshing, that there was hardly any water inside, barely two teaspoons worth; should've checked before, I suppose

I called out. 'More custard creams anyone?'

***

Meanwhile, in Milngavie, a postie whistling *You Can't Hurry Love* by the Supremes (or Phil Collins, if you're that way inclined), postbag slung over one shoulder as casual as you like, strolled his merry way towards 20 Tall Trees.

On the other side of the door was Charles Bartholomew in what was fast becoming his least favourite part of the day. He sat on the hall stairs, one more time, chewing his nails to the point he was up to his elbow.

The letterbox swung open. Charles didn't move, couldn't move, his brain was no longer in control of his body. From outside, there was the sound of scraping as packing material was being flattened and nudged through and generally made to do the postman's bidding. Then it appeared. Just a corner at first, yellow-brown, crumpled, but unmistakably a Jiffy bag.

The yellow-brown mass slowly emerged and, before you knew it, the bag had reached tipping point, falling onto the plush hall carpet.

And it just lay there, like roadkill that showed no sign of injury, that is until you turned it over and noted its innards had all spilled out like derailed spaghetti.

It was quiet, so terribly quiet. It was as if the silence, by signifying nothing, was twisted into something dark and foreboding and evil.

But the reality was that Charles Bartholomew was dressed in his second housecoat from a choice of six. All he had for company was some stationery, but not just ordinary stationery; what some in the know claimed was the vanguard of bubble wrap packaging, while others referred to it merely as a fancy padded envelope.

'It's only a Jiffy bag. It's only a Jiffy bag. It's only a Jiffy bag.' The words eddied around the hall in ever tighter circular patterns, until there was nowhere for them to go. Until they took a hold of Mr Bartholomew's head. Held him in its vice-like grip.

'Aigheee!'

It took him a full minute to realise he was screaming. He stopped himself, and not for the first time, by nibbling at his knuckles.

'Oh Lord, sweet Jesus,' he said, again and again.

A vein in his forehead pulsated, about to pop. He experienced a strange and terrible compulsion to rip off his eyelids—anything but attend to the matter at hand. The *matter* laid down at his door with his name and address scrawled on the front of it.

'It's only a Jiffy bag.'

14.

Interrogation Nos. 3 & 4

We would talk to them separately. It would save time, or so I was told. Couldn't follow the logic of it, leaving them to stew overnight, why now the sudden rush before the lawyer arrived; but there I was, without putting up a fight, agreeing to it.

It was something of a red letter day today in Helen Street with all three interview rooms available to choose from. I had Room 2. DI Fisher had Room 3. Nothing surprised me about that man, although that particular decision, all things considered, taking into account recent shenanigans, surprised me. He wanted a word with William Dreyfus and I was to spend some quality time with Ricardo. I didn't approve of this tactic, but did not object. I wasn't feeling at the top of my game. Woozy. It was all this time spent with real criminals. It was dragging me down.

I gave him this one, and it didn't seem like I was alone in doing so. He put ideas in your head. He had this ability to get your approval for something without you being aware until, too late, you were already nodding. He caught you unawares. It was never about being your friend, or garnering deference. Not inspiring, he never aspired to that type of loyalty. Soft but fair; but what did I mean by that? The polar opposite of hard, I think that's it, compelling you to step in and make the tough decisions for him.

It's the same way that nature abhors a vacuum. Without fail, you'd arrive at the decision he'd always wanted in the first place. He suckered you in. The quiet assassin; the wily operator; the prancing policeman. Where he was involved, I was still at the bottom of my learning curve, but I'd get there, I'd climb it eventually. And yet, on reaching the summit that was DI Fisher, I had the nagging feeling, the nagging doubt, even at the peak, I'd only uncover half the story.

He could have got away with murder that one.

But if I was honest, it suited me to think of him as some kind of enigma. Anything to take my mind off the lurking dread that was the prospect of visiting my mum later that night. Her blank face. I would never find, in all those lines, a meaningful expression. Her eyes would look straight through me.

I instructed my body to move and I went off to collect PC (as in Police Constable) Nimmo from one of the hot desks. I found him in front of a PC (as in personal computer) reading up on the recent arrest of The Chopper. I stood next to him and waited until he looked up. When he did so, he gave me a slow, respectful nod.

'Ma'am,' he said. 'You know your Choppers from your Cleavers.'

'That I do, PC Nimmo.'

When it all boiled down to it, we had our jobs to do. We had our places to fill. Inside Interview Room 2 on one side was myself and Nimmo. On the other was Ricardo Dreyfus. There was an edgy air about him, defiant and underfed. He had an ice pack in hand, pressed to the side of his face. I put on my most disappointed expression and hoped I wasn't over-egging the pudding. PC Nimmo inexplicably picked out one of his nostril hairs, which I was shocked to discover didn't bother me at all—in normal circumstances I was extremely squeamish about that sort of thing.

'You should let a doctor see that,' I said, motioning towards Ricardo and ice pack.

'A Doctor Heinz,' Nimmo threw into the ring.

'Fuck you,' Ricardo said venomously, looking directly at me. He then turned his attention to Nimmo. 'Fuck you,' he repeated, demonstrating he had venom to spare.

'That's very macho of you,' I said.

Ricardo slammed the ice pack down on the table. His arm snaked around the back of his head and he gently tugged at his ponytail.

'I'm saying fuck all,' he said.

With the tips of my fingers, I pit-patted my cheek. I counted down from ten in my head. The first thing they taught you at interrogation school was to know when to say nothing.

Nimmo beside me was inspecting another nostril hair.

'While we wait for your solicitor to rise from the crypt,' I said, having come to the end of my manufactured pause, 'let me tell you a story. Just as a way of passing the time, honest.'

Ricardo, as good as his word, said nothing, leaving Nimmo to break the silence. 'Love a good yarn, Ma'am.'

True to his word, Nimmo flicked away all follicles in his possession and sat up straight. At least I could rely on his full attention.

As for Ricardo, it struck me what an extraordinarily

crumpled face he had; a cross between a bloodhound and Iggy Pop. In all probability, he was communicating his displeasure, but this was a police station and pleasure wasn't in the trade description.

'It was you, William, and Bruce Dreyfus who robbed McConnell's the High Street Jewellers,' I said. 'Unknown to you at the time, that morning in fact, the deeds for McConnell's, the whole kit and caboodle, had been signed over to one Roy Lichtenstein. One of his more legitimate businesses.'

'Roy Lichtenstein aka Big Roy. You know who Big Roy is, don't you? Of course you do.'

One. Two. Three. Four. Five. I was counting the beads of perspiration that suddenly appeared on Ricardo's forehead. The more he tried to show that he wasn't a worried man, the more he achieved the opposite.

'I'm saying fuck all,' he said.

***

Before our little talk was about to commence, I listened to some whale songs on my wireless headphones. I let the soft, undulating sounds wash over me, connect with me. I was calmness personified.

It was time. With a flick of my eyebrows, the headphones popped out of my ears. Picking up the white plastic bag, I made my way to my old nemesis, Interview Room 3.

Waiting for me there was Uncle Wullie. An exchange of nods between me and the PC in attendance and off he went to take a circuitous route to the cappuccino machine.

I sat on my side of the table and made myself as comfortable as possible. I carefully placed the plastic bag down in front of me.

'Where I said it was, I take it?' Wullie said.

He trained at least one eye on the bag and, raising an arm in what seemed like slow motion, pointed at it; like you'd imagine one of the witches would do at the start of *Macbeth*. On his face, as if from nowhere, a rueful smile appeared.

'You asked for it,' he said, 'and you were pretty damn lippy about it. It's your problem now.'

'You mean this?' I rummaged around the plastic bag. 'It's called evidence, Wullie. Some nice stuff in here. Oh, and it's not a problem if you want to call me Brian.'

From the bag, I fished out a crystal tiara. Saint Laurent. Worth a pretty penny. 'Is this your share?' I enquired, even though I already knew the answer.

I was still warming him up.

Uncle Wullie was an interested observer. His head jerked up and down like he was a prize boxer, looking to clock everything his vantage point would allow.

There was nothing I had, though, that he hadn't seen before.

'That's everything, all we took,' he said.

'Didn't think bling was much your thing,' I said, carefully placing the tiara back where I'd found it. It was my turn to shift my head to and fro, although less like a boxer and more like an accountant, as I checked out the contents of the bag. There was a smattering of shiny trinkets; a decent enough stash, but I'd seen better.

'Not a lot in there,' I said. 'You in a hurry?'

'Parked on a double yellow.'

All the while, I was studying this individual seated opposite me. His exterior had hardened since Greenland. Here in custody, he was in familiar surroundings and, strangely, he seemed to draw confidence from this. He was the centre of attention. Maybe I should, I thought, limit myself to direct questions. Instead of working up to things, if there were a point to be made I should just get on and make it. I was pretty certain William Dreyfus did not do irony.

Pushing back, scraping my chair against the hard floor, I stood up, swerved, and took a step forward before positioning my back against the side of the table. I massaged my temples. The last few days were beginning to catch up on me. Fatigue was kicking in. I took a long breath, willing oxygen into my lungs.

If Uncle Wullie had something to say, now was the time for him to say it. I hoped, and then, thinking about it, sensed, and then, thinking about it, expected, he felt the same way.

And part of me wanted to scream and scream and scream and stamp all over his head and get it fucking over with.

'Okay,' I said. 'First, the jewellers, why next rob a supermarket?'

Wullie's confidence was a fragile thing. It was an optical illusion. He now stared forward, face drained. The realisation hit him like a ten-ton truck. Out of luck and out of options, he was at the end of the line. He needed a friendly face. And perhaps most important of all, a friendly ear.

'Panic,' he said. 'One hundred per cent panic.'

'We did McConnell's all right,' he continued. 'It wasn't well planned. Wasn't planned at all. We only took a couple of trays, bracelets, rings, pendants, that tiara. One miserable fucking plastic bag's worth.' Rings formed around Uncle Wullie's eyes. 'Ripping off Big Roy,' he said. 'What were the chances? How were we supposed to know he owned the fucking gaff? And bugger me if we didn't find out until afterwards. Word got round. We were shafted.'

'Ricardo tried to go into hiding, but quickly he'd used up all his favours. I suppose that's one way of looking at it, he was lucky he bumped into you at Electric Dreams and not one of Big Roy's hatchet men. I heard Big Roy had decided to make an example of us. He got to Bruce first. Bruce went missing. All that was left of him was his crowbar, much good it did him.'

'Ricardo came to me as jumpy as a fucking cat with fleas and said we needed ready cash and he had just the place in mind. I'm a superstitious sod, so I said to him, no way was I taking the crowbar, so he ended up with it, much good it did him.'

'Big Roy, Big Roy, Big Roy,' he said, 'Big Roy,' the sorrow in Wullie's voice increased with every iteration. 'Crime bosses are ten-a-penny. Every fucker these days, soon as he's past potty training is calling himself some big boss of this or fucking that. But Big Roy's different. He's a crime lord—there's only ever one of them.'

'We were shitting ourselves. With Big Roy, you just don't hand back the goodies with a note saying you're sorry. When your card's marked, it's marked. If me and Ricardo were going to run, we had to forget the stash, such as it was—we'd have more chance fencing Fanny Craddock—we needed money quick. Greenland seemed as good a bet as any.'

I returned to my chair. With me, grudging respect was ten-a-penny, I liked to share it around. So I felt some grudging respect for the man. To put things into perspective, there was only one man, Bryce Coleman—the crime boss I waved off (and perhaps a little more) at Glasgow Airport—answered to. And you've guessed it, that was Big Roy Lichtenstein.

Although, he did answer for a short time. He did answer to me.

'Hard, fast cash,' I said. 'Maybe throw in some milk and bread. Frozen peas. Half-price bananas. Heavily discounted tins of beans ...'.

Sometimes I wasn't sure I'd been somewhere. I couldn't swear; couldn't cross my heart and hope to die. Sometimes, not so much a memory, but a mishmash of recollections; the kind of disjointed flashing imagery normally associated with dreams. And as dreams went, not of the good variety. But the phrase 'tins of beans'; that's what did it for me. It all but confirmed it in my mind. Cogs had turned. Greenland, Hamilton. I had been at that place, that supermarket. It was I. It was really me.

My mouth was terribly dry.

Where was that cappuccino?

I didn't even like cappuccino. Maybe, I could have some broth? I felt trapped and claustrophobic.

There was a prickly sensation in my chest. Angst and worry. Worry and angst. I was so good at hiding it, better than most. Passingly, I shook my head and flicked my hair. Remembering why I was here; who I was here to interrogate.

'Must say,' I said, 'you don't seem that upset over poor Bruce?'

Wullie was up on his feet at this, cheering, shaking his fist in the air. It wasn't a case of restraining him, at least not yet.

'Result!' he cheered. 'Says something when an old sod like me outlives one of the young ones! Old Wullie! He still wears his pants the right way round. He still has lead in his pencil, that's what I tell 'em!'

I asked the question, I reflected, and he'd answered it. My thoughts were with Aunt Morag. Simple Aunt Morag, uncomplicated and loyal to a fault. What had she done to deserve a truly loathsome man such as William Dreyfus? Sincerely, we lived in a rotten world.

Wullie was back down on his chair, as quickly as he'd got up. A terrible smugness had taken over him. He pointed his finger, this time cocking his thumb, shaping his hand like a gun, towards the white plastic bag.

'Anyway, I say,' he said, 'atten-shoo-ate the positive. You have the stash, which means Big Roy will come after you now. That one, he puts the 'ment' in mental.'

For me, it was in for a penny, in for a pound. I could try and distance myself. I could attempt to look down at the likes of William Dreyfus, while protesting all the while that I was nothing like that. I could keep him at arm's length. Espouse disapproval with every cell in my body. But I was the crow from *Aesop's Fables*, made to look ridiculous by pretending to be a raven. This was as much my world as his. It enveloped me in dead skin, haunted my dreams, sickened and spoiled me. It was what made me what I was.

I revealed to Uncle Wullie, not for the first time, something of my other self. My mouth was crooked and my face filled out. I had puffy eyes.

'Tell me, Wullie,' I said in that second voice of mine, 'do I look worried?'

He looked at me, but this time he was cockeyed. 'A little,' he said. 'A little ... different.'

I took his conviction of before. I took his spite and arrogance and swallowed them whole. He was nothing but a hollow shell, at least to my eyes; at least to my world. My side of the table, I leaned forward.

For his part, Wullie regressed. His side of the table, he shrunk.

'You think?' I said. 'I'll tell you a secret. Anyone comes for me at three in the morning with their fists and knives, sticks and stones and oversized boots, I'll be prepared. I'll be ready for them.'

'I keep a hammer under my pillow.'

***

The solicitor, Mr Jackson, having arrived, cast his stony glare over me and Nimmo.

'Mr Dreyfus here agreed to help us with our enquiries,' I offered by way of explanation. 'Case of a missing family member.'

Ricardo shrugged. He seemed to have the attention span of a goldfish—and that was being incredibly harsh on the goldfish.

'While we're chatting, Mr Dreyfus,' I said, 'if I can appeal one more time to your sense of public, family spirit even. Can you tell me when was the last time you saw your cousin, Bruce?'

Ricardo looked across to see his solicitor hold out a hand, signifying 'halt'. Christ, he had huge hands—big hands, even for a lawyer.

Ricardo slumped back on his seat and tried to get across the impression of being completely untroubled. He needed to work on the gritted teeth, though.

'Out looking,' he said, 'for a lost puppy.'

***

Back and forth, Wullie was solemn now, hunched over, hands clasped. He could have been praying, except his eyes were wide open.

Although, was there anything to say you couldn't pray with your eyes open? If I ever had cause to pray, I'd like to think I'd keep my eyes open.

'Is he dead?' he said. 'Is he really?'

It seemed both peculiar and oddly believable that he was now questioning the fact that his nephew was dead. He'd just moments before been punching the air, extolling the circumstance of having outlived him. He had dealt initially with the news with misplaced bravado and, now things had sunk in, he was processing what seemed—at least to him—like fresh information all over again.

He was born again, reacting to the news like a different man.

'That church of his,' he said mournfully, deflated, 'much good it did him.'

***

Helen Street Police Station existed on its own terms. Outside, the seasons might change. In here, there was only one season. Sometimes it seemed to me it was removed from the rest of existence. It occupied a different plane. External to its walls, civilisation could have come to an end—be it plague, the next world war, a zombie outbreak—but Helen Street would continue on regardless, a hive of activity. There was always work to do.

The sudden appearance of the Four Horsemen of the Apocalypse would only add to the paperwork.

Enter Hadrian Jackson and the chatting had stopped. Soon after, Ricardo and William Dreyfus were removed and transported on remand to Low Moss. All that remained was for DS Spencer and I to swap notes.

'Without knowing it, they ripped off Roy Lichtenstein and, fearing reprisals, which makes sense, they've been on the run since,' she said.

I nodded. 'On the run without actually getting very far.' I studied her face. 'You seem distracted?'

'Sir,' she said. 'We got a phone call. Tall Trees, Milngavie. Another package arrived addressed to Charles Bartholomew. Another Jiffy bag. It was a severed tongue.'

'Oh,' I said. 'Oh,' I repeated. 'Didn't we put a trace on the address? Shouldn't it have been intercepted?'

'I spoke to the post office myself,' she said. 'But, you know the post office.'

'Don't know their backside from their elbow,' I said.

'Can't see the *tall wood*, sir,' she said, 'for the *Tall Trees*.'

I had to admit, even if she hadn't thought that one up on the spot, she had little time to work on it either. Tall Trees, Milngavie; the Bartholomew family home. I was mightily impressed. Didn't have much of a reward for her though.

'Sign yourself out a service vehicle,' I said. 'Go talk to Bartholomew. See if this latest development helps dislodge anything from his memory that might be useful.'

'Sir, is Charles Bartholomew a suspect?'

'Not at the moment, but I don't think he's told us everything either.'

'You not coming, sir?'

'Am I needed?'

Not for the first time, she stood there, mind working, trying to decide whether to challenge me or not. It was going to happen at some point. It was only a matter of time.

I wouldn't have wanted to, but if it came to it I was prepared to stand there all day. I was her superior, in rank at least. I was obstinate. I could sleep standing up. But it was the pull of the immediate task at hand that proved her undoing.

She wasn't the type to stand still when there was work to be done. Without further comment, she turned and walked off.

'Keep in touch,' I said.

Except that I didn't say that last thing. I kept this tiny morsel to myself. I didn't have a death wish, not today at any rate.

'Their backside from their elbow. Their tongue from their finger.' I didn't say that either.

***

There was always something about standing on the Great Western Road. The name itself evoked images of cowboys, high noon, six-shooters, and walking like John Wayne. In keeping with this flight of fancy, the sun shone high in the sky. I took a moment; eyes closed. I raised my head to the heavens and bathed in the warmth of its rays.

Minutes later, there I was, standing in front of St Mary Episcopal Church. A place of stone and liturgy. I cast my gaze approvingly over the exquisitely pointed structure. When I could, when I had the time, I would stand in awe in the presence of a church. It was the building itself that impressed me. Custodian of time; ever-present in the shifting, changing landscape which surrounded it. I was rather captivated by the idea of that. The grandeur of the building; the mystery; the secrets contained within.

That said, spiritually it left me numb, largely accepting as I was that I lived in a godless world. Still, police business called and I was just in time for the early service.

Inside, I found a decent-sized congregation. I made a beeline for the back pew. In the pouch in front of me was a bible with a bright blue cover. I gave the bible the teeniest dab with my finger as way of acknowledgement, but otherwise let it be. It wasn't until I was safely entrenched that I took a proper look around. There were arches and wonderfully expressive painted stained glass windows but, for the most part, the interior leaned on the modern side. The walls were painted white. Pulpit and altar were only a small step up from the pews.

Standing at the pulpit was an Episcopal priest. In front

of him on the pulpit was a laptop, open and ready for use. Next to him was a video screen. The priest himself was in his thirties. I tried to squash any compulsion to think too young but, too late, the thought was already out there. He wore a black priest's cloak, purple shirt, and clerical collar, no great surprises there. He was well groomed, immaculately turned out, although his hair at the back was a teensy bit too long for my tastes. Was I finding the whole display, especially the technical stuff, a bit of a let-down? Typical of a non-churchgoer, my preconceptions of what a church service should look like were entrenched in the 1950s.

'Мы очень благодарны.'

An alien voice, a child's voice, came from the laptop. On the video screen was the accompanying image of a group of children, dressed in antiquated, starched clothing, crammed together sitting on wooden chairs. The building they occupied had a wooden cabin feel to it. They seemed out of time.

A 'Rec' sign embellished the top of the video screen, signifying moving pictures, although the kids hardly moved. Still, they seemed happy—reserved but happy—their smiles seemed unforced. A young boy positioned at the front with a black bob of hair appeared to be their spokesperson.

'We are so grateful,' the priest said, providing commentary, interpreting the other-worldly words of before.

'Мы так рады.'

'So happy.'

The image changed to one of a large room chock-full with row upon row of single beds. The bedding was pretty basic from what I could tell. Which was fine by me, I wasn't criticising.

'Спасибо святому отцу.'

'Thank you, Father.'

'Спасибо за этот детский дом.'

'Thank you for this orphanage.'

A young girl appeared on the screen, all teeth and curls, waving enthusiastically for the benefit of the camera. She was dressed in what looked like a petticoat. Again, a particular decade came to mind. She could have been a child of the '50s, except for the fact that she was filmed in muted, modern colour.

The girl was obscured momentarily as the priest held out a hand and tenderly touched the screen.

'Спасибо за этот детский дом.'

'For everything you have done for us,' he said.

'Спасибо за этот детский дом—'

'For everything you have done for us—'

'Спасибо—'

'Thank you—'

The priest took away his hand. He was fighting tears. None of this smacked of a performance. He seemed genuinely moved by it all.

'Спасибо.'

'Thank you.'

He closed the laptop. The video came to an end. His congregation at this point was silent, motionless, transfixed. They were in his spell and, I have to confess, so was I.

A young deacon, barely out of his teens (his face had pimples), walked up to the pulpit. The priest handed the laptop to him and the deacon accepted it with appropriate care and reverence. The priest in kind touched the deacon's shoulder.

'Thank you, Deacon Andrews,' he said.

There was a different side to the priest now. Now he had the congregation eating out of his hand. He made the successful transition into full preacher mode.

'That we should never forget. We must never forget

the children.' He spoke on. 'As well you know, thanks to our relentless, wonderfully dedicated parishioners; your superb, superlative charity work enabled the Scottish Anglican movement to set up an orphanage and school on the Russian/Chechen border.'

'When the children decided to call the orphanage St Mary, I was filled with so much joy. We all were. I could feel God's love charge my spirit, fill my soul, my heart fit to burst.'

'We all did.'

'Such a terrible shock when, in the blink of an eye, our orphanage was gone. A Russian missile barrage over Chechnya. A stray missile, intended to quell a small faction of resistance fighters, instead hit and destroyed St Mary—in error, we are told.'

There was silence. There was nothing, an emptiness, but it meant everything. Slowly, the priest's lips began to move; it was a tremble at first.

'It changes nothing,' he said, 'because God's love does not change. It is absolute. So we forgive the soldiers who launched the missiles. As we forgive the engineers who designed the missiles and the workers who built them.'

If the eagle-eyed amongst us (me, mainly) were to look really hard at that precise moment, they might have detected the priest's mouth take on the tiniest of twists. You'd have to be incredibly observant; staring at the right place at the right millisecond. In any case, the tiniest of twists was understandable given the circumstances, in light of the terrible tragedy just related.

He was smiling now. A smile as wide as it was beautiful, projecting a piece of himself into the core of each and every one of his congregation.

'We forgive them, and we love them with every fibre of our being,' he said. 'Our very souls.'

'Amen,' he said.

'Amen,' his flock returned, in what barely registered as a collective whisper.

The congregation missed a beat in perfect unison. There was sobbing.

Heads were buried in neighbours' shoulders. From this sprang a feeling of such fortitude and strength. And I was not immune.

It would be churlish to say everything after this was an anti-climax but, unquestionably, it paled in comparison. As the act of communion played out in front of me, my mind wandered. I thought of Gary Cooper in a friendless town waiting for the clock tower to strike noon. I thought of Clydebank, my old horse. I tried not to think of dead things lying in pools of their own blood.

All done, I waited patiently as the congregation, in pockets, dispersed. My mood remained solemn as I walked towards the priest who, holding my gaze, had noticed me in return.

The priest moved away from the pulpit. You could tell by his face that he didn't recognise me, before flashing a trademark angelic welcoming smile. He held out his hand, which left me for a moment a little startled, but one, once I regained my composure, I was only delighted to take.

'A moving sermon,' I said. 'Terribly sad, and yet incredibly uplifting, Father ...?'

'Connor,' he said.

'Father Connor,' I said, pleased that I could finally put a name to the voice behind the words.

'Thank you,' he said.

There was a long pause. He cocked his head to his side. He wasn't the first, far from it, to try to work me out. In a place such as this, it was clear I wasn't a good fit. I was a fish out of water. I may have been a lost soul, but not quite ready to hand myself in yet.

I was flustered; face flushed. I suddenly became aware that I hadn't introduced myself.

'Oh, my manners, Father, sorry,' I said. 'Detective Inspector Brian Fisher. Brian please, just Brian. I was hoping I could have a quick word with you regarding Bruce Dreyfus and Amanda Bartholomew. Unrelated lines of enquiry, routine to be fair, just one of those funny coincidences, but I believe both at some point have attended this charming church of yours.'

Father Connor closed his eyes. He was in deep thought. He nodded and pursed his lips. His nostrils flared. A flicker of something came to him.

'Bruce and Amanda,' Connor said, 'yes, I pride myself in never forgetting the face of a parishioner, although I'm sure I've done exactly that over the years. If one has forgotten, how is one then supposed to remember?'

'Exactly,' I said. If this was the ideal time to jump in with a nervy, agreeable chuckle, I was not one to disappoint. Not me.

'Yes, they come to St Mary from far and wide,' he said, having waited patiently for my chuckle to dissipate. 'But I'm not sure if I can be of much help to you, Inspector. I haven't seen either of them for quite some time.'

He widened his stance, turning slightly and motioned to an arched wooden door situated at the back of the church, positioned behind the altar and to the left of a moderately-sized Christ on the Cross.

'Happy to talk, Inspector,' he said, 'but perhaps given our present surroundings, somewhere more private?'

'Yes, of course,' I said.

He waved at Deacon Andrews, who was presently some way away, hovering around the front entrance of the church. The deacon enthusiastically waved back for what seemed like half a minute.

'Once I'm gone, he'll be up at that pulpit delivering an

imaginary sermon,' Father Connor said with a conspiratorial wink. 'He'll deny it when I ask him later, but I'll know better.'

'Come now,' he said, 'follow me.'

We were at the door. With a shake of a sleeve, Father Connor produced a key. He unlocked the door, which swung outwards. He took a step or two back and there was a point where the door seemed to swallow him up, or at the very least obscure him from view. Before I knew it, I was leading the way, taking a narrow passageway which led to winding, narrow stone steps, which in turn led down.

'Down there?' I said, fully conscious of the fact that there was nowhere else to go.

'Yes,' went the voice behind me. 'The church basement. I have an office; away from flapping ears you understand.'

From behind, I could hear the top door swinging shut. There was the twisting of a key; the clunking of a locking mechanism.

In terms of light we were now dependent on a single electric bulb hanging, in humble fashion, from the ceiling. Instinctively, as I took another couple of steps down, worried that I may stumble, I reached out for support against the wall. In such a confined place, the clapping sound of footsteps on the stone surface only added to the feeling of claustrophobia.

'No problemo,' I said. 'If you don't mind me asking, how old is this church?'

Taking another step, my hips twisted a little and I glanced back at the shape following me down the stairs. About his person, around the chest area, was the glint of shiny metal. There, with both hands, Father Connor was carrying a metal cross, which in terms of context, the where and now, made perfect sense.

'Not at all,' said Father Connor. 'The present building dates from the nineteenth century, but has a history going back to the beginnings of Christianity. The cradle of civilisation, if one could be so bold.'

'Oh, yes,' I said, 'if I get the chance, I do love standing in front of churches.'

The stairs snaked to my left and I could just make out the basement door below. It was heavy and wooden, rather like my attempts at making small talk.

Perhaps it was the case that Father Connor agreed and decided to take matters into his own hands. Something metal came down hard on the back of my skull.

I tumbled down the rest of the stairs, taking the odd bump on the way, before coming to an abrupt stop next to the basement door. The pain was agonising. From nape to forehead, it felt like my head was split open. I thought I was going to die. I opened my mouth, tried to scream or shout—

And that was all I remembered.

15.

Next to No Resistance

It was pitch dark. I was emaciated. Skinless. I was floating; the soles of my feet inches above the ground. In the far distance, there emerged two car headlights, which took on a winding path; two meandering fireflies circling around each other in some weird mating ritual. Firefly in the headlights.

The life of a firefly. A life no longer ...

The headlights dipped and rose and snaked ever closer. The truth was, I was no longer scared of the dark. It bored me rigid. Filled me up so I was choking on ennui. I held out my arms, grateful for the approaching light; grateful for anything that was different, no matter the consequences. My eyes oozed slime. My lips were cold and sticky. Death metal screeched in my ears. My back was covered in cuts where flies buzzed and laid their eggs. My ankles were bruised.

The lights were closer now. Sensing their approach, suddenly the darkness had me by the neck. I was born to the dark and it wasn't prepared to let me go; not without a fight. Before it would give me up, it would rather tear me apart. If it came to it, it would reduce me to lifeless chunks. My tongue was swollen. Faster and faster and closer and closer. It squeezed.

I woke from a nightmare into a nightmare. My wrists were restrained, my head caved in. Beyond excruciating, the pain flattened me, and it wasn't for going away anytime soon.

My senses seemed heightened somehow. I was aware of a cloth or something on top of my head, presumably used to stem the bleeding. Slowly, I adjusted my head as I gauged the level of pain involved. It hurt like hell. Hell on earth.

I was in the church basement, bound to a chair. One of my eyes was closed. A line of blood emerged from somewhere above my eye. Where the line came to a stop, I did not know. All around me, I could just make out puffs of incense circulating the air. Wisps of smoke came together to make pretty, mesmerising patterns. I was dull in the head, that didn't help, but that wasn't the real reason he wasn't coming out; the *other* me. Sometimes he was just an awkward so and so.

'Nyuh.'

I was groggy, slowly coming to my senses, as if making proper sense of my present position would ever be a possibility. This should have been some kind of messed up hallucination, except that it wasn't. I saw past the fug and several feet in front of me, I observed someone else, also strapped to a chair; a woman, her features obscured by a towel draped over her head.

'Nyuh.'

My vision came back to me. My closed eye opened ever so slightly.

She was grunting, maybe drugged. Her left hand was

hastily bandaged. Could it be that some of her digits had been removed; a thumb, or at least one of her fingers? She wore a twin-set with pearls, an outfit for church, although her dress was torn and splattered with blood. For all that, the pearls remained, or so it seemed, untouched around her neck.

'Oh,' I said.

'Nyuh,' she said.

The realisation hit me like a double decker bus—as if my mangled body hadn't suffered enough.

'Mrs Bartholomew ...?' I said.

'How old is this church?' There was another voice, but the words were borrowed this time.

I adjusted my head ever so slightly. As I did so, my neck bones, collar bone, jaw, skull, all in unison, screeched their displeasure.

Father Connor was facing the wall, admiring the engravings, the ornate designs which adorned the basement. He stood by a small table. On the table were pillar candles, all lit, crammed together in such a way that they reminded me of the children from the orphanage. He reached out to feel the blood-wine sash curtains hanging before him.

His profile was illuminated by the candlelight. His face seemed to me to have taken on a change. It was a little more cruel. A little more brutal.

'This anteroom is soundproofed,' he said, 'where the priests of old would flagellate themselves. Among other things.'

'They'd whip their backs into a bloody mush. Penance for contact with the sullied nature of an outside, heathen world.' His attention moved away from the curtains, as luxurious and plush as they were. 'You are very much like me, Inspector,' he said. 'Changeable. I could see it in your eyes as soon as I saw you.'

It was then that I realised, too late, that I could see it in his eyes too.

'In my profession, I hear all kinds of rumblings,' he said. 'General chit-chat. Appeals for advice. Confessionals. And I've heard plenty about you, Inspector Brian Fisher. It's that nose of yours, apparently. You seem insistent on sticking it in all kinds of places—certain people aren't happy with you, not at all.'

'I do these things so other people don't have to,' he said.

From his mouth, I was convinced, these were more borrowed words. More shockingly so. How many times had I told myself the same thing? So many occasions, to the point of dilution, stripped of any real substance. And yet, here they were, said with conviction, saturated with meaning. The words terrified the life out of me.

'Take Mrs Bartholomew for example,' he said, 'a good, honest, upstanding, God-fearing citizen.'

The figure with the towel over her head froze at the sound of Father Connor's voice. At least she had stopped moaning.

The thing was, he was talking. He wasn't hurting anyone when he was talking, so it was good to talk; good for him to keep on talking.

'But as for Mrs Bartholomew,' he continued, 'information came my way of individuals intent on kidnapping and torturing her. Now look at her. Now they don't have to.'

On the table, there was something else besides the candles. With the angle, the smoke, the lack of light, I couldn't make out what it was. He lowered his hand and took it then, taking little steps, ludicrously small baby steps, he walked towards me.

'I want ye to change, ye ken?'

My brain was yelling at me; yes, I recognised the voice.

Disguised, heavy on the accent; laid on thick. The voice of Gerald Butler.

Instantly I thought of poor Bruce Dreyfus all chopped up and nowhere to go. If I didn't know before, then I knew I was in real trouble now.

Close now, he grabbed a tuft of my hair, making sure he had a good hold, pulling my head down, giving my brain something else to worry about. I screamed in pain. I was sick to the stomach.

'Yaargh!'

Needed to keep screaming. He couldn't do anything more to you if you were already screaming.

Nearby, this seemed to spur Mrs Bartholomew into movement. Her body rocked to and fro, at least as much as her bonds and diminished frame allowed. There was this terrible moaning which was growing in intensity. It was as much as a person missing her tongue could muster.

'Nyuh. Nyuh. Nyuh.'

Father Connor—or whatever version of himself he had become—finally revealed what was in his hand. He pressed the garden secateurs against my cheek; they were sturdy, capable of cutting through branches, vines, and the thickest of undergrowth. Moving them away, squeezing and releasing them in his hand, he accompanied this with a 'snip snip'. It was pure melodrama, but no less alarming for it.

He let go of my hair. My initial reaction was that I wanted to keep my head down. Didn't want to move my head back to its original position. Didn't want the grinding pain as a result. But another part of me won through, propelled by the need to recoil from the malevolent force standing in front of me.

He pointed the shears of the secateurs directly at my nose. The gap between cutting tool and proboscis, you could hardly fit a sheet of paper between them. The implied threat was obvious.

I was in pain. I was understandably concerned.

He was aware of such things. In this respect I was an open book.

'Change, change, change,' he said. 'I'll make you if I have to.'

Sucking in incense; it deadened the senses. I lost my centre. Skew-whiff. I was all alone.

The trick was to keep on talking. Even though my head was a little dull. 'You have the right to remain silent,' I said. 'Anything you do say may be used as evidence against you. You have the right to consult a solicitor. If you cannot afford a solicitor, one will be appointed for you.'

At this, Connor did a double take. He blinked, shook his head, his face half breaking into a smile. 'What is that?' he said, 'Are you TJ Hooker?' There was a moment's reflection. 'I don't want to be silent,' he said. 'Nor do you.'

He bent over and, using the secateurs, snipped off the ring finger from my left hand.

Efficient, over in a flash; the finger put up next to no resistance. My brow was drenched in sweat. Pain on pain rushed through me like a Japanese bullet train. I raised my head to the heavens, or as close to heaven as a stone basement ceiling would allow. Not for the first time, but with a newfound intensity, I screamed.

I looked down and saw the blood gushing out—it looked like it would never stop—and I wanted to stop shrieking, so I could laugh, before I started screaming again.

Father Connor held up my severed finger, which he'd laid on the palm of his hand. He examined it with a wistful expression. His whole demeanour was one of having experienced the kind of regret and sorrow that he could never hope to escape from.

'Just look at it,' he said, 'one minute it's animate, one of God's creations, part of a greater whole. Capable of alleviating an itch or pushing a button that condemns the lives of thousands.'

My shrieking reduced in increments, quicker than you'd have thought, to that of a whimper. In some macabre way, I could not explain why, I grew silent. I was delirious, dumbfounded.

He popped the finger into a transparent plastic bag; the kind usually seen at airport security, used to carry your liquids in. 'Now it's useless putty, inert flesh,' he said. 'The rot has already set in.'

He was back in my face. Eyeball to eyeball. In response, I squirmed and writhed and cursed my bonds. I wanted to be as far away from him as possible. At that moment in time, I would have given anything just to create some space.

He placed his hand on my left hand. Not exerting much pressure; he didn't have to. There was blood, enough to wash your face in. But on the priest there was hardly a mark, not that I could see. 'Please, please, Father ...' I said. I could barely enunciate the words. It was impossible in my current state to construct a coherent thought.

'I see this is going to take a while,' he said.

I was conscious once more of the moans coming from Mrs Bartholomew. I found myself joining in.

'Shut up!' he said. 'Shut up!'

Father Connor was poised. With the secateurs, with a flourish, he made to take a swipe at my face.

'Look ... look,' I said, gathering in everything I had, all my remaining resolve.

There was enough in my voice at the final moment to stay his hand. It won me a reprieve, however short-lived.

Firefly.

'Look, you're right,' I said, 'let's talk this through. Aah, aah ... It doesn't have to be this way. You know I'm a police officer. I'm here to serve.'

I was struggling to keep Connor's attention. The blood-smeared secateurs dominated proceedings. They had the bigger pull, clearly. He snipped them again for effect, as if the threat wasn't implied; wasn't clear to me already.

'Talk to me,' I said.

Connor nonchalantly, playfully even, circled the secateurs around one of my eyes. Stopping at the pupil, he was like the snooker player lining up his next shot. The secateurs were his cue, my eye the cue ball.

'This isn't ideal,' he said. 'None of this is. The Church has a lock-up garage in Clydebank; donated by a parishioner, now sadly departed. It would have been so much better to take you there.' He swung his arm back behind him with gusto, singling out the unfortunate shrouded Mrs Bartholomew. 'Here in this little retreat of mine,' he said, 'I keep Mrs Bartholomew drugged up to the eyeballs to ease the pain and indignity of her present condition. Tender mercies you might agree, but what of her privacy?'

He returned his full attention to me. Lowered secateurs took a grip, pinching my nostril. I was acutely conscious, thoughts rushing through me like a battering ram, that whatever I did, the choices open to me, there had to be nothing that involved sudden movement. Best to do nothing then.

Father Connor was so terribly angry. A bogeyman. A wrathful spirit. He was all over the place.

'No privacy,' he repeated, although I'd got it the first

time. 'Can you imagine? Now that is appalling!' he said, spittle curling around his lips. 'Unforgivable! Even the best of us are lacking in faith sometimes. Once I finish with your fingers, I'll scrape out your knuckles, whatever it takes—'

'So change, just change!'

And at that moment, I wanted to so much, but it wasn't happening. Inexplicably. I couldn't put my finger on it. I was in a really bad place.

***

It had been a tough enough day already, having contributed to a theme. The last several days had been rough.

As instructed, I paid Mr Bartholomew a visit in his Milngavie abode. He didn't appear to recognise me, even though I'd interviewed him along with 'Call-me-Brian' only days before. He was in a state of shock, of course. He should be seeing a counsellor (I meant to ask if he was).

What more was there to glean from Mr Bartholomew? The guy was a quivering wreck, having found his wife's tongue posted to him in a Jiffy bag. Tests were still to confirm whose tongue it was, but while sparing myself and everyone else the gory details, I was happy to accept the husband's testimony that he'd know his wife's tongue from anywhere.

Mr Bartholomew had a haunted look. He told me that he regretted the muted nature of the last exchange between him and his spouse. She said she was nipping out, going shopping, she might have other stuff to do, and he barely responded; barely registered the fact; didn't even look up from his desk in his study. Now he was wishing he'd gathered her up in his arms and taken her to Paris on a whim. But hindsight was a funny thing; fudging hilarious in fact.

And here I was, embroiled in another recurring theme, trying to track down my assigned DI again. This rocky road took me to an Episcopalian Church called St Mary. The equivalent of the Church of England in Scotland; the Protestant one where they still held mass. I knew my church institutions all right. Well, I knew of this one. My Dad's side hailed from Ayrshire, old mining stock. As long as I'd known him, when he'd had a drink, he attached an irrational prejudice to just about everything, especially if English in origin. If he was still around to see the day I walked into an Episcopalian Church, he would have turned in his grave. Not that he'd do so if he was alive, he needed to be dead, which he was, so ...

Like I said, long days, bundled up, one after the other.

Inside, the church was empty, except for a pimply youth in a wannabe priest's outfit standing in the pulpit. He seemed in a world of his own and didn't really notice me until I was standing a couple of feet away.

'Sir, umm, Father ...?' I said.

The young man appeared startled, brought back to reality with a thump.

'Oh no, oh no, I'm Deacon Andrews,' he said. 'It's Father Connor you'll be wanting—you'll be finding him in his inner retreat. He has company. A detective, I think.'

I was staring up at him. He was so young. The older you got, the younger everyone else seemed to be.

'You do seem on the fresh side,' I said. 'I tried phoning ahead. No answer. I'm DS Spencer and I'm looking for ...' I interrupted myself, as was my want. Best kept simple, I thought. 'Father Connor will do,' I said.

Deacon Andrews spun in the pulpit and pointed at a door situated at the back of the church.

'It's locked,' he said.

'Do you have a key?' I said.

He turned back to look at me. I watched on as the look of confusion grew in stages until it had taken over his entire face. Surely I wasn't the first person to ask the young deacon such a thing and, yet, then again, possibly I was.

Not that it mattered, I wasn't for waiting around. I knew you had to look at these things objectively, but I couldn't shake off the feeling that my beloved DI sending me off to the Bartholomew residence in Milngavie was his latest attempt at taking me out of the picture. Here now at St Mary, I wanted to see how much my presence would be tolerated. I wanted to see how seriously he was taking me as a partner. Maybe I could help him out with his enquiries. Yes, all of those things, and just maybe perhaps I could also noise him up. 'Call-me-Brian,' was it? 'Call-me-Arse,' more like.

'Key's somewhere around here, I think,' Deacon Andrews said.

By 'somewhere' he seemed to be indicating the whole of the church.

'Do you mind looking for it?' I said.

All the while he was chatting to me, or so I was to discover later, the baby-faced deacon was pressing a switch located around the mid-section of the pulpit. A wire led down from the switch entering the floor, traversing the wooden floorboards, through to the back of the church, down the stone steps, and into the basement. The wire came to an end at the basement wall, where it was attached to a small circular buzzer which, for the time I'd been talking with Deacon Andrews, had been buzzing like crazy.

***

Down in the basement, the buzzer rang long and hard. Father Connor continued to lean over me like a dentist hunched over a dentist's chair, but he couldn't ignore the constant droning for long. Mercifully, he withdrew the secateurs from my person. He then stared at his gardening tool of choice (which from what I could see, had never been used for the purposes of gardening) with an incredulous expression.

He fumbled. All of a sudden the object seemed so strange and alien to him. The secateurs fell with a bump to the floor.

'Why, I ...' he said, the words struggling to come out.

His features lightened, revealing a glimpse of the Father Connor, man of tolerance and forgiveness, from the sermon of before. But it was only fleeting. Connor paced up and down, hands covering his ears, trying to block out the buzzing, and the rest of the outside world besides.

'No, no, no!' he said, deeply agitated, stamping his feet. 'I need more time.'

I was grateful for the respite, but still needed to somehow get through to the man.

I coughed; had to roll with the associated collage of pain.

'Keep talking, Father,' I said. 'I'm listening.'

He stopped and, tilting his head, looked at me. I was nothing but an insect in his eyes. He had so much malice and hatred to dispense. He was unconstrained. All bellowing thunder.

'Yes, Inspector,' he said, 'let's talk and listen and roar and repent each other's sins. Let out the Beast, then follow it with some self-righteous, God-fearing anger.' He was like some convulsive whirling dervish. In a pique of apoplexy, with outstretched arm, he swiped the lit candles from the table, hurling them to the ground. 'There is no time,' he said.

In the blink of an eye, an already out of control situation grew much worse. The curtains had caught fire.

Father Connor was beside himself. 'Fire!' he said.

There was even more smoke. I glanced over at Mrs Bartholomew whose head was twitching, still trying to make sense of everything that was happening, when only madness and meaningless horror would do.

I strained against my bonds once more, one last time. As pointless an attempt as all the others, the greater the tension applied, the tighter the knot, but I had to do something.

'Fire! Fire!'

Connor kicked over my chair, which tipped, freezing for a moment in what seemed like mid-air, before sluggishly, exasperatingly, flopping over onto its side, taking my wracked and sorry frame with it.

Impacting on my shoulder, underneath the light carpeting, I could feel cold, hard stone. And there was pain, like a flood, like the ocean—it just kept on coming.

'Wait,' I cried out, and hoped the word carried with it some meaning. The fire was spreading. The heat, in irresistible, serrated waves was already upon me.

As for Father Connor, there was no sign. He had already left the basement.

***

After much scurrying and excitable facial expressions, laced with a seemingly unending litany of excuses, which I eventually gave up listening to, the deacon eventually opened the correct drawer containing the correct key.

I took the key. I moved fast. I was a blur. I didn't want

to give him time to formulate a thought, to question whether it was the right thing to do or whether, for that matter, he should accompany me.

Before one could holler 'Hosanna in excelsis', I was past the altar and Christ on the Cross, making my way to the arched doorway.

A neat combo of unlocking and opening resulted in the door swinging outwards, eating up the distance between me and it. I stepped smartly to the side in anticipation, before moving forward, leaving the key in the lock. Inside, it was dark and draughty, and immediately I decided I was not enjoying the experience. I followed a narrow staircase, which twisted down. As I descended, noise—very much unexpected—came back up to greet me. There was shouting. There was heat.

'Fire! Fire!'

Emerging from the depths was a man of the cloth gripped in the throes of panic, waving his arms in the air like a loon.

For a second, I found myself drawn to him, which couldn't be right because he was running towards me. Maybe it was the unfolding situation that gripped me, the one he appeared to be trying to escape from. I walked down another couple of steps before he barged past me, knocking me partially against the wall.

'Hey!' I said.

He had his hand to his mouth, oblivious, coughing, as he negotiated the rest of the stairs. Before I could think of anything else to say, he had ascended. He was up and gone. He was out of sight.

My attention reverted to what was happening below. There was black smoke, and I fancied this represented dark forces, having manifested, now in pursuit of a holy man. But that was just me, the product of an overripe imagination, a fascination with horror movies while not having the nerve to actually watch one, combined with eating too much cheese before bedtime as a young child.

I shook my head; shrugging off notions of the occult, forcing instincts anchored to the real world to kick in. I hurried down the steps and stuck my head past the open basement door. I tried not to gasp. Tried not to breathe in too much smoke.

DI Fisher was down on his side, tied to a chair. There was someone else, another chair, a female, her face obscured, covered.

Covering my mouth with my sleeve, I rushed to Fisher.

He was coughing, squirming. 'Car keys ... right pocket,' he managed to get out.

I rummaged around in his pocket—there were a lot of half-finished packets of chewing gum in there—found the keyring, penknife attached. Blade less than three inches in length, but sharp. I cut his straps. Blood was everywhere.

There was smoke. There was coughing. There was so little air.

'Mrs Bartholomew,' he somehow forced out, head jerking, motioning towards the other person in the room.

I skipped through isolated pockets of fire. I had to act fast. The penknife cut through her restraints. A rogue, fiery cinder jumped onto the towel over her face, and with my sleeve I quickly patted it out. It was then that I noticed that the towel was stapled on.

I scooped up her slight, unresisting frame, and deploying a fireman's lift, threw her over my shoulder.

My sight was unreliable. My eyes watering with the smoke. I smelled burning. I tasted it. All my senses were in the grip of it. The flames were rising, streaking across and demarcating the room. My legs had changed from light as a feather one instant to the next, the heaviest they had ever been. If we didn't vacate the premises right now, we never would.

I needed to keep Fisher engaged. 'Come on, DI! Move! Move!'

He was on his feet. He was using his good hand to apply pressure to the mess that was his other hand. He was in shock, but I hoped still mobile.

'Come on,' I said. 'Come on!'

I climbed the stairs with Mrs Bartholomew slung over me like a ragdoll. I had to trust that Fisher wasn't far behind. Deprived of oxygen, my head could no longer differentiate shapes properly, was no longer working the way I wanted. I had no idea where my footsteps and ragged breathing started and his ended.

Deacon Andrews was at the arched door as Mrs Bartholomew and I emerged. He seemed to freeze at the sight of us, all the energy sucked out of him. He just stood there, his mouth open in the most pathetic of ways.

'Miss ...' he said latterly, his voice hardly making an impression, such was the roaring in my ears.

I took a huge breath and coughed up some lung in turn. It would take all of my strength to lower Bartholomew down onto the church floor. Up here there was no sign of fire, but real or imagined, and it didn't really matter one way or the other, I could feel the heat on my back.

I couldn't stop moving. I was gripped by fight or flight, coming down decisively on the side of the latter. Mind you, with the former, I had the funniest of thoughts, who was there to fight? The deacon? My DI? The woman I carried my back? It was ludicrous. Really, if I had the inclination, I could die laughing.

My surroundings were a blur. I hurried along the church aisle, as fast as my leaden legs would allow, towards the front doors. Deacon Andrews ran with me.

For something better to do, he curved out one of his arms protectively around my back, while not touching, like he was some fey guardian angel.

I just concentrated on putting one foot in front of the other. When we got out into the fresh air, all of a sudden it felt like I'd entered some parallel universe where danger no longer existed. My brain wanted to relax. I wanted to lie down and sleep. But it wasn't over; it was anything but.

I was conscious of Mrs Bartholomew's towel flapping in the wind. I laid her down on the ground on her back.

I got on with it. I got down on my knees, applying heart massage. She was rigid; not moving.

I bent over her, my head close to her, but couldn't hear her breathing. Having come to a decision to remove the towel, I gritted my teeth, went for it; tugged until, with a tearing sound, the fabric gave way. I could hear the staples ping.

'Keep it together girl.' I said this for the benefit of myself. 'Keep it ...'.

I examined her face. Her mouth was a twisted, puffy, purple mess. What had the bastard done to her?

Taking a deep, long breath, all the dust and muck I'd inhaled made my throat and lungs growl like a car engine starting.

Subconsciously, I couldn't help it; I contorted my mouth in the attempt to mirror hers. I gave her mouth to mouth. Her lips were hard, congealed shut, but I tried to get some breath inside her. I willed it.

***

Fuzzy. Everything was a haze.

I did my best to follow DS Spencer. Lagging behind, measured in terms of tens of seconds, wary of putting too much strain on my ankles; of stumbling, falling, never to get up again. A nightmare happening in real time. But even so, eventually, mercifully, I stumbled out of the church.

Outside, the first thing I saw was the deacon from before, just standing there, in reaching distance. My hand clasped his shoulder as I looked to steady myself.

Deacon turned and gave me a quick glance, a nervous little smile, before returning his attention to DS Spencer several feet in front of us giving Mrs Bartholomew the kiss of life. Spencer stopped, straightened up, and employed cardiac massage, trying to jolt life into the still frame in her care.

'I'm losing her,' she said. 'Come on come on come on.'

'Can I help?' Deacon Andrews called out to her from the sidelines, while demonstrating zero willingness to move from the spot. It was the best he could do. He was part of a world where the only promises were empty ones. 'Can I help?'

Down and down, hands cradled, exerting a rhythmic pressure, stopping to check for breathing, then returning to it, down and down again.

'Phone an ambulance, the fire brigade,' she said. 'Shit, phone the police ...'.

I tried to take a step forward but was let down by knees of jelly. The ground was unsteady under my feet.

Meanwhile, Spencer was getting nothing. She looked up and stared at me, then Deacon Andrews. She was devastated. The trick was to be selective, to choose carefully which injustices of the world you allowed to get to you. Frustration was a dam; it wasn't healthy to keep everything in all of the time; sometimes you had to pick your moment and let the barriers burst; let the walls come crashing down.

Deacon Andrews held his mobile phone to his ear.

'Phone the fucking coastguard,' Spencer said.

My right arm moved over to my other arm, slid down to my damaged hand. I could acknowledge pain, it was there okay, I could feel it, but it was of a disconnected and distant kind. Pain by proxy. It was only a reminder, an approximation of what pain actually was. Like, I had left it all behind, and all that remained was residual, a painful memory. I was woozy and faint. I was muttering to myself.

'We let him get away,' I said, but my words seemed equally far away; distant, echoes of the past; those spoken by a dead man.

I tried to focus on the church building. I used to enjoy that, didn't I? Was fascinated by it. Took it all in: the grandeur of the building; the mystery; the secrets contained within.

He was gone. Father Connor had waltzed out of the church just like that. He did as he pleased. How were we to know?

Numb inside and outside. I couldn't keep my head straight. My neck gave way, my legs buckled. I didn't feel good at all.

***

She was gone. I couldn't save her. I tried so hard. The kiss of life, external cardiac massage, but it was useless.

I looked up and started shouting all kinds of rubbish at the deacon. At least he was on the phone.

I howled my frustration. My whole body shook and I wasn't sure if it was ever going to stop.

Fisher was there, also, on the public path, some feet clear of the church. He was bug-eyed, on the lookout, but not in a way that suggested he was searching far or wide; already resigned to the fact that what he was looking for was no longer there. He looked terrible, chalk white. Insubstantial; like he was a ghost.

His head went, then his legs, before collapsing entirely down onto the concrete.

It was all a mess.

16.

Herringbone (Sum of my Parts)

To make sense of the person I was and the person I could have been. Isn't that what we were all trying to do? Make sense of it all. The madness. The badness. We were the sum of our parts, but not necessarily the master of any of them.

I was in a place. I occupied a space. I was a space that filled a space that filled space. On one side of me was a hotel, on the other side a saloon, right next to the haberdashery. Dominating the townscape was the clock tower, which read twenty to noon.

Someone was coming for me. Something was coming for me. The sun was exactly what it is; a huge fireball eating up a chunk of the sky. I could feel the heat baking the nape of my neck. Rivulets of sweat trailed over my face, having started at my brow, finally to dribble into my mouth. The sweat stung my chapped fat lips. The taste of salt began small before taking hold of my mouth, before shooting up and taking hold of my brain somehow.

I had arrived where I wanted to be, I was sure of that. I climbed down off my saddle and tied my horse, name of Clydebank, to a hitching rail. I gave Clydebank a pat, took a step away, exerting all my willpower to fight the compulsion to go back and pet the horse again. For me it had to be the high way; no hesitation. It had to be onwards.

The ground beneath my feet was rutted, upturned by the many tracks that criss-crossed through it; this was evidence of a busy thoroughfare. As I looked around me, there was no one to be seen. Right now, at this moment in time, the whole town was deserted. I announced my arrival, at least to myself, by digging my spurs into the dirt. I drew a line. I noticed I had a hole in my shoe.

In the rippling heat, an easterly gust of wind whipped up a dust cloud of eye-bothering grit.

'OK,' I said in my best Texan drawl, talking to myself, conscious of time and what it may represent; the clock tower was my guide. 'You have twenty minutes, I guess.'

Suddenly, there was a leaping man. He leapt on my back; snarling, jaws snapping. He was like a mad dog; feral, trying to bite my face off. Such was the force of impact, my cowboy hat flew off. I twisted and pushed back, fending off my attacker's jaw.

He didn't say a word. He grabbed my hair. He wore Panamanian latex gloves. I pushed some more, until his head was at an angle and I could see his ear. On his ear-lobe was a tattoo or transfer, or something similar, of an elderly woman with mushroom cloud hair. Somehow, I sensed that the tattoo had psychic powers, that it had gotten through to my attacker; that it was making him do its bidding. Now, through him, it was getting to me. 'It' was a 'she'—the tattoo was the old lady.

It made sense because it was nonsense. And here, non-sense made sense.

I didn't want to get married because I was certain that after an indeterminate number of happy (borderline tolerable) years, it would all turn sour. Before I knew it, I'd be waking in bed, only to discover she had cleaved parts off me. Mentally, physically, forensically. I would be a bit part, an incidental, victim of a would-be serial killer with a poor choice in plastic gloves. Individual pieces of me wrapped in newsprint and buried in a shallow grave in the back garden.

But that wasn't going to happen, not to me. I'd vowed never to let anyone that close, so I stretched my neck to the point of dislocation until the offending earlobe, which carried the mad feisty female's visage, was in reaching distance. Thereon, it was a case of following instinct. I took the ear in my teeth and bit so hard it tore away, like it was several layers of lettuce. Earlobe tumbled into my mouth and with a gulp I swallowed. I did it so that *she* could never again lure anyone into a life of doomed, ill-fated domesticity. Pray, find me one lofty, misguided soul prepared to mourn a world with one less black widow. One less praying mantis.

Sucking the marrow from my bones.

No? Yes?

I threw my attacker, minus his ear, down to the ground. Undeterred, on all fours, he began sniffing, licking feverishly, shoving his tongue through the hole in my shoe. I couldn't stand it. The invasion of personal space was killing me.

'Go away,' I said.

And he was gone.

The wind died down. I inhaled long and hard. I coughed into the palm of my hand and, looking down, saw there was black gunk. A mixture of ash and dust and dead bits of skin.

There was a swirling, whooshing sound that moved

fast through the air. I spotted, of all things, a lobster, which was flying towards me. Propelled through the air, pincers clicking, making the noise of a cooling radiator (patent pending). I was alarmed. I didn't fancy the prospect of those claws getting close to my tender parts. I executed a forward roll a drunken ballerina would have been proud of. In the process, I scooped up my cowboy hat and, in the same extended movement, I turned, arms high in the air, and caught the flying lobster in my hat.

And so it went on. It was one incoming lobster after another; a procession of prickly, pinching marine crustaceans. I looked across and spied the man who was launching them at me. Or, to be more precise, not a man, but a half-man, half-cat. He, or it, was wearing a leather jacket, sleeves rolled up to the elbows. His exposed lower arms were covered in thick, predominantly black fur with some white markings. He had pointed ears, and human eyes, and long and wiry whiskers. As appearances went, a strange, deformed, half-human, not all there. That's how I saw most people. That's how I viewed myself.

Man-cat stopped to groom one of his hairy arms. It was in his nature, programmed into his DNA, so he couldn't help it.

Criminals are terrible creatures of habit.

Taking advantage of the break in proceedings, I tensed my shoulders and rushed at him. I picked up speed, faster; I was going at him like I was one of his speeding lobsters. Suddenly, Man-cat was aware, alert to the incoming threat. He turned and legged it. Before you knew it, he was at the front wall of the town's undertakers, claws out, ready to scale the wall, climb over, and be lost forever. He didn't get too far, though, before I grabbed his leg and pulled him back. He gave out an ear-crippling mew. With both hands gripped securely around his ankles, I began spinning like a hammer thrower, spinning him around. It was a scene of pure slapstick; cartoon carnage.

I turned and turned and turned him, to the point he was horizontal; a whirling, twirling, gyrating set of speedlines.

Along the way, his rotating, flailing frame just happened to collide with a group of schoolkids daubing graffiti outside the Old West Photographers. It was collateral damage.

Subject to the full force of a Man-cat and flung to the far corners, the various children, still in their school sweaters, spun off into the horizon, rotating, caught in gusts of wind. Slowly, they were completely enveloped, until they themselves became little individual whirlwinds. Fledgling cyclones.

The upshot of this was that the graffiti was unfinished, interrupted, and read—

'Rosebud was a S ...'.

Which got me thinking, Rosebud was a what? A movie reference? I didn't quite get it. For the life of me couldn't complete the phrase. Rosebud was a sling? A snake? A slight mental edge?

'Why is the answer to this suddenly so important to me?' I said aloud, not realising I had an audience.

DS Spencer stood there wearing straight cut trousers and a dark blue blazer. Her hair was in a bun, a couple of stray locks having fallen away. A hairstyle, I guessed, showing care not to come across as too strict, too cold. Despite her best efforts, she didn't look like she fitted in. She stuck out like a sore thumb because this was my game, this was my town.

'No,' she said. 'That can't be the question, because no one cares about the answer.'

'I care,' I said, dispensing with the Texan accent, which

on reflection, even to my tin ear, probably wasn't the most convincing anyway.

'No you don't,' she said.

She gave me a shrug, so large, so precise, I wondered if she had any French blood in her family. Then I wondered nowadays, if you could think such things without being considered racist? Didn't the French shrug their shoulders anymore? Or eat garlic? Or hate vegetarians? Suddenly, I was gripped with worry—this was the kind of thinking that would get me in trouble with the thought police. I was on the verge of hyperventilation; but I calmed down with the realisation that the thought police hadn't been formed yet. They were still some years off.

'No,' DS Spencer said, 'no French connection at all.'

'But it's not that,' she said, furiously rubbing her temples. '*Citizen Kane*,' she said. 'The closing shot. Orson Welles. The greatest movie of all time, so say a small group of film critics, who apparently know about these things.'

I was aware; I could feel it in my mouth, my tongue unilaterally tying itself into knots. It took every ounce of my brainpower to untie it back again.

'*Citizen Kane*?' I said. 'Heard of it, of course, I mean who hasn't?' What do you take me for? I'm not a complete philistine. It's got that immortal line, '*Play it again, Sam*.''

She didn't react. It was as if she'd been freeze framed. A glitch on a TV screen.

'Wait, isn't that a black and white movie?' it dawned on me to ask.

Normal service with DS Spencer resumed. She rolled her shoulders in fast time. It was then that I noticed her eyebrows tended to move up and down a lot, especially when building up to a point she wanted to make.

'Yes,' she said after a few moments. 'Why do you ask?'

'That's my blind spot,' I said. 'Or to be more accurate, other peoples' blind spots.'

'Colour TV license,' I continued. 'Because certain people—the type who write or tweet or phone in, or post on their local MP's Facebook page—complain when a black and white movie is shown in a prime-time slot, no matter how classic it is, or even if it's starring Jimmy Stewart. "I don't pay for a colour license for the BBC to show something in black and white—"'

'What about *Schindler's List?*' she said and waited for me to react.

Yes, there were exceptions to every rule, but that didn't invalidate the rule. I wasn't prepared to get into that anyway.

'So, if the BBC respond by only showing the likes of *Citizen Kane* at non-peak times, like half twelve in the afternoon, or four in the morning,' I explained, 'I'm never around to see it. I work those shifts; the antisocial hours.'

She smiled at me. She smiled in a way that said she knew something and I didn't. I didn't like that smile. In fact, I hated that smile.

In any case, this couldn't be considered an excuse nowadays, when you can buy a disc, or indulge in some streaming, or tape it onto the hard drive of your TV box. You didn't have to be a detective to figure that out.

You could download it straight into your cerebral cortex. Wait, like the thought police, that was still some way off.

You know what, next time someone asks me, I'll say outright I don't watch black and white movies and leave it at that. I had nothing against them. If they tell me I'm missing out on some of the best movies of all time, I'll simply nod in terms of acknowledgment and then I'll tactfully change the subject. Talk about the weather, or the Royal Family, or the latest violent crime statistics. I just don't do black and white.

It was like DS Spencer knew I didn't want her too close. I'd engineered scenarios to ensure we kept our distance. I'd say things to her, to not rely on her; but when it came down to it, if you look past the excuses, the verbal diarrhoea, now she was here I didn't want her to leave.

No, my mistake, my world turned upside down. *Did want her to leave.*

She took off her blazer and folded it. Dropping down on bended knee, she laid the blazer on the ground. It was then I noticed the herringbone design on her shirt. To confess, I was spooked by the white twilled nature of her blouse. I was fearful of where all this might be heading. Please, let me be reading too much into this.

'Must everything be so black and white?' she said.

'Do you have any friends?' she said.

'Know of any family?'

'Do you struggle with the term associates?'

'How close am I to finding you out?'

'Do you think we're all out to get you?

'Do you feel threatened by me?'

So many questions, who did she think she was? Words poking at me like sharp sticks. My head was spinning. Fit to burst; the weight of it was oppressive. Crushing. My ears were ringing. I had this feeling, if I answered her, maybe I could alleviate the pressure. I needed to force out a response. No Google, no coffee establishments with free Wi-Fi here in the Wild West, so it was up to me to grope around the inner vestiges of my mind to see what I could scrape up. 'Rosebud was a—'

I must have picked it up from somewhere. If it was such a big deal, someone on colour TV or radio would surely have made reference to it. Had to be there, somewhere, tucked away in the pointless-and-unconnected-trivia-that-one-day-might-save-your-life section of one's long-term memory.

'Rosebud was a sledgehammer,' I stammered.

I looked for DS Spencer, but she was gone. All that was left was her blazer. I had this feeling wash over me of both relief and disappointment. And then hunger. I realised I probably hadn't eaten for days.

I glanced back up at the clock tower. It was still twenty minutes to the hour. It was as if Father Time was refusing to move on; to accept or acknowledge the crazy stuff that had gone on before.

Hunger had never been a problem to me. It was a demonstration of self-control; that I was the master of all my inner urges. But on the other hand, it was tricky. It was all a question of balance. I didn't necessarily want to starve myself to death either. I had to eat some time.

The trails in the thoroughfare resembled tracks on a junkie's arm. Occupying the centre of town was a tent, and each trail led to it. It was a food tent and waiting to serve me was Francis Telfer, appearing as shifty as ever. He was wearing food overalls, which may at one time have been pristine white, but now were a murky yellow.

'Commandeered any nuclear submarines lately?' I asked him.

'They haven't been invented yet,' he said in a deadpan delivery, which would suggest this wasn't the first time he'd been asked that question. 'I mean this place might be the Wild West, but it's not *that* wild.'

'What's your poison?' he went on to say, instantly brightening up.

'I'm starving,' I said. 'It wouldn't surprise me if I was fading away right in front of you. What do you have?'

'Just the thing,' he said.

From behind him, he brought out a stonner kebab, sizzling away, a Glasgow delicacy. It's a saveloy wrapped in strips of doner meat, coated in two layers of batter, and then deep-fried to an inch of its life. It came in at a hearty one and a half kilos and, just count them, every one of those one thousand calories. It carried a world health warning. Incidentally, it's called a stonner because it so resembled one's manhood in a state of arousal.

But beggars can't be choosers, so I took it in both hands, this slab of transmogrified kebab flesh, and moved it slowly and purposefully towards my welcoming open mouth. My mouth was as accessible and wide as the Clyde Tunnel. I could smell the batter, the seasoning, the re-processed lamb. I was drooling unconstrainedly. Slobber fell on stonner, softening it up, all to aid the mastication process. The stonner was caught in a trajectory beam of my mouth's making, and there was nothing I could do to change this, although part of me did regret, and not for the first time, the decision I made in 2012 not to turn vegetarian.

I was aware there was someone else in my vicinity, which coincided with an elbow in the ribs courtesy of a big man called Roger. Roger had arms of granite, given cause to use his bulk in a certain way.

I lost my grip of the stonner kebab, the impact of Roger causing me to involuntarily toss it up. The kebab was spinning in the air. Roger, demonstrating a balance and poise you wouldn't immediately associate with a large man, caught the kebab mid-air. Revealing as unrepentant a set of big man's gnashers as you could ever hope to witness, he took no time at all to tear a big chunk out of my stonner.

'Noooooo.'

My kebab was taken from me. I was distraught, beyond tears and anguish. I fell to my knees, both hands clawing at the ground.

Roger's granite hand moved abruptly to his throat. Just

as suddenly, he joined me in collapsing to his knees. Quietly but violently, whole body shaking and gyrating, he was choking on the unedifying gristly matter that was his last bite.

I got up and circled around behind him. I wrapped my arms around his ribcage, taking secure hold of the arch of his back; aware of sweat dripping down to the tip of my nose.

Walking towards us was Bryce Coleman. His body was hunched, his movement hampered. He needed a walking stick. Injuries sustained, I would have thought, from his encounter at Glasgow Airport with yours truly (or was it *his* truly). There was no love in Coleman's eyes, no compassion, no feeling of kinship towards the likes of yours truly. Of course, this was a basic requirement; Bryce Coleman would never have attained the position of feared gangland boss without having so much hate to give. And he had a mountain of it.

Roger continued to choke and writhe in my arms. He was a handful.

Bryce Coleman shuffled closer, making ground in a broken manner, his stick leaving an irregular pattern on the dirt. His whole belaboured body movement gave me the heebie-jeebies. Mouth tight, jaw clenched, like nails scraping down a blackboard.

I felt trapped and claustrophobic.

Unhurriedly, in calculated stages, Bryce Coleman raised his walking stick high above his head. The hate had taken over him, transformed him. His body was a collection of sinew, of muscle. I could see through him. I could see the blood pumping in his veins. He was meaning to hit out.

I applied the Heimlich manoeuvre on Roger. On cue, the fragment of kebab lodged in Roger's windpipe flew out of the big man's chops. Coated in saliva, moving this fast, it was a missile. It pierced Bryce Coleman square in the eye. Coleman put his hand up to the compromised eye socket, but he was just going through the motions. It was all window dressing (perhaps a little salad dressing), there was no thwarting the kebab. Bryce Coleman keeled over, a hunk of processed meat lodged in his eyeball.

Roger's head jolted; came back up at me, smashing into my chest. Before I knew it, I was belly down on the thoroughfare, half-blinded, a bloodied face for company. It wasn't safe out here, on open ground, I decided. Arduously, I began to crawl towards the saloon.

I wriggled past a ne'er-do-well who sat on the ground, legs crossed, eating a pasty, before spontaneously combusting. His body was engulfed in flame, just like the burning monk Quang Duc.

The spectacle left me with a thirst. I wanted a Diet Coke.

It seemed to take an age. Squirming and breathless, I was panting when I reached the swinging saloon doors. A figure strode through the doors and offered his hand. I took it and was duly helped up to my feet.

'Much obliged, sir,' I said.

The figure was Henry Roberts; killer, desecrator of Lindsey Handley, wearing a black t-shirt, stretched at the neck before its time.

I could smell her on him.

I recoiled.

A combination of shock and dread imprinted on my face, I moved in a sort of half-pirouette action into the saloon proper. It was some achievement, given the extent of my injuries, but all that mattered to me was that I get away from this monster.

I was at the bar, which was long and wooden, chipped and festooned with spittoons. Cowboys had used pocket knives to scrawl curses on the wooden finish, against sworn enemies, corrupt lawmen, overzealous cowhands, and ex-lovers.

'Diet Coke?' went the barman. A brace of words intended for my ears only. It was Father Connor, dressed halfway between a barman and a preacher.

'You're probably wondering why a priest should find himself working behind a bar,' he said. 'If people want to find hope from a bottle, some kind of solace, then the least I can do is make sure they hear my voice while they do it. I'll tell them, no matter what they are going through, it will be okay. Sometimes they just need a sympathetic ear.' There was a twinkle in Father Connor's eye. 'And, if they want someone removed, or badly beaten or tortured, or all of the above, as God is my witness, then I'm obliged to do it for them. I'm the preacher-cum-barman of this two-bit town. I do it so no one else has to.'

I couldn't stand it.

I moved away from the bar, took one step backwards then another step, until I bumped into a shotgun-wielding Uncle Wullie. Wullie was terribly nervous, body shaking.

Henry Roberts and his narrow face came at us, silently, soundlessly, noiselessly.

Wullie, suitably freaked out and generating enough noise for both of them, pulled the trigger, emptying both barrels and blasting Roberts to smithereens.

Father Connor vaulted the bar in spritely fashion, only for Wullie to swivel on his heels and release another thunderclap. Father Connor, filled with buckshot, was done for before he hit the floor. I did my best to stifle a cheer.

Uncle Wullie was on a roll. It was a procession. A deadly procession. I backed off. I held up both hands in surrender. Uncle Wullie aimed his gun at one of my hands, and then adjusted his aim towards the other. He had a frightened mongoose look about him; easily spooked, especially deadly.

'Easy there,' I said, 'we're friends, remember? I let you keep your dentures, didn't I?'

This was a genuine question. I wasn't quite sure myself. Would have welcomed clarification on the dentures front.

He fired both barrels, an example of overkill if there ever was one. It was a thunderclap. It blasted my left hand, which exploded into smithereens. All that remained was a mangled stump.

'It wasn't supposed to be this way,' I said to myself, tears streaming down my face, biting my lower lip to the point it was bleeding again. Without thinking, using my bloody stump, I tried to wipe away the blood, tears, and snot from my face, making the problem a hundred times worse.

It occurred to me that I should be screaming; howling in pain at an imaginary moon up in an imaginary sky, but then a better idea presented itself. It was at my feet. Among the swill and spit of the saloon floor was a jigsaw man consisting of various body parts, fished out from the River Clyde. The body parts were arranged just as described to me by DS Spencer.

Even so, there seemed more limbs and organs than I was expecting. I counted two hearts for a start—and three hands.

I dropped down to examine them one by one by one. There was a torso, all puffed up, a knee, a thigh. There was a second left foot, which was no good to man nor beast. Then I found what I was looking for—a left hand—which I placed ever so carefully over the open bone sticking out of my bloody stump. Forcefully but diligently, I pressed down until with a satisfying click, the hand connected with my wrist. It was like two plastic building bricks, having spent an eternity apart but ultimately destined for each other, finally brought together.

There was nothing more to do but to take a moment to admire and examine this new forelimb of mine. I flexed and rolled my fingers which, to a digit, danced exotically, like bellyless belly dancers. Everything seemed fine until it was time to take a stock count and excluding the thumb I only counted three of them. To my utter horror, my ring finger was missing. It had never occurred to me before, but they called it right. I was never to wear a wedding band (at least on the correct finger; maybe instead I could wear it through my nose). I was destined to be with no one, which in truth had always been the case, but I felt wronged, robbed, and cheated now the decision was taken out of my ...

Hand.

Still, I thought, damaged goods were damaged goods. So I sorted through the various bits and bobs of the jigsaw man. You see, I wanted to make a complaint in the strongest possible terms directly to the head; no other appendage would do.

I scrambled around until I found it, grabbing it by the roots, so to speak, and hoisting it to eye level. The hair was black. My mood was black. Once I sorted out my feelings, I had nothing but revulsion for it, for it was my own dead face staring back at me. Except for the fact that there was no staring. The eyes were closed. Skin white and bruised. The bruises—the most prominent on the left cheek—were a deep dull purple. Contusions. Welts. Ringed, concentric circles that appeared to spiral on forever. The rot had already set in.

I ran, could you blame me? Through swing doors, I escaped the horrors of the liquor house. On leaving, I looked back for only a second, but enough time to make mental note of the name of the establishment. A sign in big, bold letters read Electric Dreams.

I was back outside, standing on scorched earth, the rutted thoroughfare, the dirt and the grit. I breathed in some of my surroundings and I breathed out some of me. None of it seemed real, but it was like I belonged anyway.

The three Wise Men stood before me. One covered his mouth; another covered his ears; another obscured his eyes. Was it also worth mentioning that each of them was dressed in stripy pyjamas?

I decided today was not the day to explain myself to them, or anyone. To me these men, wise or not, comprised nothing more than an obstacle course.

I sprang towards them. I was climbing, looking for a foothold. One foot wedged into a knee then shoulder, the other a stomach then a Wise Man's face. I didn't have to do it—could easily have walked around them—but I wanted to show I could do it. A swing of the hips and I was clean over.

On the other side, lying in wait, or maybe ambush, was DS Spencer, again. No matter the nooks and crannies I tried to hide in, she was never far away. And here she was, dressed incongruously in a white herringbone shirt, except I knew that I couldn't be right.

She had an uncertain look on her face. She took a deep breath as way of building up to ask me something; another question, one related to the others, but more pertinent perhaps; a continuation of a theme.

'Do you seem me as an obstacle?' she said.

Furiously, I shook my head. It wobbled for so long and with such ferocity, I was sure the only way this could end was if my head dropped off. But, frantically, I was thinking, that was all wrong; that wasn't the right question. That. Was not the. Right ...

'Can you still do any good?'

Standing there, it wasn't DS Spencer, not anymore. It was Dr Dawn. And while accepting the change didn't make perfect sense, I hoped it would make better sense. She unbuttoned her top button as final proof, at least to me. Dr Dawn, utilising her cool words and cooler mind; she was the one to rescue order from chaos, to dab away the tears and mop up the spillages. I was happy to put all of my eggs in the one basket. In Dr Dawn I was prepared to trust.

'I'm good at my job,' I said.

'That's an answer to a question,' she said,' but not the answer to *the* question.'

She was good.

She was pushing me further, forcing me to dig deep, to peer into myself, to finally come to terms with whom or what I really was.

'I ...'.

I hated that word. I despised everything it represented. I was jealous of a person who could say 'I' with anything approaching complete conviction—to speak wholly for him or herself. The reality was something different. The word 'I' was cruel and malicious. It wiped your nose in it.

Dr Dawn waited patiently for my considered response. Except, she was no longer quite Dr Dawn.

Blood started to appear, seeping out of her chest. Red lines coursed down, forming diagonals, until they met at the bottom, forming a crimson V-shaped pattern.

Herringbone.

She had a perplexed look on her face. She would have been scared if only she could have accepted the logic of what was happening to her. The downright strangeness of her surroundings.

'I'm sorry,' I said.

The seepage continued, but I hoped for her sake, not for much longer. It wasn't as if I set out to make people suffer. And even then Dr Dawn would be the last person I'd want to see go through that.

There was a tearing sound. It was the sound of crows set on fire trapped inside a man-made tunnel. The sound of self-loathing, misery, and hate. Through bone, fat, and skin, my head had burst out of Dr Dawn's chest. Or, I should say, the head belonging to the *other* me. He looked confused; eyes moving rapidly, but his peripheral vision was hampered by the proximity of Dr Dawn's shuddering frame. And I hadn't dared to look at Dr Dawn's face. I hadn't dared look at all.

'I thought you were gone for good?' I said to my other self. 'I thought the bad things that happen around me—around *you*—would stop. I could draw with my heel a line on the ground. I could move forward and put all past misconduct down to *you*. Things would turn out a certain way for me now. I'd do everything by the book. I could exonerate myself. Wash my hands of it; the nightmare ended. The fear of being recognised; of getting caught. People would accept what they see with their own two eyes and not disbelieve. They'd not feel the need to explain it away as something else. Adding two plus two and coming up with something that's not five. I could say 'I' and know where I truly stand. I'd have a clean slate.'

'It wasn't me, I could tell them,' I said. 'It was him.'

I pointed a finger. 'It was *you*.'

It was all so desperate, but I had to be heard. I had to say the words and I had to listen. For my ears alone; I wanted so much for the words to mean something. To become something transcendental. To lift body and soul.

The 'other me'—the other 'I'—no longer questioned the strange setting he found himself in. Instead, he focussed on my face. Our face. His face. The sum of my parts.

He seemed much surer of himself. His countenance went dark. Dr Dawn's blood in streaks began to run down his cheeks. He smiled the kind of smile that could crack an egg, or skin a penguin.

'Rosebud was a—'

'Strike,' he said.

As soon as the words left his twisted lips, it had turned noon and the bell of the clock tower rang out. I swallowed as hard as I ever had and braced myself for what was to come. It was a new beginning, and for all that, no less daunting, no less terrifying; the stuff of nightmares.

And then I woke up.

***

When I woke, things seemed no less hazy than they did before. I was in a white room. In with the needles and disinfectant.

I was in a hospital bed. Pain encased me like a block of concrete, but not sufficiently enough, apparently, to warrant a morphine drip. Next to my bed on a side table were daffodils in a vase and a paperback, *Crash* by JG Ballard. I had no recollection of how they got there. I wasn't sure if either of them weren't someone's idea of a bad joke.

I had dipped in and out. It was all a dream of course, but as it played out, there was this strange sensation where I could have sworn I wasn't completely asleep, not the whole of the time. Case in point, I tried to shut my eyes for a minute, tight, to exorcise a bad thought, but there was no measurement of time available to me except for the counting of seconds in my head. And to be alone inside my own head, I found this intolerable, too much like mental torture.

I couldn't ignore it anymore. I lifted my left hand to inspect it. Tightly bound in frost-wrapped dressing.

White, bulked up; recognisably hand-shaped, except for one missing digit.

All I could do was wait. I had a thought. If I changed and became the monster inside, became the other me; let all the fury and hate bubble to the surface, kicked some doors in and shouted out a selection of well-worn obscenities, changed outside as well as in, what then? A complete transformation? That my finger would grow back? Would I be whole again?

A chair suddenly came into play; shepherded next to the bed; someone had entered the hospital room. I was no longer to be alone with my thoughts. Good thing, bad thing, who could decide?

'Hi,' she said.

17.

Tiny Facts of Kindness

'It's Julie,' she said.

The name threw me for a moment. It swam about inside my head, caught in a whirlpool of the cerebellum. The vortex stopped temporarily in order for me to fish something noteworthy out of it. Julie = DS Spencer = someone I don't really need near me right now. I had no idea, when I started that thought process, that it would end on such a sour note, but that's the way the mind works sometimes.

However, it quickly turned out that I did have need of her. There had been a phone call made; the conveyance of specific instructions. A call that came from this hospital room. One I didn't remember making but I must have, because there she was. She carried the holdall I'd asked her to fetch for me from the station—from under my desk, in fact.

Everyone—everything—had a story. I had one. So had she. So had the bag.

***

I'd put a bag together in advance of a stake-out I had planned, or rather had a notion to plan, should I ever receive a tip-off on this Roy Lichtenstein crime lord fella everyone was talking about (myself included). An unofficial stake-out, I should say. If it came to it, I'd take a couple of days leave. It would be simpler that way, less red tape, less chance of aggro from one's superiors.

Anyway, my stake-out holdall covered as many eventualities as I could think of—change of clothes, Thermos flask, a Kit Kat. It then occurred to me, for the benefit of prying eyes (it was a busy office) that I should make it appear more like a travel bag. So in went the pyjamas and travel pillow. And where the pillow led, another—essential—item was sure to follow.

'Anyone comes for me at three in the morning with their fists and knives, sticks and stones and oversized boots, I'll be prepared. I'll be ready for them ...'.

***

DS Spencer placed the bag on the side table, which effectively hid from sight both flowers and paperback. She reverted to the plastic moulded hospital chair. The idea of visiting didn't seem an alien concept to her and she seemed pleased to see that I'd woken up. Still, there was a tension in the air, which became apparent in subtle, covert ways. The more she tried to hide it, the more noticeable the stress lines on her face.

'How do you feel?' she said. 'They tell me they put three stitches in your head,' she added, a comment not necessarily designed to lighten the mood.

I tried to shift my body a little towards her. It seemed the right thing to do, but then I felt a sudden, strange, unclassifiable twinge that only served to heighten the general sense of unease which gripped me. So I took the executive decision to stop short and keep my frame where it was.

'Sore,' I said.

I checked on my damaged left hand. It had been roughly a minute since I'd last done so.

'Mrs Bartholomew? Father Connor?' I said.

I couldn't help but inject a hopeful tone into my voice. As way of contrast, my better judgement was preparing me; while things might be grim now, in all probability they were going to move in one direction only. This was the best it was going to get.

'It's a mess,' Spencer said, falling in line with the 'better judgement' camp. She clasped her hands together as in prayer, brought them up to her nose and mouth. She tried to bury her face in them. She was exhausted.

'She didn't make it,' she said. 'Combination of shock and Christ knows what he did to her. Although I could make a stab, for want of a better way of putting it, at piecing it all together; I guess we'll have to wait for the post-mortem. Just as well I got to you when I did.'

She smiled at me, without the expectation of one in return. It wasn't that kind of smile. 'Connor is missing,' she said.

She widened her eyes, fighting the lethargy to the point, momentarily, she looked like a ghoul.

'We're holding the deacon, Andrews, for questioning. Poor sod's all over the place,' she said. 'He claims Connor liked to surprise him—test him—calling out for him unannounced to pray at various times of the day. It was on such an occasion that Andrews assumed Connor, having initially invited Mrs Bartholomew into his inner sanctum, had then seen her out. He hadn't of course.'

'He thought Connor had retired downstairs to the

basement for some privacy; some peace and quiet, to compose his thoughts, prepare the next day's sermon.'

'And there was you. All the time I was talking to him, Andrews was ringing a buzzer to let Connor know he had another visitor. He thought it perfectly innocent, and you know what, I believe him.'

She leaned forward. My head was stuck to an unyielding hospital pillow. It had me in its vice-like grip. But there she was, all of a sudden in my line of sight, and it seemed like the ideal opportunity to watch her (I wasn't going anywhere) and get a fix on her. It felt like I was properly seeing her now, clamping my eyes on her for the first time. She was sombre, and it wasn't all to do with the present case. It was something more than that. A deep sadness infiltrated her, resided in her bones. I could see inside.

And then, as these things tended to, the moment passed. Equally so, I had moved on. She was next to me, but still she eluded me.

'Ask him about a lock-up in Clydebank gifted to the church,' I said. 'I'm fairly certain Mrs Bartholomew isn't the only victim.'

And I was thinking, it was Clydebank twelve years ago—and now a different Clydebank twelve years on.

'It's a bad situation,' she said. 'A bad, bad situation.'

'No better or worse than when we got up this morning,' I said.

Spencer massaged her shoulder; the one she'd used for lifting the unfortunate Mrs Bartholomew. She was past the stage of being annoyed, no matter how much, under normal circumstances, my comment would have irked her. Her mood was neutral by default rather than design.

'If you say so, DI,' she said.

'Connor has contacts throughout various churches and charities based in Eastern Europe. We think he's heading there. We're checking out the ferries, airports, buses, Eurotunnel. He's probably already a stowaway in the back of a lorry somewhere.'

My body felt like it was stapled to the hospital bed. Not for the first time, I could feel gravity pressing down and I could have sworn it was much heavier for me and my fragile crumbling physique than for the next person. You could say my mind was elsewhere, anywhere but here.

'Yes,' I said, my voice croaking, very small, 'use every available resource.' There was a tap, tap, tapping noise. I wasn't sure if it originated from inside or outside my head. 'DS Spencer,' I said, 'you'll have to excuse me, I'm really tired.'

A moment passed. It was a moment of unpredictability; I was unsure how things would pan out.

'Of course, sir,' she said. 'Just before I go.' She broke into the biggest and friendliest of smiles, holding up an old friend. 'Rescued this from your desk as well.'

I hadn't noticed it before; up until now it hadn't been in her hands—she must have had it squirrelled away somewhere. It was a decent enough gesture on her part. That was the main thing.

'I thought I'd bring along your diary,' she said. 'You were right. That's how I knew you'd be at the church. It was all in there. Name, place, time. Old school. Respect.'

She flicked through the pages until she came to today's date. At least I think it was still today. She held up the relevant page, which read, 'FATHER CONNOR, ST MARY'S, BEFORE, MAYBE AFTER LUNCH'.

She lifted the holdall and placed the diary on the book and then lowered the bag. She did so in slow, distinct movements, like the objects around her were the most fragile things in the world.

I caught sight again of the daffodils. They really would have to go. I resolved to eat them in my sleep.

She afforded me a quick curious glance before heading for the door.

She'd come with gifts. It seemed damned uncharitable of me to send her off without at least one conciliatory remark. 'At the church, you turned up because you wanted to talk to me about something?' I said.

She reached the door before turning to speak. It was pretty apparent at this point that she had been looking for an excuse to leave anyway. 'It can wait,' she said. 'Get some rest, DI. I'll send one of the uniforms to check up on you later.'

If a PC did appear, old habits die hard, I would have sent him out for a cappuccino I had no intention of drinking. But DS Spencer didn't need to know that.

And then she was gone. The needles and disinfectant now had a companion. There was a sense of anti-climax in the air.

***

I climbed the hospital stairs. It was a concrete, clinical experience. Keeping close to me was my ever-faithful companion, a muscled, besmirched mass of moving darkness on four legs. It was the shape of a devil dog and went by the name of Duke.

The Royal Hospital was an old Victorian building. A back door was known to me; used by members of staff slipping out for a sneaky cigarette break. My experience of hospitals at night was to avoid the maternity wards and then you stood a good chance of avoiding detection. You keep to the empty regions of space that separate the wards. Typically, areas curtained off, with vacant chairs, abandoned bedpans, and unused machinery for company. You need to weave and scamper between the various sets of stairs.

By the time I had reached the twelfth floor I was perspiring lightly. I was still in my clerical clothing. Duke was panting slowly. It still amazed me that dogs could not sweat; cooled down by circulated air generated from panting; which didn't seem enough. Although I had later learned that, apparently, technically (I stood corrected), dogs did sweat, but only through their paw pads. Truly, the Lord moves in mysterious ways.

At the top of the stairs, I grabbed the handle of one of the double doors and pulled it towards me. The door complained with an innocuous squeak. Even so, I turned to Duke, my faithful shadow up to this point. Bending forward, one hand rested on my knee; from my other hand I brought a solitary finger up to my lips, making a silent gesture. Duke peered up at me attentively, taking it all in. He would have nodded if such a thing was in his purview.

Light of foot, we slipped into the hospital corridor. We were like ghosts that had not passed over to the other side, at least not yet. We still had God's work to do.

We were an unlikely couple, the holy man and the devil dog. We glided along in perfect synchronicity and found ourselves in a single room ward, seeking out, successfully as fate would have it, one room in particular.

Having entered, Duke dutifully set his not inconsiderable bulk down in the corner, waiting for his next verbal command or hand signal. Not that I thought, in this instance, anything of the kind would be needed.

A man in his sixties lay in a hospital bed; I couldn't tell if he was sleeping. His head lay on its side, facing away from me. As I walked towards the bed, I passed a spare pillow on a chair. I grabbed it and sat on the side of the bed, pillow rested on my lap, waiting for the patient to stir. This I was pleased to do, having the patience of a saint.

It was only a matter of minutes before he moved his face towards me.

He opened his eyes, squinted, and tried to focus. He executed as much of a double take as the confines of his hospital bed allowed.

'Father?' he said; his voice was croaky. I wondered if I was the first human being he had spoken to today. 'Is that really you?'

'Hullo, John,' I said.

John was terribly frail. His head was virtually bald except for a few strands of hair, hanging loose and free and pleading for a comb over.

'Yes it's me, Father Connor,' I said. 'I was passing through and thought, while I'm here, I could call in and offer some moral support. How are things? You were sleeping.'

'Only for a wee while,' John said. His voice was trembling and uneven.

He tried to lift his head, and for a moment, it was just hanging there adrift. But it was a losing battle, and back down it went again.

'Op went well, you know,' he said, 'but all that patching me up, only to open me up all over again ... fucking Paki doctors, never shutting up and you cannae understand a word. A lot of pain, I don't sleep that well, Father.'

I knew a confessional when I saw one, but I was on a tight schedule. There was plenty of work to get through tonight. It was a case of as needs must.

'Shush now,' I said. 'Спасибо.'

'You don't need to explain, ye ken,' I said. A change had come over me. I took a firm grip of the pillow on my lap. 'Shush now.'

There was a lack of understanding from John. No comprehension. When the reality of what I was doing finally registered, it was impossible to see his face, now covered by the pillow.

I pressed the pillow down from both sides. I leaned over, directing all of my weight as I smothered the life, precious as it was, out of him.

'I already know.' I spoke the words through gritted teeth and clenched jaw. My brain was on fire.

His body shuddered slightly. In terms of a fight for life, all said it was a poor show. I tried to level my thoughts and counter the disappointment, the mundane nature of it all, the minimum resistance so encountered. He could have put up more of a struggle. Life had to mean more; hadn't it?

***

Here in my sickbed, I had never felt better. It was like they'd put me on steroids; they might have, how was I to know? I was alert and restless. I was full of energy and dynamism. I had swallowed whole one of those uranium fuel rods. Steam was coming out of my ears. My eyes were eight different shades of red. I was a hospital infection's fucking nightmare.

I was back and what better way to prove my rediscovered vein-popping, organ-entrancing vitality than by lying completely still. To be so aware of every part of me, down to the last molecule. The need to spring into vigorous kinetic life became a demonstration of the ultimate in self-control by then not budging an inch.

I was dressed in stripy pyjamas, which I'd rescued from my holdall. I was assisted in this by a spritely middle-aged nurse on her ward round called Anna.

I'd arranged for everything on the table to be moved to the corner, with one notable exception. I managed to rescue from the bag the Thermos flask, embellished with a traditional tartan pattern—a red tartan—which now took pride of place on the table. Like a tartan phallus—a red tartan phallus.

I couldn't help one thing, though, that tic, that periodic event – I kept checking on my left hand. Where my ring finger should have been, there was nada, the void, literally nothing. There was still fuck all. I grinned like a schoolboy.

'I knew it,' a voice said that was not my own.

He was at the door, the whacky finger-pruning priest. And with him for company he had a big, black fucking Hound of the Baskervilles.

The priest's face lit up like he'd discovered a long-lost pal washed up on shore next to a pirate's treasure chest crammed with, you guessed it, treasure.

'Why change now?' he said.

'After all we've been through?' I said. 'Why the fuck not?'

We could talk all night for all I cared. I had changed, but nothing had changed. It wasn't as if I was in a rush to be anywhere else.

'I knew you'd come,' I said. 'It was a certainty, running through my bones. I knew any notion of unfinished business would burn a hole in your piss-poor excuse for a cranium. You're the kind that will never let sleeping dogs lie.'

I was the mouse who had not only fucked off with all the cheese, but his next door neighbour's mouse-wife as well. I would have patted myself on the back, if I could've been arsed.

'Sleeping dogs,' Connor echoed; the sneer in his voice very much to the forefront, leaving meagre pickings for the background. 'I like that.'

He moved forward, slithering like a snake. He came to a stop at the foot of the bed and, in a blink of an eye, fell into a trance; like he was miles away. When he finally returned from Moon Base Alpha, or wherever he had gone to, he threw a dismissive hand in the air.

'As for the other stuff, that's all weak assertion on your part, idle speculation,' he said. 'Don't flatter yourself.'

You could sense he was about to let rip and I tried to give him my full attention, but I couldn't help keeping at least one eye on the black mass of panting fur in the corner. It was the blackest black; a version of the abyss. I knew where the dog's face had to be, but still, I couldn't quite pick it out.

Connor's gaze lowered to the flask, which stood proudly on the side table.

'It's empty,' I said, not that I owed him an explanation, 'I like looking at tartan. I find it strangely calming, but not too soothing. Sexy, but not too sexy. I mean it's all relative. You wouldn't know where I could get some quality cotton tartan pyjamas, would you?'

'Call me a detective,' I added, in a mocking tone. If I could have irony for breakfast, I fucking would.

Connor, legs pinned together, swayed a little forward then back. It was almost as if he was taking a moment to remind him who I was, who he was, why he was here.

'Paid a visit to one of my parishioners down the corridor,' he said. 'A bitter, small-minded racist. Don't pick me up wrong; he was never a regular, he just turned up to Christmas and Easter services. The ones everyone goes to.'

'It was only a matter of time,' he said, 'before the children he abused would go after him. You could say I saved them the trouble.'

The monster-dog had his head cocked, big flappy ears up, listening attentively. He was anticipating, waiting for something.

'You see, I'm a sin-eater,' Connor continued, in full

flow, waxing lyrical, nothing would hold him back now. 'I intervene. I prevent the sins of others. You heard of Roy Lichtenstein, Inspector? 'Big Roy' I think people call him, if they're brave enough to refer to him at all. He's certainly heard—or so I've heard—of you.'

'Pollice verso' was the Latin phrase; from ancient Roman times, referring to a gladiator having been defeated in the Coliseum discovering his fate. No one really knows if it was the thumbs up or thumbs down that spared the gladiator's life, but you could be sure that one of them did. Father Connor gave the thumbs up and behind him, instantly, the monster dog was up on its feet. I had a feeling though—a very strong feeling—a very strong fucking feeling—that the thumbs up in this context was not the preferred option.

It was the voice. I couldn't help but be entranced; be lured in by it. Connor continued his sermon for one.

'You see,' he said, 'I can't do it all myself. There is so much of it, sin. I could be immortal and do what I do and still I'd only make a slight difference. I'd go on and on. But all I ask, as God is my witness, as I call on His support, love, and forgiveness, by tiny measured steps, I can make the world a better place.'

'The way this case is going, we might have to call God in as a witness,' I said, seeking to show I was paying attention—and not the reality that I'd just beamed down from Planet Gibberish.

Connor stared at me, nonplussed. 'It is a matter of faith,' he said, mustering a seriousness of tone I'd normally associate with a Chief Constable. Albeit one with an evangelical streak. 'Without faith, where are we?'

Connor's eyebrows were raised, then suddenly he looked sheepish. 'And here we are again,' he said. 'His name is Duke.'

Monster-dog was on the move.

'Looking for your finger? Still harbouring some vague hope they might be able to sew it back on?'

Slow, ponderous, and all the more terrifying for it, the dog had reached the side of my bed. The left-hand side. My left-hand side.

'Still hoping?' Connor said. 'Sorry.'

Gritting my teeth, I forced myself to sit up in bed. I slipped my right hand under my pillow. I grasped for the only protection I had.

'Fed it to the dog,' he said. His words were tiny but, once inside my head, like a psychotic ear worm, would not let go.

Monster-dog was ready to pounce. Snarling. A massive pair of balls slapping together. In killer-mode; bearing gloriously cruel teeth.

The fucker, all talons and saliva, flew at me.

Swinging the stubby claw hammer which I'd just retrieved from below my pillow, I met the bag of pus and fur midway. The head of the hammer connected sweetly, hitting the beast square in the noggin.

There was a smacking noise, a slurping, as the hammer embedded itself nicely between the eyes. The dog's bulk swayed to the left, then right, undecided as to which way to fall, but it wasn't over. Duke suddenly came to life, drawing on a second wind, displaying teeth on teeth.

Lunging forward, snapping, curling spittle drizzled on my face like some fucking Caesar vinaigrette, I tightened my grip on the hammer, applying leverage, twisting for dear life.

There was the growl, like a drill, like regret, like a broken promise.

Duke twisted and I had to twist with him. The hammer swivelled in the wound. It was a war of attrition and the cards were stacked against me.

The beast pushed forward, neck muscles extended,

head against hammer. Flexing, muscled, black mass of fur; this was all I could see. It was up on the bed. Jaws so close I could smell the halitosis; could practically taste it.

Twisting, twisted again. My left arm snaked out towards the side table. Fingers grappling, what remained of them, I grabbed the flask.

The thing with dogs, if you get stuck in a holding pattern with them, it won't be long before they've worked it out; before they try something different. I had to be one step ahead. Letting go of the hammer, changing the emphasis to my forearm, which I now pressed against its throat. I adjusted my heft, forcing the dog down under me.

It was wriggling. I adjusted. Heat. I could feel something give way in my back.

Claws scratching me in the chest and flank, tearing fabric and skin. It would be seconds before the monster canine squirmed out of my hold and bit my face off, or any other extremity it took a fancy to. One bite and I'd be lost; there would be no coming back.

I raised the Thermos flask in my other hand.

Swooping. Grunting, grinding. One last fucking hurrah. It wanted to rip out my neck, tear my throat into strips. Dog's idea of a square go. Red. A red tartan.

I brought the flask down on the dog's head. Wielding it like a tartan cylindrical club. Again and again. A series of dunts. Picking up one dent after another, the flask lost its shape, but still, it held itself together.

Melted, spastic time. The dog was stunned initially, but I was relentless. Down the flask went. No mercy, no quarter. A gash opened up to me, a crevice, a yawning chasm, a red rag to a bull, and I kept on going. I spoke no words, all the while cracking the dog's head wide open. As far as I could see. As far as I wanted to see.

I broke it.

No longer to be used as a weapon by testosterone-filled macho men and evil bastards, Duke lay there, quiet, at peace I'd like to think, his brains bashed out on the bed.

'Good doggy,' I said.

I retrieved the stubby hammer from the crimson farrago that was the beast's skull. There was also a dented, misshapen tartan flask to be found around there somewhere. But I had the hammer, that was enough.

Hammer in hand; dressed in blood-spattered, tattered stripy pyjamas, I climbed out of bed. The whacky priest was square in my sights.

Connor was done. He had just watched his monster pet dismantled by the classic one-two of claw hammer and tartan flask. He stood there, dumbfounded. Not for the first time, his mind seemed elsewhere. Moon Base Alpha possibly. Chechnya probably.

I wasn't done though, far from it. 'Right, you,' I said, my intentions pretty plain.

Connor took some steps back; backed up against the wall.

I raised the hammer—fragments of dearly departed Duke still stuck on there—above my head.

Connor realised he was in swinging distance. In response, he bowed his head, compliant, hands clutched together, ready for whatever brand of justice was at hand.

'Do what you have to do,' he said.

My head was in the grip of vengeance and fury.

Hammer remained in the air, became an extension of me; it stretched time. I was ready to strike, ready for something to give.

I already could see it. It was there, on the tip of my nose. Strike number two. I could have this one, and then no more. I had to be practical about this.

'You—'

Hammer swerved past Father Connor's head, slamming, lodging into the wall behind him.

He just looked at me, completely mystified. For him, it wasn't supposed to be this way. Sometimes I had to admit I surprised even myself.

Somewhere along the line, in the last few vital moments, Connor had unravelled. He was untethered. He'd lost the fire and crucially, so now had I. We could see it in each other's eyes.

I was calm, although I needed a second to confirm the sound of whale song was happening inside my head and not coming out of my mouth. I had his full attention.

'I'm still looking,' I said. 'All the misery and suffering; all the anger and violence. A production line of pain. Someone needs to listen to me. *I* need to listen to me. We are so tiny. I'm still searching for proof that this isn't all just a complete waste of time.'

Never leaving my gaze, he nodded, indicating that he understood, at least after a fashion. 'I can see you now,' he said, more in whisper than anything else.

Still, you could see he was emboldened by this. He was smiling, beaming, arms held out as way of welcome, of supplication. He was in awe of me, like a child, an angel, the holy man he once truly must have been. And he looked like he might hug and kiss me, rather than torture and kill me, and it made me feel like one of his precious dead Chechen orphans which, personally speaking, was no kind of payback at all.

Thoughts turned to tartan.

And I was back again. A shadow consumed three-quarters of my face. I took his arm, twisted it around, and arrested the wanker.

'You have the right to remain silent ...'.

Truth was I hoped he wouldn't be silent. Increasing the pressure on his arm, pushing it up against the socket, the only mercy I wanted to afford him was to put him out of his misery by ripping the fucking thing off.

Father Connor's feet shuffled. He started squealing. At least he gave me that.

***

There was a strong police presence outside Glasgow Royal Infirmary. It was proving a busy night.

Worthy of particular note were two pockets of activity. First, an outsized canine was carried out on a stretcher. Secondly, a relatively unscathed and handcuffed Father Connor was led out by two police officers. One of them I recognised as PC Nimmo.

The atmosphere was flat, understated; purposefully so. They had caught the bad guy. End of. That's all that really mattered. The exhilaration would have to come later.

They reached a police car, door opened. Nimmo placed his hand on top of Connor's head as way of steering the prisoner down into the backseat.

'Doesn't anyone want to hear me out?' Connor said.

'Not tonight, it's late,' Nimmo said. 'There's always tomorrow.'

Watching on, listening on, I liked that. I liked the fact there would be a tomorrow. To underline the point, the car door was shut with a reassuring thump.

As I watched the car drive off, Connor was looking straight ahead. Unlike Lot's wife, he did not look back and therefore, if the Old Testament is to be believed, did not change into a pillar of salt. Intuition told me his expression was instead one of puzzlement and disbelief. He was dealing with Glasgow's Finest, so he'd best get used to it.

Through the car side window, I could read his lips and

piece together his words at the moment the car peeled away.

'God made me do it.'

I was dressed in my suit and I was ready to roll. There was a definite nip in the air.

To combat the night-time chill, I put my hands in my pockets and scrunched up my shoulders. A simple enough act, but in my present condition, it was not without a good deal of pain. But I told myself I should be used to it by now. And if I wasn't, after all I'd been through, I'd need to sit down and ask myself why.

Now the car was gone, my line of vision was dominated by one Detective Sergeant Julie Spencer.

She wasn't in the best of moods. Her back was up. If tension was currency, she'd have enough to buy the factory. To be fair to her, I did have some explaining to do, but not now, to be equally fair to me, I wasn't feeling up to it.

Plus, I had this awful unbending feeling of déjà vu. Hadn't we been here before?

'I've discharged myself,' I said. 'I'm feeling better; more like myself. I'm going home.'

She was angry and wasn't prepared to even think about trying to hide it. I suppose we'd gone past that stage.

'Well, bully for you, sir,' she said. 'What happened in there? We've got a dead dog—the size of it—and ... and a hammer, for God's sake.'

'I kept a stubby hammer inside the flask,' I said. 'You don't have to tell me how odd it sounds, I know, but I can't sleep without a hammer under my pillow.'

'As it turned out, ironically enough, in terms of self-defence, the flask proved more effective than the hammer.'

She was blinking furiously. Her head had been reeling,

but now her mood was changing. I realised then that she was more in a state of shock than I was.

'Did you know he would come after you?' she said. 'Was there anything at any point, sir, any information you were prepared to share with me?'

'I don't know,' I said. 'I don't know if I have the answers you need. Dog came with Connor. I was stuck in a bed. At no point did I think it was all about me.'

She seemed appalled. She looked ill. 'It was never ...' her voice trailed off. 'Who are you, sir? Who are you really?'

So many questions, one after the other, like a Gatling gun on speed dial. My head spun, my jaw was clenched tight; I didn't appreciate where this situation was going. So I walked, gazing ever-forward, not looking back and, before I knew it, I had already walked past her. I knew her eyes were on me. I tried not to flinch.

I came to a halt, just for a moment, and nudged my head a little to the side. 'First and foremost,' I said, just loud enough for her to hear, 'I'm a person, DS Spencer, just like you. Just like anyone.'

I resumed walking. The greater the distance I put between her and me, the lighter the load I felt on my shoulders. Don't ask me to explain, but undeniably the combined stresses of the day began to lift.

A part of me wasn't content merely with walking away. It was the part which wanted me to skip my feet and damn the pain and discomfort. Happily for all involved, I resisted the impulse. It was dusk. It was dark. Every one of us; we were all under a lot of pressure.

From several feet behind me, a voice came back at me; not a shout, but clear enough for me to hear, certainly.

'Like fuck you are,' she said.

18.

Twisting the Knife

It was always going to come to this. Looking back, it was inevitable that I would end up in a certain place.

That morning, I visited my mother in her care home. I probably said the exact same things, the exact same way, word for word, pause for pause, as I did during my last visit. And I never stopped talking, terrified of the prospect of empty space.

'I love you, Mum,' I said.

There was only silence in return. A wall of silence. A wall I didn't hit, rather it was the reverse, it smacked into me. I felt bloodied by it, inside.

Times like these you ask yourself, what would I do to hear from her? To have from her any kind of acknowledgement? To see some sort of recognition in her eyes? That I could hug her and she would respond, hug me back, not unsure, not unfeeling, not oblivious; not asking who was this other person in the room.

What would I do? But, more likely, it was a case of what I wouldn't do. Not change anything, because life wasn't like that. I wasn't a fanciful person. I wasn't by nature an 'if only' type of person. I didn't join the police so I could live a life where I could get away with thinking like that.

I left my mum none the wiser and placed my broken heart in a safe place so no one could get at it, especially me. By the time I returned to Helen Street Police Station, my head was clear. I was focussed.

My first port of call was the first floor, where nothing much happened. It was a cold, largely uninhabited level, subject to strafing, unexplained icy drafts of air. Here, there was one place of real interest, not that you would ever admit to such a thing. Just because you knew of its existence didn't mean it was up for general discussion; didn't mean you mentioned it to anyone. The sign on the door read 'Anti-Corruption Unit'.

There wasn't any point putting it off any longer, the circus, so in I walked. Inside was a solitary chair with none of the trimmings, which made perfect sense. Anti-Corruption wasn't about placing you in your comfort zone. The chair faced three Wise Men, all present and correct as they sat at a long top table. I took everything, the spectacle, the set-up, with a pinch of salt. Of course, everyone knows that 'wise' and 'man' is a massive contradiction in terms.

Initially, my surroundings were a little unclear, resulting from my eyes having to adjust to the room's dim lighting. The men were a band of elasticated greyness, except for the more prominent parts of their faces, which obligingly stuck out. I settled myself, put on a show of trying to get comfortable in the chair, and bought myself a few moments as I made the transition.

I wasn't going into this blind. I knew what was expected of me, of what I expected of myself. It wasn't about being brave, or embarking on some well-meaning fat-headed moral crusade. I was set on doing the right thing. That's what it was all about, and we would just have to see where that got me.

'Ah, Detective Sergeant Spencer,' a Wise Man said. It could have been any one of them. 'So, what can we do for you? What can you do for us?'

To me, these men represented a single body with multiple heads. They weren't for giving away anything of themselves, which I could understand, but here I was expected to pour my heart out to them. It's not as if I'd ever be friends with any of them outside of police 'corruption' hours. To me, they represented the three ages of Scrooge, given the caveat that Scrooge was nothing else but old, just about decrepit. No point in trying to distinguish one from the other.

There was an air of looming serenity about them, an air of calm, which came with the experience of the job you'd think, while at the same time they managed to project onto you a pressing, urgent requirement for a quickfire response. Piled up on their table were various stacks of folders and documents.

'Sirs,' I said.

I sat up.

My back could not have been straighter. The tension was palpable, like a cat on a hot tin roof, jumping from my shoulders onto my neck.

With an elaborate sweeping motion, one of the Wise Men picked up what I surmised to be a copy of my report. As he opened and read, one eyebrow was quickly raised, swiftly followed by the other. It was all very mannered; it was coming across that he was only reading the contents for the first time, which surely couldn't have been the case, could it?

'This report,' he said. '*Your* report. Been up typing all night, Detective Sergeant?'

For effect, he leafed through the rest of the pages in

short order. I'd swear if he was trying to make a point, it was the most pointless point ever.

'Very neat. Very precise. I'm sure there's a lot in there,' one man said.

'Talk to me, but keep it recent,' said another one.

He carefully placed my report down on the table, keeping it perfectly straight; all terribly neat and officious.

So here we were. It boiled down finally to me giving a verbal report. They'd asked for it and they were going to get it.

'There was a robbery,' I said. 'All the places, times, and dates are in my report. A neighbour heard banging from next door and phoned the police.'

'When DI Fisher and I arrived at the locus, we found a seriously injured woman, name of Margaret Sykes. Upon discovery of a robbery in progress in her home, she had apparently intervened. The robber reacted to the encounter with the use of excessive force.'

The images remained lodged in my mind. Sykes was a diminutive woman in her fifties. We found her lying face down on the living room carpet, not moving, but there were shallow breaths. We did the best for her. Her attacker had nearly killed her. She had multiple fractures. She was defenceless. For someone so small and frail, there was a lot of blood.

'She was hospitalised for over two weeks. Eight pints of blood were required to see her past the first night. I'm told she'll need a metal plate to hold her face together.'

The Wise Men listened and waited for a natural pause. I had to breathe at some point. They just had to get their own deep breaths out of the way first.

'Shocking,' a voice said. 'But with respect, DS Spencer, I suspect your description of the victim, as graphic as that was, is not the reason why you are here. Anything to report out of the ordinary?'

'DI Fisher,' I said. 'While we waited for the ambulance to arrive, he waved to summon me into the hall.'

It was his left hand, I reflected, as point of fact, wrapped in white strapping.

'He had resisted any attempts to take time off,' I said, 'and recuperate from his recent attack in the church basement.'

Yes, now I was thinking, he was insistent. He had this knack of putting his case across at the right times to the right people. He had lost a finger in the line of duty and claimed it didn't affect him. It wouldn't be there tomorrow, same as today. It didn't hurt. And in any case he was right-handed.

'There was the offer of a desk job on the table,' I said, 'and he assured everyone that he was considering it.'

My throat was dry. I fought the compulsion to cough.

I don't know how he got away with it, but I chose not to get involved. Didn't believe much of what came out of his mouth, but crucially for him, someone did. Genuinely, after all he had been through, a part of me couldn't help but be impressed to see him back so soon, even if I wasn't that pleased about it. I kept out of it; it had to be someone else's call. I regret that decision. I regret it all now.

'So,' I said, 'we were in the hall—an ambulance was on its way—and DI Fisher leaned forward a little and asked me to give him a minute before walking back into the room where Mrs Sykes was.'

'What did you do next?'

'Nothing, I just waited in the hall. I gave him a minute.' I could feel my face crumpling into a hundred thousand folds and creases. 'No, not quite—not waited,' I corrected myself. 'The living room door was ajar. I took a peek in. I saw DI Fisher looking down at the victim. Much like the victim, he was completely motionless.'

'And ...?'

'And, I stayed in the hall. I closed the door.'

With both hands, one of the men propped up his head. As actions go, he made it look laborious, like his chin was made of marble. None of them were giving anything back; barely collectively mustering a passing interest. Well and truly, I was being Scrooged.

'I've seen the file,' he said. 'Her face as you say, unrecognisable. An outrage. A tragedy of course.'

Another voice. 'As is the case with someone with her type of injuries, the victim was put in the recovery position. Perhaps DI Fisher was listening out for her breathing. If not this, what are you trying to say, Detective Sergeant?'

I looked up and saw three wizened faces lording it over me. Before I knew it, I had a smile on my face. An enigmatic smile. A big girl smile. One that said I'd tell them in my own time and in my own fudging way. 'I'm getting to that, sirs,' I said. *Softly, softly, catchee monkey*, I could have added quickly, but *quickly* decided against it.

'A couple of days later, DI Fisher and I were driving along a residential road. Again, times and places ...' I pointed a hooked finger in the direction of the pile of paperwork on the table facing me, my signature buried away in there somewhere. 'Following our car was a clapped-out Skoda. I took a sudden left to see if the other car was staying with us.'

'Did it?' a man asked.

'It did,' I said. 'Sykes' family were understandably angered by the assault. We'd previously interviewed a family member who must have recognised our car. In the hope of being led to her attacker, to presumably mete out their own brand of vigilante justice, they took to following DI Fisher and myself in the course of carrying out our investigations.'

'I made the decision to stop the car.'

This I did, I'll at least admit to myself, after a short period of me driving round in circles and them following. I needed a different approach and I hit the brakes hard. Have to confess, I didn't warn DI Fisher, but sometimes in the car it's difficult to know if he's asleep, or in a trance, or whatever it is that he does, so I think—if I'm honest—I wanted to put that to the test as well. The car came to an abrupt stop. DI Fisher experienced a sudden jolt, but that said, so did I.

'I could hear from behind us,' I said, 'our shadow vehicle screeching to a halt also.'

'I got out the car and approached the Skoda and its occupants.'

Etched in my mind, three local males dressed in tracksuits, all tumbling out the car, all members of the Sykes family tree. They were already on the road to meet me. I was not in the best of moods. But nor were they.

'We exchanged words,' I said. 'I tried to avoid swearing. They were not so selective. I told them to be on their way.'

'That was as far as it went where I was concerned. The oldest member of the group, Tom Sykes, in his fifties, wasn't finished though. He turned his attention to DI Fisher, who had quietly emerged from the passenger side of the car.'

'Tom Sykes was pointing and shouting abuse at Fisher, something on the lines of, "Hey you, police, call yourself a man? Letting a woman give out orders. Your cock drop off or something?"'

Okay, I admit it, I reported this as much for effect as anything. Give those sticks-in-the-mud something to really chew on. It didn't seem half so bad reporting other peoples' bad language; telling it exactly how I'd heard it. I was thinking I had stumbled onto something here.

The things you learned about yourself. I had paused at this point in proceedings, maybe in order to better gather my thoughts or for more dramatic effect. You could take your pick.

'And?' a man said, not as remotely flustered as I might have hoped for.

'DI Fisher just stood there, said nothing,' I said.

In fact, thinking back, his shoulders were hunched, arms crossed. To all intents and purposes he was his usual detached self. Perhaps he appeared more fed up than usual, if anything, but it had been a long day.

'The outcome of it all was that the Sykes family got back into their car and drove off,' I said. 'DI Fisher took a note of the license plate, informing me that he'd put it through the system; see if any irregularities came up.'

'By the sounds of it,' a man said, 'the least he could do.'

Finally, and a little unexpectedly, I was in receipt of a supportive comment from the Wise Men, presently cocooned in their stiff shirts and embroidered epaulettes. Finally, this whole exercise wasn't feeling like a complete waste of time.

***

'Mum.'

'It's me, Mum. Julie, your daughter.'

'Mum.'

How could you explain it? You could grasp at straws. The random nature of it. Of all the things that made people mad, if you let it under your skin—but, then again, where else was it supposed to go? Suddenly, she was in my head. My mum. I was staring, but there was nothing in there to stare back at me. What made that part of my brain kick-start now? Why think of her now? The timing was bad. It was terrible. It was human.

***

'Are you still with us, DS Spencer?'

I blinked. This was followed by more blinks. My eyes had moistened.

'We have another meeting,' a man said, 'scheduled in twenty minutes' time, could stretch it to twenty-five.'

I got the hint. I got straight back into it. 'We found the robber,' I said. 'It was a day later. A landlord called in, report of a knifing in one of his flats in Westerton. There were items found in the flat linking the occupant to the Sykes robbery.'

'It was a bedsit; one room and a bathroom. We found the occupant, by the name of Anthony Dorrans. It being only one room, he wasn't difficult to find. He was in his twenties, topless, bare feet, wearing pyjama trousers, seated on the floor, legs splayed and back slumped against the wall. He wasn't moving; not sure if he was breathing. He had bruising and lacerations around his face and upper body. There was a knife buried in his chest. Someone had got to Dorrans first, obviously. You ask me, Dorrans' attacker was tipped off.'

'DI Fisher and I were in the communal hall waiting for an ambulance to arrive.'

Thinking back some more, you ask me, the Sykes family had the right idea following us around. Frankly, it should be a matter of policy for an ambulance to tail DI Fisher and I all the time. We did seem to be drawn to the badly wounded, the fatally injured, various bits of dead people, or for that matter whole dead people.

'Fisher turned,' I said, 'and asked of me, in that very low and precise way of his, to give him a minute. He returned to the bedsit, door left ajar. I'd been in this situation before. We'd both been there before.'

'I stood and put my hand on the door handle; had

every intention there and then of pulling it shut, but I hesitated this time. A split second of indecision, that's all it was. Instead I looked in. DI Fisher was standing over Dorrans, one was as still as the other.'

'Then, there was movement. He was down at Dorrans, positioning his ear at his mouth checking, yes you'd have thought, for signs of breathing. No idea if he heard anything, but there was certainly a reaction. With his left hand, he gripped the handle of the knife that was sticking out of Dorrans' chest.'

'I tried to shout, my mouth was open already, but everything was happening too fast for me, I couldn't wrap my head around it. I couldn't keep up.'

'I'll tell you what I saw. I saw DI Fisher twist the knife. I saw Anthony Dorrans' head flop to the side.'

There was a sound, that's what I remembered, like a long sigh, a marker, indicating any trace of remaining life in Dorrans' body was gone. Perhaps it was that, or that he'd gone already and it was just the release of dead air.

'Another thing,' I said, 'he used his damaged hand to twist the knife. His other hand was gloved. Maybe he was making some kind of twisted point. I don't know.'

'I was shocked. It was like something had shut me down. It was then that DI Fisher turned his head, noticed that I was at the door. Except that it wasn't DI Fisher.'

From the table, there was the sound of the turning of pages. Apparently the written version of my report was back in vogue again.

'I'm reading here,' a man said, with no attempt to disguise an incredulous, unpalatable tone, 'you allege that Detective Inspector Fisher tipped off the Sykes family as to Anthony Dorrans' whereabouts. Furthermore, with a twist of the knife, while you watched on, he finished off what Dorrans' attacker had started.' The tone continued. 'He turned and looked at you. "*The face of a crazed man*," it says here. "A *contorted and evil face*." Does this sound like DI Fisher to you?'

There was a tiny voice at the back of my head, counselling me, urging me to stand up and admit to having made a mistake. It was easily done. I could just say that none of this actually happened. That would be the easiest solution. To bury my head in the sand. To just will it away. Having said that, I was in the process of discovering there was an even easier option available, and this was to be ignored and dismissed by three shapeless Wise Men.

A Wise Man put my report down. He placed his hand, fingers spread emphatically, on the covering sheet.

A man was speaking.

'Are you sure he was even in the room?'

'You two don't get along, do you?' someone continued. 'We don't need to read it in your report. It's implied by the look on your face anytime you mention his name. It does not paint a particularly gratifying picture. Not where you are concerned.'

'You understand the seriousness of these allegations, Detective Sergeant? Allegations in respect of a fellow police officer; one superior in rank no less? Allegations with no real proof. It's not even his fingerprints on the knife that killed Anthony Dorrans. Smudged, not a full set, yes, granted, but even so, there are no points of comparison. Your case, your allegations do not hold up, do not fulfil the burden of proof.'

Was it my turn to speak? I was sensing, not quite. The next man to talk did so while looking up at the ceiling.

'I'm concerned,' he said. 'It is worth reiterating, are we talking about the same Fisher? Where are the written warnings? Where's the documentation? It's all hearsay and anecdotal, this great troublemaker of yours.'

I was aware that one Wise Man had given way to

another, but I had to confess I was struggling to differentiate where one voice ended and another began. 'Would green-lighting another investigation into an officer with an outstanding—and unblemished—record not be seen, justifiably I might add, as something of a witch hunt?'

I realised then that I should have brought my pointy hat.

'But that's just one instance,' I said. 'The most recent one. There's the Connor case, the missing ear. He was allowed back on duty too soon. Ridiculously so. There's a lot more. It's all in my report.'

'I'll tell you one thing that's in your report, both verbal and written,' a man said, lifting the document, now folded in two. 'A degree of unnecessary cursing. If I didn't know better, I'd say these are the actions of an officer under pressure.'

'Tell us about your mother?'

And there it was. Suddenly it was no longer about him.

'Sir ...?' I said. 'I don't see what ...'.

I didn't have enough in my armoury to deal with this. It wasn't something I could just shrug off. I wasn't built that way.

'Dementia, isn't it?' he said. 'She no longer recognises you? Bad business all round.'

Were there still three men? Three heads in front of me? I could no longer count them. It was all a blur. I wanted to scream at them. *Don't tell me what it's like! You have no right!*

But where would that have got me?

'Two weeks,' one of the three said. 'Take two weeks compassionate leave. Full pay. Use the time to sort things out. We'll make all the arrangements our end.'

'We insist.'

Raining down on me, one body blow after another. It

wasn't compassion, that wasn't the point. It felt like I was being clubbed to death.

Once the bludgeoning was over, it was conciliatory looks all round. I knew I should have done something when I saw that twist of the knife. I thought I was doing something right now. I thought I was being brave. But it wasn't enough for me to just leave. I needed to be seen to run away. They wanted a full capitulation and they so didn't want me to disappoint.

'And not to worry,' one of them said; it didn't matter who, 'we have your report. It can keep. There's nothing here that will go away. If you want to return to the case at a later date, another review, Detective Sergeant, not an issue. We can certainly arrange another meeting.'

It wasn't a case of not having enough fight. That wasn't the reason I came here. I was a professional and they weren't going to take that away from me.

I wanted to stand tall; up until the point I realised, after the fact, that involuntarily I had dipped my head. My resolve wavered and that, I was sure, was enough for them. They had exacted their pound of flesh.

'Two weeks not enough for you?' a voice said.

I looked up. Was two weeks sufficient, I wondered? Was that enough time to find something about me, to rediscover and rekindle; to make me fall in love with being a member of the force all over again?

'No, I ... that's more than enough,' I said.

None of that mattered, though. They had to drag my mum into this—now that was unnecessary. That was just cruel.

'If that will be all, then.'

'Sirs.'

I pushed back on the chair with my legs, causing it to scrape along the floor.

I got up.

I tried to do the right thing, my conscience was clear. Or so that's what I told myself; that's how the noise went inside my head, around in a loop.

I walked to the door. The present always had an exaggerated effect on things. In time, when I could look back, this might shed a different light, but in the here and now, with no hint of recall, it felt like the longest walk of my life.

'Oh, and one more thing,' they said in near unison.

As I left, the three Wise Men occupied the corner of my eye. The muted lighting in the room could have been playing tricks with my eyes, but each of them seemed to have undergone a change; a strange transformation. Like the pigs at the end of a book I read at school, *Animal Farm*, but in reverse. The men had become pigs.

Police officials as pigs. The irony of this was to occur to me, but only later. Red-eyed, twisty pot-bellied creatures, but pigs nonetheless.

'Close the door, would you,' they said, 'on your way out.'

19.

Appointment No. 4

Here was the news; I was back again to being a one-man band, at least as far as the next two weeks were concerned. I was liberated. I was *Free As A Bird*.

I genuinely hoped that, at some juncture, DS Spencer and I would find a way to reconcile our obvious differences. We'd started off on a series of wrong foots, but if we were going to work it out, nothing was going to happen overnight. If I'm honest, I had more immediate concerns. I needed to make a decision and choose who I wanted to see first. Lots of questions; loads of criteria to be filled; oodles of boxes to be ticked. Like, for example, to whom would I reveal more of myself to? And who could glean more of the truth from me?

I spun an imaginary bottle in my head. It had to be Dr Dawn. I hardly knew anything about her and I very much hoped we would keep it that way.

I called, without an appointment, to Cuthbert and Associates and, to be fair, she didn't keep me waiting for long. A tall, bald man appeared from her office. As he was about to pass me, he gave me a look, one with widened eyes. I assumed this was some kind of statement on his part; expressing his displeasure at my arrival coinciding with his session being cut short. My theory was immediately put to the test, though, when he did the exact same thing to the lady at the reception area, and then to the coat stand next to the front door.

Before you could say 'antidisestablishmentarianism', Dr Dawn appeared at her office door to usher me in. She was wearing cream trousers, but more to the point, today there was no shirt or blouse, only a sweater. Nothing in the way of herringbone at all. It was all I could do to hide my disappointment.

She held out her hand, and I reciprocated. Her grip was gentle, as was mine.

'To business?' she said.

She waved her hand, directing a little swipe towards the chair and I promptly sat myself down. In this, as in everything that had gone before, she was uber-relaxed. She was the bee's knees; utterly professional.

'How long do we have?' I said.

'We have as long as it takes,' she said. 'You talk and I listen. I only have the one question, as you well know.'

For the first time in what seemed like ages, there was the universe, the start and end point and everything you'd hope to find between, all back in order. She leaned back on her chair, legs crossed. She gave me the tiniest of smiles which, I have to say, had a profound effect on me. I wasn't sure where any of this was going and the uncertainty was rather liberating.

As long as it took? It might be worth going with this. Put to the test even the patience of Saint Dr Dawn. We would just have to see.

I began.

'What you need to understand about me,' I said, 'is

that I need to control myself; to be constantly inventive. To stop the lost, angry man from venting his bile and frustration at the bad world he sees around him. Maybe my thoughts, my instincts, are a little heightened. I'm too self-aware, oversensitive, but ultimately I don't think this sets me out as that different from anyone else. Who doesn't have their moments? Who doesn't tune into the six o'clock news with its shopping basket of tragedy and horror and not know rage and despair to the point you can hardly move, you can hardly think? Who doesn't watch *Strictly Come Dancing* on the BBC on a Saturday evening and not want to gouge their eyes out at the sheer banality of it all?'

'And it's a lot more real to me. I deal with criminals, traffickers; murderers of their own sons and daughters. When they come to my attention, I can't simply switch over to another TV channel, you see? And they take a place in your head, they lurk in your memory, and you can't shift them.'

'There is nowhere for them to go.'

'It doesn't end, not with the conclusion of your investigation, not with your statement to the procurator fiscal. And some investigations are never ended; some are never caught; the faceless ones, they still find a way to burrow into your head all the same. We have to deal with them, all of them, we have to find a way somehow. We scream in our sleep, in the dark. We turn to drink and drugs, embrace whatever poison, personal demons; whatever it takes and in our own particular way. We hit out, sometimes literally, at the ones we love. We scrabble around for self-preservation. Something is trying to consume us. It's a coping mechanism.'

I was sure Dr Dawn would have her own stories to tell, but was equally certain she would never share them with the likes of me. I feared I'd have to content myself in my own time and in my own mind by making some up just for her.

'I diet,' I said. 'It's a strict routine, fruit and natural yoghurt for breakfast, poached eggs for lunch, and pasta with a light accompaniment for dinner. I try to avoid meat. I avoid alcohol. It's regulating the little things, avoiding snacks, the odd sneaky glass of wine or a bacon sandwich, all those temptations. I eat Brussels sprouts. I build my life on abstention, fortitude is my only indulgence. Zero tolerance. I know if I do these things, then I can stop my other self from emerging. Well, that's the hope anyway. That's the plan; the stab in the dark. I'm not saying it's not difficult. It is gruelling. Grim. It is a grim existence.'

'Grim existences all round,' I continued. 'I'm reminded of—must have been more than a year ago—it was something like half six in the morning and I was called out to Allardyce Farm on the road to Stirling. A man in his sixties had been involved in a freak accident while out walking his dog. Trampled to death by a herd of cows. Big, heavy, stupid beasts; something must have startled them ,and before the victim could react, they were on him. His dog, went by the name of Shep, or so I recall, escaped unharmed.'

'It was a tragedy of course, but there's always room for gallows humour and while out on the field, literally in this case, one of the officers joked we should match up the hoof marks imprinted on the victim's body. Having identified the cows which committed the trampling, we'd take them in for questioning. And while everyone laughed, and I too was going through the motions, a snicker here, a snigger there, I found myself staring at the herd and wondering how much meat was packed in each of them? In my mind there was a visceral explosion; of hanging dripping carcasses; red parcels of meat. And

I had this mad compulsion to bite a chunk out of one of them. Raw, the taste of flesh and juice bouncing and dancing in my mouth. And I would just chew and chew.'

'But I fought the temptation. Of course I did. I mean, we've all been there, haven't we?'

I was aware I had asked another question, but this time a determination came over me to sit it out and wait for a response from Dr Dawn. She complied, but only in terms of another tiny smile. There was nothing more meaningful to be had; nothing more enlightening. This was my confessional, after all. It was up to me to decide ultimately how far I was prepared to go. My determination all but faded; I continued.

'Then there was this other incident. I think it might even have been later the same day. I arrived at the scene of a car crash; a Ford Fiesta had hit a curry delivery van straight on. The van driver wasn't wearing a seatbelt, probably considered it too much of an inconvenience, got in the way as he popped in and out delivering one curry after another. Such was the impact of the collision; it had sent him flying head first through the windscreen. Several boxes for delivery had been stacked on the passenger seat and they'd followed him out also, so the bonnet was covered in fragments of Tikka Masala and Chasni, as well as glass, blood, and various body fluids. There it was and my mind was working overtime and I couldn't look away from this curried human detritus. It whispered my name, carried it in the light breeze, like some spiced-up siren. My tummy rumbled fiercely and I swear if I had some naan bread to hand, I would have scooped up that bloody curry concoction right then.'

'It was like I had been taken hostage by food and strange appetites. The notions, temptations; the pull of it, it got evermore crazy, evermore bizarre. The feeling followed me around for weeks.'

'Like the time I checked in on a man named Nigel; he had returned from the holiday in Hell or, if you will, the Australian bush. A mishap with a compass had seen him get lost in the middle of nowhere. It was like something straight out of Hollywood, hapless, confused, he had randomly hooked up with a German Shepherd named Bruno. Nigel—and Bruno—spent the next weeks searching for help, teetering on complete dehydration and starvation. When Nigel was eventually found, he had lost five stone. There was no happy Hollywood ending, though, he had eaten his companion.'

'The choice in front of Nigel had been pretty simple; it was either that or starve to death. When he returned home to Scotland, he received an inordinate amount of media coverage; multiple death threats, social media mainly, from dog-lovers everywhere. Not least from Bruno's former owners back in Australia. So I checked in on him periodically to see if he was okay and ensure, online bluster apart, that the dog-lovers of the world were keeping a safe distance. Sometimes Nigel would invite me in for a cup of tea and talk about his experiences lost in the bush. Obviously still traumatised, he would talk about Bruno, the dog he ate.'

'Tasted like aardvark, so he told me.'

'That's the thing, it was everywhere I looked—and didn't look. All the crazed, zany people walking their aardvark-flavoured dogs on streets, and in parks, and in the countryside next to herds of tasty cows. All that time, I really tried to think of our canine friends as anything else but potential snacks. Chihuahuas for elevenses. For me it was all about focus; to demonstrate the mental resolve not to cross a line.'

I shifted uncomfortably in my seat and looked down at my hand and then my feet.

'There was one dog I definitely didn't want to eat,' I

said. 'In fact, he wanted to eat me. Even made a start on me. But that encounter came later, much more recently in fact, while I was in hospital, but that's not what I want to talk about right now.'

'You know what,' I said, straightening my head to stare into the piercing brown eyes of Dr Dawn.

She never flinched, never once diverted or withdrew her gaze. She never let me down that way. I could rely on her like a spider and its web, a drunken sailor and his cider.

In her company, I never once glanced at my heavily taped damaged left hand. And nor did she.

'You can fight off the temptation ninety-nine times out of one hundred,' I said. 'It's the one solitary indiscretion that creeps up on you. It only takes that one time, you lower your guard, give into weakness, an uncustomary lapse; you've not properly thought it through. So it was when I was faced with investigating an incident in Glasgow's only Michelin-starred restaurant, I knew I was in big trouble. Genuine fear took hold; it was like I was about to face my most difficult case yet.'

She did not flinch, even though I gave her cause to do so. As I changed, I held this stupid grin on my face. Just like last time, our prior appointment, it was a partial reveal, the *other* me from inside of me. I—one of us—still maintained a level of control. Or the illusion of control. When it came down to it, wasn't it the case of both of us, the *good cop*, the *bad cop*, wanting the same thing?

But Dr Dawn wasn't to know that. (Was she?)

Too right, her pupils widened at the sight of me. I had her by the teat, at least professionally speaking. She didn't show much, but she showed enough. She was fucking delighted to see me. But, where was I?

'Glasgow hasn't had a Michelin star restaurant in over ten years,' I said, 'which, if you ask me, is a disgrace.

This is the city, for Christ sakes, that gave us the "steak bake", deep-fried pizza supper, not to mention the thousand calorie stonner kebab!'

'The term "Michelin star" is supposedly the hallmark of fine dining quality. So, in all fairness, we're not talking chicken burger and chips, but crab and salmon mi-cuit and fuck-me roast pheasant and grilled foie gras. Foie gras, the process before slaughter of fattening the animal until its insides are fit to burst. Basically, the only way to go. Torture on a plate.'

'So when I was called out to investigate an alleged assault at The Flying Duck, the first Glasgow restaurant in half a lifetime to be awarded the fuck-aye accolade that is a Michelin star, I did so with a heavy heart and an empty stomach.'

'Half a lifetime?' Dr Dawn interjected.

I shrugged. Wrapped around the interjection was a fair point. 'Only applies to those with a life expectancy in their twenties.'

She nodded. She seemed okay with this.

'It had been raining all day,' I said. 'This brought a freshness I didn't normally associate with the city, which unnerved me. So it was a relief then, when marching into the plush confines of The Flying Duck that I was hit immediately by very different scents and smells. No point trying to fight it; with all the food fumes kicking about, I was already out of my fucking box. My stomach rumbled and I swallowed enough spit to put out a forest fire. In my head, lobsters were crawling out of pots and my chest was smeared in creamed polenta while I was biting the arse out of Highland Venison. My brain was crammed with phrases like *À La Carte*, *Degustation*, and *Du Marche* and I swear I was aroused; it was giving me a stiffy; I was Mount Vesuvius. Even the mention of sweet potato puree might have been enough to tip me over. I needed to remind myself several times over that I was there on police business.'

'I was taking a statement from Augustus, the head waiter, who had witnessed earlier that evening the alleged attack on a daytime television presenter named Esther Smart, by her ex-daytime television presenter husband, Barry Savage. Both Augustus and I sat at one of the tables. I did so cross-legged with a napkin on my lap. "In your own words," I said to him.'

'Both had ordered roast fillet of red mullet, he told me, but there was tension in the air. Augustus went as far as to say he could taste it.'

'Taste it?' Dr Dawn said, 'The waiter actually said that?'

'Cross my heart,' I said, although neglected to carry out the action.

And I was thinking, another interruption. It felt to me like she was building up to something. But that couldn't be right. It was me who should be building up to something. Like, what the fuck?!

'As Augustus talked,' I said, trying not to snarl, 'I was handed a plate of food by a passing waiter. I looked down and staring back up at me was slow cooked beef cheek with all the trimmings. I assumed this was a token of the restaurant's appreciation of the relentless and sterling work done by the boys in blue. But who cares anyway? I ordered a half pint of brandy, for lubrication purposes, and then I descended with gusto.'

'"They started arguing," Augustus said, "about politics, about fashion, about politics *and* fashion. Ms Smart mentioned something about Mr Savage being famous when she first met him and how she wasn't—and how the roles were now reversed. She said as a couple they had lost their vitality. They had lost their spark."'

'Augustus was on 'topping up', wine duties, when all

this kicked off. Apparently Mr Savage just blew up, said something like '*I'll show you a spark*,' before grabbing her by the neck. I recall Augustus saying, "He squeezed and she was turning a funny beetroot colour—which doesn't go at all well with red mullet."'

'Anyway, Augustus tapped Mr Savage on the shoulder and instantly he upped and left. Five minutes later, Ms Smart left and hailed a taxi. Sometime between, the incident was reported to the police, anonymous caller.'

If Dr Dawn was wondering where I was going with this, she didn't show it. If I was wondering where I was going with this, I didn't know it.

'As statements go,' I told her, 'I could not deny it was pretty comprehensive. The realisation was sinking in; my duty here was done and I no longer had reason to remain in the Flying Duck. It was fucking heart-breaking!'

'Then, suddenly, strolling into the restaurant, completely out of the blue, was Barry Savage. Apparently, when he stormed out of the restaurant from before, he left behind his umbrella, and was now in the process of asking for it back. Before you could say "*wop bop a loo bop a lop bam boom*", I was up on my feet arresting the man Savage. In fact, as I was apprehending him, I think I did say, "wop bop a loo bop a lop bam boom". I handcuffed him and sat him down on the chair across from me, only just vacated by Augustus. Savage looked perplexed. His lips were twitchy.'

'If you'll picture the scene, I looked him straight in the eye and told him, "I don't like you. You're a prick. Your time as a TV presenter, you had one high profile interview and you blew it. You were a Teddy Bear to Tony Blair."'

'Then, as an afterthought, I warned him if he grabbed or went anywhere near my neck, I'd rip his fucking head off.'

'I sat back in my chair. While it was important to be seen to enforce the full extent of the law, the cold, stark reality was that I hadn't had my dessert yet. On cue, swooping onto my table was chocolate and hazelnut mousse and pear sorbet. All that was missing were some Brussels sprouts.'

As punchlines go, it wasn't my finest moment. In terms of finesse, it wasn't up there with the statement of Augustus. I longed to hear Dr Dawn laugh. I longed to touch her hair. Two seconds on, I couldn't bear the thought of her laughing. I hated the idea of anything about her hair.

She leaned forward, and it didn't seem like the leaning action was going to stop anytime soon.

I was gripped by movement all around me. The walls closed in. Everything was blown up in my mind. Puffy. Distended. It disturbed my equilibrium. I felt giddy. I felt small. I'd moved beyond the realm of justification. But wasn't this why I was here? If I had a solitary need, wouldn't it be to have a platform to justify myself?

'Can you still do any good?' she said.

And I was back to normal—or at least, as normal as I had any right to believe myself capable of. And it seemed the cold-hearted reality of the situation was sinking in; it was Dr Dawn who was in control. It had always been Dr Dawn. As facts go (I was on stronger ground here) this had literally just 'dawned' on me.

'It is only the bad who see me for what I truly am,' I said, 'the corrupt and the wicked. It is the good and virtuous who look away.'

'Doctor,' I said, 'what do you see?'

For the first time during our time together she retreated. She leaned back in her chair. She wasn't even taken aback by the fact that, since our last appointment, I was one finger down. Didn't question it. I was sure she must have noticed it—she saw everything—but like the professional she was, didn't give it a second glance.

Now, now was the time. Cometh the hour, cometh the man.

'You've answered a question with a question,' she said. She looked almost positively cross-eyed. She sighed. 'No matter,' she said, 'if that's your answer, and I've waited long enough to hear it, that's what goes in my report.'

She placed both hands on the arms of her chair and lifted herself out.

'Our fourth session is done now,' she said. 'Many thanks for your cooperation and excellent time-keeping. I wish you, Detective Inspector, the very best for the future.'

I found myself mimicking her actions. Before I knew it, I was standing facing her. It was over now, without fanfare, nothing left outside of professional courtesy and the replenishing of fresh breath in the lungs, as it always had to be. And it occurred to me, as it invariably does at a certain point in proceedings on so many occasions, that nothing exists in a bubble. Who was Dr Dawn reporting to? The thought again that she was Scotland's version of Deep Throat. Was it too late to enquire? Should I just accept that I had missed my chance? But if this indeed was the end, no comeback, no future chance meeting, no forgotten umbrellas, if I had to know, I'd need to ask soon enough. Sooner than I was ready.

We were all bags of liquid; vessels of information. Some might call it intuition, the more knowing among us a stab in the dark. But we all had to get our info from somewhere. Everything was tentative, on tenterhooks. The session was finishing and our relationship, such as it was, was also finishing. Now, now was the time.

'By any chance, it wouldn't be a group of men you report to?' I said. 'Three in particular?'

Her expression in response was expressionless, but there was one thing, one instance of crucial punctuation. Blink and you'd miss it but from Dr Dawn, for the most nimble of moments there, it was her trademark tiny smile. I was blinking, but no blinks coincided with the fleeting upturn of her mouth. If one of them had, it would have been forever lost to me. I always maintained for this to work, she had to give something back. It had only been a firefly of a moment, the briefest of smiles. Taken in context, in terms of timing, it was massive. It was good enough.

Dr Dawn did not look away. Initially I was heartened by this, then realised the fact she hadn't was perhaps no cause for celebration. I was walking now; and kept on walking. The last I saw of her, a glance barely, she was a blur. All I could make out from the general murkiness that enveloped her was her distinctive, attractively so, snub nose.

Dashing past reception, I made my leave of Cuthbert and Associates. I didn't look back. It felt like it, because indeed it was—it was the end.

20.

Take your pick: Appointment No. 5/ Interrogation No. 5

'*Can you still do any good?*'

As much as I might have wanted, I couldn't afford the luxury of dwelling on things. DS Spencer; Dr Dawn; it wasn't a case of shrugging these people off. But I was a fatalist in every sense of the word and, like Sinatra, it was 'my way' to dust myself off, put my head down, and just get on with things. It wasn't in my DNA to stop, or look back, or take stock. Where would any of that get me?

And I didn't fancy much going home either. All that waited for me back there was a PS4 still in its box, a horrendously unmade bed, a lobster carcass hidden under a pile of old newspapers; that and my old friend, dust. My flat was in urgent need of attention of the housework variety. I kept on telling myself I was too busy to do it, but at the same time, wasn't prepared to pay anyone else to do something I could so easily do myself. It was the domesticated version of immovable object and unstoppable force. It was the road to insanity.

But the dust; invasive particles and spores, like microscopic swarming killer bees, carrying the faeces of dust mites; it made you sneeze and gave you a runny nose and itchy, watery red eyes. Dust was everywhere, but who cared to be reminded of the fact.

There were so many things I tried to blot out, like nostalgia for example. I did not consider memories to be my friend.

I was alone of course. No one was waiting for me back up the road. Most spouses and partners of members of the police were nurses or other members of the police. It was the nature of the job; the shift work; the antisocial, otherworldly work cycles. It shaped everything about you; your outlook on life; a dislocation, setting you apart from the general public (the people you were expected to serve). The make-up of the job prescribed your choice of partner. You needed to work those types of shifts in order to understand what it was like for others who worked those types of shifts. Not that any of this, where I was concerned, was relevant. I could never abide it; the thought of anyone close. I already had someone to share my life with. A caged animal trapped inside my skin.

So, it was to the Bar-L, then. Or as it was more officially known, Her Majesty's Prison Barlinnie, located in the north-east of Glasgow, specifically the small town of Riddrie (not that the good folk of Riddrie liked to publicise the fact).

Dotted around the world were concrete pens packed to the rafters with as much scum and villainy as a cartographer of crime could shake a complex diagram at. In this regard, the Bar-L would not disappoint. To coin a phrase, it was hoaching with all kinds of psychopaths and head-bangers. It was Glasgow's answer to Arkham Asylum.

On entering the building, I was greeted by a prison officer called Gordon (funnily enough, if you know your Bruce Wayne), who seemed overly cheerful (I wondered if he was on happy pills) with a fondness of twirling with his fingers an impressive bundle of keys of all sizes attached to his belt.

There was no great need for formal introductions, so we set to it right away. I was led through one corridor after another. This signalled the procession of one metal-plated door slammed after another. It wasn't long before this created a kaleidoscope of circular thunderclaps, so much so, you couldn't tell if the banging and slamming was coming from behind you, or out front.

Prison officer Gordon was chatty, especially in the sphere of facts and figures. 'In total, post-war, up until the '60s, between these walls,' he said, 'ten official judicial executions by hanging.' He unclipped his keys, after jangling them first, from his belt. He had the keys to the kingdom. Without fail, each twist and turn resulted in a clang, like an out of tune chime from Big Ben. A call out to every lost and dismembered soul. A door would swing open. Latterly, he looked at me. 'State executions. The good old days,' he said, his eyes twinkling.

After much pounding and thudding, I was escorted into a small room. A visitor's room. It was outside official visiting time, but I wasn't here in an official capacity, and this could hardly be referred to as *visiting*.

Already seated, waiting for me at the table was Father Connor. Outside of owning the box set of Channel 4 sitcom *Father Ted*, I was no expert on ecumenical etiquette, so I wasn't sure when implicated in mass murder and torture if you were stripped of the title 'Father' (probably not). But at least he was no longer wearing his dog collar, dressed instead in a bog-green sweater, standard prison issue.

I turned to Gordon. 'Give me ten minutes,' I said. I shook my head and muttered to myself something even I found indecipherable. 'Make it fifteen,' I said, my words much clearer now.

The officer vacated the scene, trademark keys rattling in hand. The closing of the door bringing on another sequence of crash bang wallop.

The table was bolted to the floor and Connor was tethered to the table. He was composed, serene. It was as if he had already played this scenario out a hundred times in his head.

'I'm glad you came,' he said.

'Your lawyer was insistent,' I said. 'This is all off the record. I'm just passing through. Maybe we'll talk. Exchange the speediest of pleasantries. It's no skin off my nose.'

'Did he tell you I plan to plead guilty to all charges?' he said. He shuffled his frame as much as the chains holding him in situ would allow. 'I confessed to all. There were other lost souls you didn't know about. I did it so no one else had to ...'.

At this, I lifted my bandaged left hand. 'You already told me that part while you snipped off my finger.'

He looked genuinely apologetic. 'Sorry, I was making a point,' he said. 'You're right-handed, are you not? It could have been worse.'

'Point made,' I said.

'Your secret is safe with me,' he said.

It was a head spinning moment. I thought he wanted me here in the Bar-L primarily to gloat. Or to tell me he'd changed his mind about the guilty plea. Or both.

I wanted to show him that he hadn't won; nothing had

changed for me; that I was still the same. At least that was the scenario I'd played out in my head, I wasn't expecting this. All the while Connor continued. And I just shut up and left him to it.

'I am not insane,' he said. I wasn't sure if this statement was more for his benefit than mine. 'I remain sure of myself and of my work. I have my instruction. I have faith. But I have changed. I am reformed. By the grace of God, the *changeable* aspect of me has gone. No more funny voices. In prison there is so much frustration, ignorance, and despair, allied to the sheer brutality of living of course. In here, I think I can turn this around.'

It wasn't the case of not giving them the satisfaction of a reaction. It's just that I didn't have the energy.

'Do you know Adam Walker?' he said. 'Of course you do. You bit his ear off when you interrogated him. Well, *one* of you did. And I cut your finger off. You, him, I; we are a trinity of sorts; connected. We are a version of the Eucharist; engorged on the flesh of the other. We dance on tiptoes on the heads of pins. We pollinate the air.'

'I have not physically suffered, but I should have,' he said. '*Bang, bang, Inspector's silver hammer.*' He made a tapping noise on the table with one of his fingers. 'But I have endured all the same. Have I not been incarcerated? Did I not experience the trauma of seeing my dog's brains bashed out on a hospital bed?'

'With a tartan flask,' he added quickly. 'And everything else, piled up like so many sheets of paper, the height of a bible. I can exorcise the past, but I can't wish away the present.'

'*We pollinate the air ...*' I was not sure who he was trying to fool, but surely not the two people, him included, in the room. His was a nonsense cocktail of drivel and psycho-babble. I could put an end to it anytime but, it seemed to me, far too much effort to interrupt. Let him say his piece and let me count down the minutes. It was his time; his point to make. Or not if it came to it, or didn't come to it. Let him kill it all on his own. I said nothing.

'Adam Walker is in this prison too. His cell is not far from mine. He has found religion, so it makes divine sense, don't you think, that our paths should meet? A man of few words. Believe me when I say, everything you need to know is written on his face.'

'He has turned away from the wickedness of his past. He has disowned it. From this day on, his only concern is for the sanctity of human life. Such an epiphany came about when he met you, Inspector; when he was attacked by you. At one point there was no light in you, and in the moments of calm after the terrible, wild, frenzied storm, you talked, and the light returned to you. Through its absence, it dazzled all the more.'

'The significance of this he was to fully comprehend only later, while inside these prison walls. When you showed him your true self, you pointed him to the way to salvation. From something so forsaken, so irredeemable, he saw an aspect of the divine in you, so projected on himself.'

'Adam saw it, as have I. He will never tell the authorities what happened in that room, will never press charges, or make accusations, or claim police malpractice, at least not where you are concerned. And I, too, will never tell. Your secret is safe with us. You know what that means, don't you?'

'I just wanted you to know,' he said. 'You owe it to yourself and to others who know you, who have taken the positives and had had their lives turned around. It is in your gift that it falls to us to spread the light. It means you can go on and on and on.'

Then suddenly, written all over his face, there was a

look of realisation. His eyes had widened. He was the priest from the sermon at the church all over again. If he had encountered a crisis of faith along the way, such doubts were now utterly dispelled. A thunderous, exotic, and relentless fire returned to his gaze. Across from him, there sat a different man to the one who had entered the room.

'It's you, isn't it?' he said.

I banged my head on the metal table. Another crash bang wallop; the sound echoed around the room. It hurt like Jesus. It opened up an old wound. I felt a single sliver of blood re-emerging from the resulting gash.

The room was spinning. It seemed to shorten the space between us. It made the room smaller. Everything seemed that much darker. He never once took his eyes from me. You had to hand it to the guy, he had made his fucking point.

'Again,' I said. 'Ask me the question again.'

21.

Inside and Out

This wasn't about me; it was about the work. I couldn't shake the Connor case off. Something was still bothering me and that's why I'd agreed to see him.

At Barlinnie, our time was up.

Connor never had the opportunity to repeat anything he said, and this left me feeling neither happy nor sad. After the fifteen minutes I had with him, I was all washed out, a spent force. Exhausted. It was difficult feeling any kind of emotion.

When prison officer Gordon appeared, I put my hand up to my brow, made a show of adjusting to the light beyond the door (not that it differed much from the light in the room) before hitting my head against the jamb of the door. I now had a (to be fair, pretty unconvincing) explanation for the gash on my forehead. Gordon was a good sport about it, so long as I zoned out the strange looks. He handed me a handkerchief embroidered with his initials. I applied it to the wound, exerting pressure on my forehead and immediately felt much better for it. I made a mental note to launder the handkerchief at some point and mail it back to him.

It was a mistake to see Connor. He had no answers. He claimed to be reformed and maybe he was in a way, I gave him that. But if you ask me, he just wanted to trip people up and speak mumbo jumbo, make it look like he had the answers. Religion has its place, you had to respect the views of other people, up until the point they break the law and you have to put them in prison. Father Connor had crossed that line, that was a given, but that wasn't what was troubling me; following me around, making me edgy, jumpy, paranoid. An uneasy feeling that dragged my whole body down with it, disturbing my whole equilibrium to the point I felt permanently giddy.

It didn't matter. He was a killer and he had to pay.

It was clear, then, it wasn't Connor, that it was something else. Something that perhaps only I could fix. There were thoughts, compulsions; feelings taking shape. Three strikes and I was out and that would fix everything. But the truth was, the spectre of it, oppressive as it was, followed me around not some of the time, but all of the time, and I had grown hardened to it.

It didn't matter. I was a killer and I had to pay.

But, no, despite everything, that wasn't what was bothering me either.

***

I gave Old Jock a quick call. If there was a canine held in a Scottish dog pound anywhere to be found, then he'd know about it. And in this instance, he did not disappoint, he knew all about it. All three of them in fact.

I drove to the pound at Aitkenhead Road. In one of the pens, all tangled up for warmth and emotional support, were three Staffordshire Bull Terriers. The handler opened up the pen, and in I walked. In my presence, prompted by the nuzzling, gently growling dominant female, the dogs untangled before all sitting in a line. The Boss lady had taken the middle position.

The dogs had been found in Connor's lock-up in Clydebank, starving and abandoned. They had licked up a fair amount of various victims' blood, discharge from the torture and dismembering which had occurred there. But blood splatter always finds a way and, thankfully, for evidence purposes, some arterial spray had landed out of reach of their stumpy legs.

Now they found themselves at Aitkenhead Road, where the surroundings were less icky, but where the bedding was basic and the food even more so. Cold, but dry; there was an unmistakable canine smell about the place. As kennels go, it was functional, but couldn't be called a home to these dogs. Surely we could come up with something better.

I placed a hand on the top of the dominant female's head; finger scratching the back of her ear.

'Ladies,' I said, 'I'm springing you out of here.'

***

Once I had signed out the dogs, I ushered them post-haste into the back of the car. This proved an error in judgement. In my hurry to vacate Aitkenhead Road I hadn't enquired into the last time they had spent a penny—and it was something of a mini-trek to Milngavie. Lord knows what they'd been feeding them at the dog pound, probably something a tad too basic; clearly it was not agreeing with them. It was unspeakable; it was carnage; it absolutely covered the back seats. As way of warning there had been some whining beforehand but, in my eternal wisdom, I had chosen to ignore the signs. The stench nearly caused me to run off the road at least a couple of times.

Once I reached my destination, I opened the back door and the Staffies were as keen to get out of the car as I was to see the vehicle evacuated (there had been enough evacuations of another kind already).

'Out you go,' I said.

After jumping out of my car, the trio of pooches just stood there. The odd sniff at the cracks of the pavement under their feet besides, unsure of their next move. My mind wandered a little. Threes. And twelves. The numbers that seemed to follow me around.

'On you go,' I said.

The dominant female shot me a little cock of the head, the tiniest of looks, before scampering off, the other two following in tow. I closed the car door and made a mental note to contact a car valet firm next available window I had. In the meantime, I crouched next to the car, using it as cover.

The dogs headed in a particular direction, although seemed to lack basic road sense, weaving in and out of residential tarmac as they went. It hadn't occurred to me to check on this either. If I'd ever wondered whether I was a suitable person to own a pet, I felt now I'd answered this several times over. Luckily there was no traffic. The street was as quiet as the inside of a coffin.

The dogs continued on their way, navigating a bend in the road. In terms of walking distance, they were a good minute or so away, but I could still see them well enough from my vantage point.

The dogs gravitated to a certain door. It was as familiar to me as it was to them.

The Boss lady scratched at the door for a little while. There was no barking or howling, or any signs of agitation. It was all terribly restrained. Describing the scene as relaxed was perhaps stretching things, but there wasn't much in it. I was in no hurry to stray from my present spot, and nor were the Staffies.

Charles Bartholomew, dressed in his customary housecoat appeared at the door. He, on the other hand, seemed to be in an agitated state. You didn't have to be psychic to work out what he was thinking, or muttering to himself, before he reached the door: 'Who can this be? At this late hour?' (We were losing light.)

He seemed highly irritated as he looked to the left, then right, then down. He trained his sights on the three Staffordshire Bull Terriers. 'What?'

'Hmm ...' He opened the door wider. 'Come on, then.'

And in the dogs trotted, the front door closed securely behind them.

As I sprang to my feet, about me I had a renewed sense of purpose. I followed the dogs' path—not literally though, I kept to the pavement. My every intention was to pay Mr Bartholomew a visit, too.

I was thinking. My mind was racing. You see, I had finally worked out the thing that had burrowed its way into my skull and, as of now, was threatening to explode, taking my head and shoulders with it. Borne of previous notions; the compulsion to plan a stake-out. My intended target was Roy Lichtenstein, or so I had thought. But Big Roy was a smokescreen, that was clear to me now. It was all to do with the subconscious. Seriously, I was better than that. I just needed some joined-up thinking. I'd gone to the lengths of preparing a holdall. Always at the back of my mind, now at the forefront, the thing that was bothering me was Charles Bartholomew.

There was something about him. When we talked, he was a man whose wife was posted missing, so why spend so much time in your housecoat, sitting quaking on the stairs, waiting for the mail to arrive? Was he wracked with concern for his spouse? Or was it more than this, the product of a guilty conscience? Was it something along the lines of wanting his wife out of the way, but the idea of torture, it might have been mentioned at the off-set, but was all heat of the moment stuff surely? Like following the dogs' path, not to be taken literally.

Father Connor, by comparison, he was literal to a fault. He did it so you didn't have to.

With every step, the door loomed nearer. My pace both quickened then, mid-step, slowed right down.

He didn't have the nerve to do a Mrs MacPhellimey; to murder his spouse himself and make a plan to bury her in the back garden.

I wanted to get this over with. I wanted to savour every moment.

I was aware of footsteps coming from behind me. Tantalisingly so, there was no time for me to react. Not for the first time, with crushing force, I felt something hit the back of my head. There was a crack. It was like there was a target painted on the back of my head, irresistible to every passing psychotic bully boy.

There went the stitches. A doctor's healing touch ruthlessly undone. Sound and pain became indistinguishable. After that, I wasn't thinking anymore.

***

When I came to, it was either going to be a bright light shining on my face or no light at all. It turned out to be the latter. I couldn't see a thing. I'd been black-bagged.

Aware of movement. Abruptly, a granite grip took hold of both of my shoulders, then manhandled me out of a car. I was hauled into what seemed like open space. A car park, maybe? All I could say was that there was no noise. My lumbering captors besides, no evidence of any living things anywhere nearby. The wind nipped at my clothes. It tugged at the bag covering my head.

Someone else, an additional pair of hands, took hold. I was divvied up, as they took a side each.

'I don't feel well at all,' I said, voice muffled through the bag.

This was true, I was woozy, my head ached. I was the boiled egg cracked open, soldier dipped into the yoke, then put together, taped up, only to be cracked open one more time.

'Good,' someone said, standing in front of me. All told, including myself, it was another, a fourth, individual—all male.

The voice—if only I could have concentrated. If only I could rise above the surges of pain. I was sure if I could, I would recognise it. The voice washed over me.

'I see you're a loner again. One man. Jimmy no mates. Bad timing for you, good for me.'

'The banker may be of some use to me,' the voice continued, 'so it wouldn't do for you to lay your trotters on him. You could say I've decided to bank the banker.'

There was laughter from the two goons holding me upright. They seemed to find that last remark genuinely funny. They weren't putting it on. Really, it took all sorts, I supposed.

'Maybe,' he said, 'I've grown averse in my old age to the good people of Milngavie being harassed by policemen clearly acting above their station? Maybe, I've become a self-appointed protector of citizens, men and women of the 'burbs, to the right to a quiet life?'

'All I know is that I have several upset parishioners, ex-members of Father Connor's flock, to console. Who are they going to rely on now, a wee word here, a huge sob story there, to do their dirty business?'

The voice moved in a semicircle. As it did so, it came to me at different levels; ebbed up and down presumably to coincide with an uneven gait. And now it was behind me.

'Between you and me, Detective Inspector Fisher, there are so many scores to settle. A score of scores.'

I sensed he was going to stretch this out until he had proof that I recognised him. Until I said his name. He mumbled; his voice was dreary and monotonous—and the muffling effect wasn't purely down to the bag over my head. This was a man who didn't see the need to enunciate his words, or make an effort to be easily understood. It took a lot of effort; a straining of the ears, but it was proving tedious; providing an antidote to the obvious danger I was in. The pain in my head had gone numb.

'*Ottoman Empire* my arse,' he said.

Suddenly, night became day; clouds separated and a huge yellow fireball burst out of the sky. The sound in my ear was less tinny, much clearer. Easy when you knew how. At last I could put a face to the voice and, as already established, it was not a pleasing voice.

Black-bagged or not, I could see it now, those hairless eyebrows. 'Bryce Coleman,' I said.

'Some call me Samurai,' he said, as gruff as you like.

From my lower left leg, there was a stabbing sensation. A blade, big enough to be a sword, slashed and made its merry way through a collage of tendons and nerves. Pain and numbness; numbness and pain. I cried out. My leg went dead. The goons either side of me prevented me from dropping to the ground in a miserable heap.

I was dragged into a building. It didn't seem like Bryce Coleman intended to join me but, in truth, I was spoiled for company anyway.

Of my two escorts, no one seemed concerned that my bleeding leg must have been leaving a ruby red slug's trail behind it. Maybe that was their intention? Maybe that was the point?

'We not using the lift?' one of the goons said.

'No, stairs. Orders,' the second goon answered. 'Christ knows if the lift even works in this fucking dump. Mind the steps for needles.'

So I was hauled, pushed, and jostled up many sets of stairs. Twelve in total; I counted.

A door clanged open and I was greeted by the wind once more. But this far up, the currents were stronger, more turbulent. More foreboding.

I was shoved forward to the point I could be shoved no more, it seemed. For all I knew I could have reached the end of the world, a short drive from the north-west of Glasgow. There was a stretching sound as the bag was removed unceremoniously from my head, so I could see for myself.

First impressions, I was no longer in the plush residential surroundings of Milngavie. I was on top of a building four or five storeys high in a run-down part of town. Given the situation I now found myself in, it seemed an inefficient use of time to search for distinctive landmarks.

Up so high, it was all so clear. It wasn't as tall a building as they would normally use. But they needed somewhere secluded, I was assuming, somewhere in a hurry. It was a case of beggars not being choosers, or something along those lines. They wanted it done with the minimum of fuss and they wanted it done fast. I should be taking it as a compliment.

'Please,' I said, 'I don't want to ...'.

In perhaps my greatest moment of need I wasn't for changing. And that may have been the problem. Too much talk of three strikes and you're out. The terrible irony was that I hadn't even got that far. Two to go—or was it one—did twisting the knife on Anthony Dorrans count? Wasn't he dead already? My memory was fuzzy on that point. See, I couldn't keep on top even of that anymore. Maybe *he* just wanted to have the last laugh, go out on his own terms. I couldn't even hear my heartbeat; drowned out by all the laughter. In my head.

It was up to me, then. I needed to quick-think, fast-talk my way out of this. Me and my one working leg, I was out of options. Where was there to hop to? I lifted my head to look at, to plead some more to my captors, only to find a granite hand placed on my back, pushing me forward. At that point there wasn't anyone to look at. It was just empty air, moving really fast. I was falling.

The faster time moved, the slower it seemed around me.

Down on the ground was Coleman. He clutched a walking stick, brought about by injuries from you-know-who, sustained in our only other meeting. He was looking up at me, following his usual fucked up MO. His face was etched with cruelty; perhaps a little older, animated as ever by sheer bloody cold hatred. Hairless fucker. What he was looking for, who could say?

He had a bad leg, but so did fucking I.

Falling. It was like each side of the brain was yelling opposite things. Scream; don't scream. Flush; don't flush. Fall; don't fall.

Falling down the best of five storeys, who the fuck had time to speculate? The man with the fucking cheerless voice waiting down below was welcome to whatever godforsaken, awful, dismal thoughts that filled the gap between his ears.

Down, down, down, whistling as I went. My bulk had adjusted. My eyes had reddened. My cheekbones less defined. As I hurtled down, did my life flash in front of me? Which life would that be?

My last thought: so glad I hadn't got around to making

that next dental appointment. Saved me the job of cancelling it.

My—definitely this time—last thought: '*Some call me Samurai*.' The nutsack below was having a laugh.

My—oh, never mind—last thought: Dr Dawn, it was never meant to be.

Perhaps it was his injuries that slowed Coleman down. He wasn't at his most sprightly. Maybe, there was something about my face; the way it changed mid-descent. It now told a different story.

Whatever the reason, Coleman just stood there, transfixed. He didn't budge a muscle. There was nothing he could do, but watch.

I was heading straight at him. My arms were out, cajoled by gravity. Good leg—bad leg—neither slowing me down. All there was to do was fall. The air pushed back on my face; my lips were moving. I mouthed one word. 'Strike.'

There was a whack. Skin on skin, bone on bone. Spit on spit. A fucking almighty smack.

Then it went black.

Then, there was nothing much at all.

Editor: Elinor Winter
Proofreader: Kirsten Murray
Production: Jim Campbell
Cover by Alex Ronald

Thanks to Ed Murphy, Nathan Robinson, Steve MacManus, Luke Cooper, Gary McLaughlin, Aaron Murphy, Will Pickering, Jane Quigley, Linsey May, Liz Small, Scott Lindsay & John McShane

Love to LC

Contact Jim Alexander at planetjimbot@gmail.com
Follow him on twitter @JimPlanetjimbot

Contact Elinor Winter at elinorwinter01@gmail.com
Contact Kirsten Murray at hello@kirstenmurray.co.uk

We're on Facebook:
www.facebook.com/groups/planetjimbot
Check out our shop online:
www.etsy.com/uk/shop/PlanetJimbot

Lightning Source UK Ltd.
Milton Keynes UK
UKHW011839101218
333781UK00001B/89/P

9 781916 453500